WHERE I CAN SEE YOU

WHERE I CAN SEE YOU

LARRY D. SWEAZY

SEVENTH STREET BOOKS®
AN IMPRINT OF PROMETHEUS BOOKS
59 JOHN GLENN DRIVE • AMHERST, NY 14228
www.seventhstreetbooks.com

Published 2017 by Seventh Street Books®, an imprint of Prometheus Books

This is a work of fiction. Characters, organizations, products, locales, and events portrayed in this novel either are products of the author's imagination or are used fictitiously.

Cover image © Getty Images
Cover design by Nicole Sommer-Lecht
Cover design © Prometheus Books

Inquiries should be addressed to
Seventh Street Books
59 John Glenn Drive
Amherst, New York 14228
VOICE: 716–691–0133 • FAX: 716–691–0137
WWW.SEVENTHSTREETBOOKS.COM

21 20 19 18 17 • 5 4 3 2 1

Library of Congress Cataloging-in-Publication Data

Names: Sweazy, Larry D., author.
Title: Where I can see you / by Larry D. Sweazy.
Description: Amherst, NY : Seventh Street Books, an imprint of Prometheus Books, 2017.
Identifiers: LCCN 2016035168 (print) | LCCN 2016048541 (ebook) |
    ISBN 9781633882119 (paperback) | ISBN 9781633882126 (ebook)
Subjects: | BISAC: FICTION / Mystery & Detective / Police Procedural. |
    GSAFD: Mystery fiction.
Classification: LCC PS3619.W438 W48 2017 (print) | LCC PS3619.W438 (ebook)
    | DDC 813/.6—dc23
LC record available at https://lccn.loc.gov/2016035168

Printed in the United States of America

To John Helfers

Never say goodbye because goodbye means going away and going away means forgetting.

—J. M. Barrie

CHAPTER ONE

"You know how it is at that time of year; the days seem to last forever. It was as perfect a day as you could imagine—until she left.

"One minute she was there waving to me, telling me to be a good boy, then she climbed into a shiny black sedan and sped away behind dark windows. If I had known it was going to be the last time that I ever saw her, I would have run after her, grabbed ahold of her, and held her back with all my might. But I didn't budge. I waved and went back to what I was doing, just like it was another day."

"You still miss her."

"Wouldn't you?"

~~~~~~~~

The walls were bare and in need of a fresh coat of paint. Ghosts of pictures, diplomas, and an oversized dry-erase board glowed gray and looked like lost pieces of a puzzle waiting to be put back together. A herd of dust bunnies congregated in the corner, demonstrating no fear of being swept away anytime soon. The room smelled like a mouse had died in the wall, rotting away slowly, one whisker at a time. There was none of the sterile institutional aroma most often encountered in a police department headquarters. Funny thing was, the office hadn't been vacant that long.

One fluorescent light buzzed overhead and flickered like an ancient disco strobe. The other tube was burned out. There was no window, no distracting view of the world beyond, which was just fine with Hud Matthews. He wasn't there to daydream.

"It's not much." Paul Burke stood shoulder to shoulder with Hud, staring into the office. There was no evidence of shame or embarrassment on Burke's pockmarked face. Even though they were close enough in age to have been boyhood friends, Burke looked as if he'd walked headlong into a hailstorm all of his adult life, and any effort to grow facial hair of any kind looked to be futile. His face reflected a permanent, angry, expression, whether he intended it or not.

Hud squared his shoulders and straightened his spine so he was as close to equal in height as could be to Burke—nobody called the chief, Paul, not even his wife. "I'm just glad to be here."

Burke looked him in the eye. "It's not too soon?"

Hud dropped his shoulders again. "The wounds are healed; I need to get on with it. How many times do I have to tell you that? The shrink said I was good to go. You got the report."

Burke shrugged, didn't blink, and stood with his arms crossed as though he was waiting for something more. It was a common expression and stance with him, especially in an interrogation. Paul Burke had the consummate skill of being an asshole without ever having to say a word.

"I'm not dead," Hud offered.

"I can see that. All right. I still have my reservations, you know that."

"You've always had your reservations about me."

"I've known you for a long time." Burke paused, looked away from Hud quickly, then back into the dismal office. "I won't coddle you."

"That's why I came to you for a job when it was obvious that Detroit didn't really want me back."

"That's the only reason?"

"Sure, what else is there?"

"Old business." The words echoed inside the office and bounced off the cold damp cement walls right back at Hud.

"I'm just glad to have a job," he said, as he stepped into the office and nodded his head with approval. "This'll be fine, just fine."

~~~~~~~~~

It was the perfect kind of day for someone to find a dead body: gray, overcast, a slight mist hanging in the air. Two county squad cars blocked a narrow lane that led down to the lake. Hud could see the smooth water as soon as he got out of his car—a six-year-old black Crown Vic that, according to the garage mechanic Lonnie Peck, was on its second engine and temperamental as a back pasture mule. Times had changed. It seemed as if the whole department had been recycled and was held together with nothing more than duct tape, duty, and the eroding will to serve and protect.

Hud flashed his badge at the female deputy standing guard just beyond the bumper of a county cruiser. She was blonde, tall for a woman, had the lithe muscular body of a martial artist; obviously the kickboxer that Burke had warned him about on his way out the door. Her face held a scowl like she'd been personally done wrong by Hud, but he didn't know her, didn't recognize her from the past, didn't care what grudge against the world she held. She was at least ten years younger than he was. Their paths would have never crossed in places that mattered.

"So, you're the new one," she said. The other brown-and-tan cruiser was empty. "Another one of Burke's old pals come to save the day. Got lucky. Caught your first case three days in. Some people have to wait a lifetime for that around here."

Hud shrugged and stuffed his badge back in his pocket. The wallet was new, just like the badge. Didn't have a scratch on it. Only time would tell if it would show any wear. He didn't feel lucky. "She down by the lake?"

He was in no mood to explain to the kickboxer that he wasn't really new at all, that he'd worked plainclothes for a long time. Detroit would teach her a thing or two about justice just like it had him. Not that it would matter. Hud knew animosity when he heard it. The deputy was ambitious, had her eyes on detective grade as the ultimate prize. It would have been easier for her to stay in the ring, or dojo, or wherever she trained and fought. A title might have cost her a tooth, but it'd be worth it in the long run, easier on her soul.

The deputy nodded, twisted her lip and bit it, held back, restrained herself for now. "Yeah, half in, half out, a single gunshot to the head. No easy answers that I could see."

Hud exhaled and walked on. He knew he was right about her ambitions. She wouldn't take his advice—*try another department, maybe the city police instead of county*—if he were willing to dole it out. He wasn't. She wouldn't be the first woman to think he was aloof, a sonofabitch. He didn't give a shit what she thought.

The water smelled distantly fishy, but not in a dead rot kind of way. The smell just announced that aquatic life was present and plentiful; he knew it immediately, knew it like a simmering stew on the stove. It was the smell of his childhood summers, the smell of home. He was immediately comfortable and uncomfortable at the same time. He had missed that smell, longed for it deep in his sleepless nights, but now it made him want to puke.

There were no boats on the lake. It was vacant and lonely, smooth as glass. The air was chilly, and most of the vacation people had packed up, shuttered their cottages, and gone back to their real lives after the Labor Day weekend.

The leaves were starting to turn color: fiery red, dangerous orange, fragile yellow. On a sunny day their decay would be a splendor to see: a beautiful impressionist painting, something to hang on the wall and reminisce about, or a line of poetry to write, if one was inclined. Hud wasn't.

He pushed forward, slowly, from the farthest perimeter of the crime scene toward the center of it, toward the victim.

After the initial impression of the path, it was easy to ignore the state of the trees and shrubs on both sides of the lane as Hud searched the ground before him. He was looking for anything out of place. A broken branch, a lost shoe, a fake fingernail torn off in an attempt to flee, things he'd seen before, things that had helped him solve murders in his previous life.

All the while, Hud listened intently: a blue jay chattered in the distance, not alarmed, just enjoying the sound of its own voice; there were no hawks about. Beyond that there was silence. There was no wind to clatter a screen door open or closed, and there seemed to be nothing, at least on his first pass, that stood out on the ground before him. Nothing seemed unusual; nothing out of place caught his eye. He wasn't surprised. It usually took more than one pass to see things clearly, to spot something that held meaning.

Three men were gathered at the water's edge, looking down at the ground as though they were in prayer. The shroud of first responders was always dark and mournful, that moment before mass or some other formal ceremony was set to begin. Conversations on the radio had told him that one of them was the CO, the Conservation Officer, who had found the girl; another was the first deputy on the scene, who had most likely arrived in the cruiser next to the kickboxer's; and the third was the coroner, who had just arrived minutes before Hud. Men accustomed to seeing the worst of what humans could do to each other and to animals but who never got used to it. At least Hud never had.

He stopped fifty yards from the trio and surveyed the lake. If he were being honest, Hud would have confessed that he avoided the water, looking the other way whenever possible. Seeing and smelling it was like being in the presence of an old lover who had betrayed him in a deep and profound way. *You took something from me I can never get back.*

The water was smooth as black ice, drinking in the mist after a thirsty, dry summer. A wedge of Canadian geese suddenly honked with anxious fortitude on the other side of the lake, cutting south in a hurry, ready to leave the lake like the rest of the part-timers, like they were late in their departure.

Abandoned cottages on the opposite shore looked small, and the wedge even smaller, like the stroke of an artist's brush pushed through thin black paint into a perfect V. Hud had forgotten how big the lake was. It covered almost a thousand acres, with fifteen hundred miles of shoreline on its edge.

"Detective Matthews," the CO said, pulling out of the group. He walked toward Hud with confidence, as though he was in charge. They met on the path and stopped to face each other. "They said you were coming. It's just you?" The department was small. Three detectives besides the chief, Burke, eight deputies, and a handful of reserves. The surrounding towns had marshals, some deputies, mostly part-timers. They pitched in, along with the state police, when there was a need.

"Do I need backup?" Hud said. He stuffed his hands into the pockets of his overcoat. He'd left his thin winter gloves behind, hadn't remembered how a day like this could chill you so deep you thought your veins were going to freeze.

"Not that I know of. It's just this is a little disturbing. First murder we've had around here in a few years. Last one was an easy case, the result of a domestic dispute."

"I'm the only one on shift. Department's stretched a little thin," Hud said.

"Aren't we all."

"How do you know this one's not?"

"I'm sorry?"

"Domestic? How do you know this one's not a domestic?"

"I guess I don't." The name badge over the CO's right breast pocket said SHERMAN. It was old but highly polished. The man had a fair amount of gray at the temples, and his uniform was stiff and starched yet faded enough to be comfortable. He'd worn it in regular rotation over years of service, not months. Of the three men, he was the only one without a hat. His hair was glued to his head from the light mist that hung in the air, but he didn't seem to mind the dampness. Hud had to look up to make eye contact with him. "I was surprised when I heard they'd replaced John Peterson when he retired," Sherman said, like he was anxious to change the subject.

"I came cheap."

"I bet you did."

Hud settled his neck so he looked ahead, beyond Sherman to the girl, to the other two men—who had taken their attention off the ground and were watching the conversation between the detective and CO.

"Tell me what you've got," Hud said.

CHAPTER TWO

Demmie Lake had been dug deep by an ancient glacier that had dropped down past the Great Lakes in the long ago Ice Age. Springs had broken free from the fertile ground and run into the permanent gouge left in the earth, filling it with cold, clear water that would prosper and flow for eons to come. Over time, the water had spread and connected the big lake to nearby smaller lakes, creating a navigable chain of waterways that became a perfect getaway for fishermen, boaters, and vacationers in the twentieth century.

The place had really began to boom after World War II. Before then, there'd been a few collections of rental cottages, a hotel or two, and a boardwalk that had popped up a few years before the Great Depression. In the mid-1940s, the soldiers came home from the war and went to work in the factories fifty miles away and beyond. City people and factory workers needed a place to escape. The crystal-clear waters, mournful call of migrating loons, and plentiful panfish drew in hoards of the new middle class seeking to get away from it all, looking for a place to recharge themselves, to escape to. The drudgery of work was distant on the water.

Restaurants sprang up along the revitalized boardwalk. There were ice cream stands, miniature golf courses, merry-go-rounds, go-kart tracks, and a lakefront Ferris wheel that could be seen from miles away on a clear night. It looked like a star had fallen in the water and stayed afire summer after summer.

The lakes were the place to be—until the factories started to close years later, then disappeared altogether, and people in the city couldn't afford to keep two houses. Hard times came after sixty years of affluence. It didn't take long for the wildness to gloat with redemption;

weeds grew fast and tall, cement cracked and left potholes deep enough to test a boat motor in, tax revenues dropped, and the cottages became low-rent housing for desperate folks who had nowhere else to go, who were just trying to hang on. The Ferris wheel was rusting away one rivet at a time.

Someday the cycle would swing back, and a new generation of weary seekers would be able to pick up a post-war cottage on the cheap. But that didn't look to be happening anytime soon. All Hud Matthews saw was neglect, depression, and a whole lot of ruin. It was hard to say that he was happy to be home. It looked nothing like he remembered.

～～～～～

"You were never in that house. You wouldn't know."

"Try me."

"Nothing ever changed. Especially after that day. Gee just stopped living."

"You called your grandmother Gee?"

"Yes. Is that a problem?"

"Just clarifying."

"Gee put a lock on the door to my mother's bedroom, but I knew where she'd hidden the key. I'd go in there sometimes just to see if I could conjure an image of her, hear her voice, smell her perfume. Before I knew it I was thirteen and she'd been gone for five years. But I always kept looking for her to walk in the front door like nothing had ever happened. I could never quit doing that. I could never quit hoping that she would come back."

～～～～～

"The call came in about an hour ago," CO Sherman said. "Lady thought it was a deer that had washed up on the shore overnight."

"She didn't come down to check?" Hud said. The deputy and coroner stood guard over the girl. Neither had offered to join in the conversation.

"Obviously not."

"How often does that happen?"

"A phone call like that?"

"No, a dead deer washing ashore."

Sherman shrugged. "I guess I might've seen it once in thirty years. But there's more deer around here now than there ever was before. I didn't rush right over, but I headed this way once the call came in. I was curious. I found her just like this." He nodded over to the girl.

Hud didn't follow the CO's gaze but watched his every move. Who knew what the truth was? It was a skill he'd acquired a long time ago—maybe even before he knew it was a skill. Don't make any assumptions. Question everything. "You talk to the caller?"

"She didn't leave a name. Dispatch said it was a local call, but the ID was blocked or didn't exist. Probably one of them pay-as-you-go phones that you can buy for a few bucks down at the Walgreens." There was disdain in the CO's voice, a recognizable dislike of technology, of how things had changed. It was a middle-age disease that Hud was uncomfortable with but could feel metastasizing under his own skin. Change came too fast.

Hud looked over his shoulder, away from the CO, down the lake-front for as far as he could see. It was lined with cottages. He knew he'd have to canvas the whole cluster of them before the day was over, might have to employ the kickboxer to help, or call in some of the reserves for backup. If this wasn't cause for that, nothing was. "But it wasn't a deer?" he finally said.

"Nope," Sherman said. He shook his head and looked at the ground. "A girl, mid-twenties, a single gunshot to the back of the head."

"Execution style?"

"Could be I suppose. I didn't think about that."

"Let's go take a look."

The CO led him to the girl. Hud had nothing to say to the two men who stood in wait. His eyes were to the ground, looking, searching, for anything out of place. He stood above her for a long five minutes, just listening to the wind skim across the lake, the three men breathing, road noise in the distance, behind him. He finally leaned down and shined a pen-sized flashlight into the girl's brown eyes, then looked up at the coroner. "How long you figure she's been dead?"

"Hard to be exact, but she's stiff as a board. Between twelve and twenty-four hours. I don't think she was in the water long, though."

"Why's that?"

"Turtles hadn't got to her yet."

The coroner, Bill Flowers, was old enough to be Hud's father. Flowers's family had owned a couple of funeral homes in the county for as long as anybody could remember. He was a tall, thin man, rickety with arthritis, and he had the coldest hands Hud had ever encountered.

Flowers also held the biggest and best Fourth of July party on the lake. Fireworks, a hog roast—a big pig cooked in the ground, luau-style—music that played deep into the night and floated across the dark, smooth lake. There were more beautiful women at those parties, tanned from worshiping the summer sun, than you could shake a stick at. Hud had never been invited to any of the Flowerses' parties but his mother had. Of course his mother had. He'd only listened to the music alone in a boat, smelled the food as it wafted on the breeze toward him, and dreamed about all of the pretty girls, especially Goldie, the coroner's only daughter, the princess of the lake. He'd had the biggest crush on Goldie, but she acted like he didn't exist, even when Hud tried to talk to her at school. She became his fantasy girl. The thing he couldn't have. The face he saw in the middle of his hard, lonely teenage nights. All he'd ever wanted was a chance to show her what he could do, how he could make her feel.

"So you think she was dumped here?" Hud said.

The deputy, Bob Varner, stood back out of the way with a glare on his face. He was a stranger to Hud and hadn't said two words to him after their initial greeting. More animosity. The air was thick with it.

"Hard to say," Flowers said. Tiny pebbles of moisture had collected on the coroner's black lapel like they belonged there. "They could've dropped her right here with a high-powered rifle. Doesn't look like a point blank shot to me, but again it's going to be hard to say for certain until I get her in and conduct the autopsy. Strange things turn up that we can't see right away once we're under some lights and can pull back the skin. I don't see any obvious powder burns, residue that would be left behind from a close shot."

Hud stood up. He restrained himself from showing any sign of agreement, though he knew the man's words to be true. The coroner's speculation about the rifle didn't sit well with him. The girl had on jogging shorts, a T-shirt, and no shoes. She wasn't dressed to be outside on a day like this. He thought she'd been dumped there, even though there was no sign on the ground that suggested such a thing. "You get the pictures we need?" he asked the coroner.

Flowers nodded.

"Good. Let's get her covered up." Hud stared at Bill Flowers, waited for the man to get on with it.

Instead, Flowers just stood there and stared back at him petulantly, like a stubborn child refusing for the pleasure of it. "I was sorry to hear about your grandmother. Are you staying at the house?"

"No," Hud said. "I've got a room at the hotel."

"That place is going to fall down on itself one of these days."

Hud nodded, turned away from the girl, and headed back up the path, the way he'd come down. His grandmother had requested to be cremated at an unknown and untested funeral home two counties over. She'd never had any use for Bill Flowers or his kind.

CHAPTER THREE

By the time the ambulance arrived, a small crowd had started to gather against the yellow police tape. They were mostly older, retired full-timers, lips closed tight, hiding their stained and crooked Social Security teeth, more scared than curious. It was a weekday. Any kids or teenagers who lived nearby would still be in school—or should have been. Two overweight EMTs struggled to get a gurney down the path to the lake. They looked angry, as if they'd been pulled away from a video game against their will. Hud watched them disappear, then started toward his car for a fresh notepad. The crowd would be easier to canvas than knocking on the doors of vacant cottages.

"Who's in charge here?" It was a woman's voice.

Hud stopped just in time to hear the kickboxer say that he was. Without any hesitation at all, the woman, hair as gray as the sky, eyes as black as the lake at night, pushed the tape out of the way and headed straight for him.

"Hey, you can't do that!" the kickboxer yelled.

The woman paid her no mind, and Hud didn't either. "What's the matter?" he said, reading the panic on the woman's face.

"The boy, he's missing." She stopped inches from Hud. She was wearing a morning housecoat and smelled of cigarettes and canned tuna. Her feet were bare, save the faded blue slippers that looked thin as a newspaper and old as the scratched up wedding ring on her finger.

"What boy?" Hud asked.

"Hers." The woman nodded toward the lake.

"How do you know that?" Everything around Hud had ceased to exist. He was in a vacuum, focused entirely on the woman and what she had to say, on what she had to show him.

"Has to be her, the way she lives. Men in and out at all hours of the night and day. Not too many others around here these days anyways." The woman stepped forward, craned her neck upward to inspect Hud a little more closely. She was a little bug-eyed. "You're that Matthews boy, ain't you?"

Hud's instinct was to step back, react to the invasion of his personal space, but he held fast and nodded. "I am. What's your name?" The muscles in his face were as hard and petrous as the ground he stood on.

The woman eyed him suspiciously. "Danvers. Harriet Danvers. I knew your grandmother. And your mother, too. Such a shame about Georgia Mae. Sorry about them both. That why you came back?"

Hud steeled himself. He had known he was going to have to face an inquiry sooner or later. More than once. This was just the start. "The boy, ma'am. What about the boy?"

"They never found her? Your mother? They never found any sign of her, did they?" the woman continued, ignoring Hud's question. Her eyes were glazed over, her mind in the past, her trembling right hand in the present.

No, you crazy old bitch, they never found her. Not one fingernail, nothing. Is that what you wanted to hear? Luckily the words stayed where they belonged: under his tongue, in the pit of his soul. He'd had plenty of practice at keeping his mouth shut.

Hud shook his head slightly, then looked up at a rattling ruckus that was heading his way. The EMTs were having a harder time coming back up the path than they had going down. "Can you identify the girl? Can you tell me who she is, where she lived? It'll help us find the boy, if he's really missing."

"Things have a way of disappearing around here, in that lake. It's deeper than people think it is," the woman said. "Divers went down into it 'bout thirty years ago, said there was catfish as big as men. Monsters. Maybe one of 'em crawled out and did this ugly deed. Wouldn't surprise me none at all. No sir, it wouldn't surprise me none at all to have monsters walking among us." She stepped back and followed Hud's gaze to the closed black body bag on the stretcher. "I'll see her if she's not too bad to look at. I know it's that Pam girl. I'd be surprised if it wasn't."

"She's just dead, not very much blood," Hud said.

"All right. I've seen that before. I've seen dead before," Harriett Danvers said.

<center>~~~~~~~</center>

The kickboxer's name was Joanne Moran. She said Hud could call her Jo, but he wasn't interested in being on a first-name basis with her. He needed backup. That's all. Nothing more. Deputy Moran it was.

He followed Harriet Danvers to the trailer where she said the girl had been staying with her eight-year-old son. It was old, probably manufactured in the late 1950s or early 1960s, ten feet wide and about fifty feet long, the color of a dead oak leaf: dull rusty brown and just as fragile. Black rain streaks reached down from the roof in thin, gnarled fingers. Holes in the screens were big enough for a bat to fly through. Two fifty-five gallon drums sat at the rear door and overflowed with trash that had yet to be burned. If it hadn't been for the rainy mist, the flies would've been feasting on week-old chicken bones and getting drunk on the fermented sugar left behind in the empty soda bottles.

Hud had instructed Harriet Danvers to give the other deputy a description of the boy and to stay away from the trailer. Surprisingly, she'd given in, stood back like a submissive dog, and done what she had been told to do.

He stopped next to the screen door of the trailer, raised his .45 to the ready, and listened for anything out of the ordinary. He preferred the .45 to the Glock 9mm Burke had wanted to issue him. Hud liked the reliability of the Colt, the history of the government-issue 1911 design. He didn't trust plastic.

"You don't even know that *that* woman was telling you the truth," Deputy Moran said in a low whisper. Her tan windbreaker was soaked with a thin layer of mist. It didn't seem to bother her. She held a black

Glock, hadn't had the choice he'd had. Hud wondered if she was any good with it. He hoped her ambitions were true.

Hud shook his head, dropped his voice to meet hers. "Doesn't matter. If she lied about a child in peril, there are consequences for that. You want to take the time to check out everything she said first?"

"The boy can't be far if he ran out on his own."

"You don't know much about eight-year-old little boys do you?"

"No, I don't."

Silence returned between them with a chill and a glare. Hud regretted his words as soon as he said them. Animosity had been replaced with a distant but raw hurt. He looked away from Moran and caught a whiff of something familiar, a mix of chemicals that couldn't be mistaken once they'd been smelled. "Somebody's been cooking meth."

The deputy shrugged. "No surprise there. It's an epidemic here."

"It's an epidemic everywhere." Without any further hesitation, Hud pushed inside the trailer with as much muscle as he could, leading with the barrel of his gun. "Police! Everybody down!"

Moran pushed by him, leveling the Glock, sweeping the small front room as she went. It was empty save the trash on the floor. There were no living beings to be seen. No roaches, no mice; nothing.

The trailer rocked under their feet, unstable, out of balance, not leveled. A burning sensation immediately assaulted Hud's eyes and throat, but he hustled to the back of the trailer, yelling and kicking open what few doors there were as he went. Moran checked closets and under beds.

Five minutes felt like a lifetime trapped inside a toxic cloud, but that was all the time Hud could take. His lungs felt like they'd been soaked in drain cleaner, and he feared if he stayed inside the trailer another minute his skin would start to peel off. Moran followed him out the door.

They both crumpled to their knees coughing, choking, gasping for air like unlucky fish yanked out of water. Their state drew Deputy Varner to them. "You all right?" He spoke directly to Moran, ignored Hud completely.

She nodded and coughed. "It's empty."

Hud got his breath, stood up, and tried to get his bearings. He looked beyond the trailer, tried to remember what lay beyond it, even though he didn't want to. "The Dip still up the road?"

"No one's there," Varner said. "It's been closed for a few years."

~~~~~~~~

"What about your father?"

"What about him?"

"Where was he?"

"Dead. He died before I was born. All I had were pictures and a story of a perfect whirlwind romance. You could see it, even in black and white. She loved him and he loved her."

"How did he die?"

"A car wreck. She was with him; carried a scar on her ankle and up the back of her calf for the rest of her life. It was all she had left of him. The car burned up. She was lucky to be alive. She told me that a million times."

"And you believed her?"

"Why wouldn't I?"

CHAPTER FOUR

The Dip was one of those places that had popped up after World War II, almost instantly becoming an institution. The onslaught of vacationers had made it a viable enterprise for fifty years, selling soft-serve ice cream cones and penny candy to kids, and cigarettes and bags of ice to their parents. It was a destination not to be missed on any visit to the lakes, but now it stood, unsurprisingly, in disrepair. The roof had buckled inward, waiting for the next heavy snowstorm to come along and cave it in the rest of the way. Orange and white paint, in alternating stripes, was faded, peeling off the cement-block building in flecks and bits. It looked like a million miniature leaves had fallen from the roof to the surrounding ground. Hud was surprised the place was still standing.

He and Moran had walked up to the Dip from the meth trailer, navigating the road slowly, cautiously, eyes peeled, just like on the path to the lake, for a sign of certain evil or something out of place. He wasn't sure if he was heading in the right direction or not, but if he were an eight-year-old boy, he would head for the allure of ice cream, or at least the promise of it, maybe find a place to hide in the old lion's cage. A kid would know about the place. Hud was sure of it.

The road was bordered by a popcorn field on one side. It was flat and harvested; only stubble remained, poking out of the brown ground like the remnants of a giant's beard. The other side of the road was nothing but of collection of driveways that led back to cottages and ultimately to the lake. Most were marked Private. Hud stopped and examined every piece of litter along the way.

"I thought you were in a hurry," Moran said, halfway there.

Hud let her words drift away into the mist unanswered. He was concerned about the boy, but he was in no hurry to revisit the Dip, no matter the reason.

The road sloped down into a deep ravine, dropped off like the first hill of a roller coaster, flattened out briefly, then climbed back up the other side so the ground was even with the initial drop off.

The little ice-cream shop sat at the bottom of the ravine, squarely in the middle of the dip in the road. It was a clever name with the placement of the business, especially since it was located on the main road that skirted the lake, guaranteeing a steady flow of traffic at the height of the tourist season. But it was what was behind the cement block building that had caused most of the vacationers to really stop to visit. For an extra quarter, vacationers could visit a small zoo that stood behind the building. Only it hadn't actually been a real zoo, just a haphazard collection of freestanding cages holding an old male lion, a female tiger, and three ostriches. Ducks, Guinea hens, and peacocks roamed the grounds untethered. Old gumball machines dispensed dry dog food, a nickel a handful, to feed the tame fowl. Starlings and a variety of sparrows hung around for a free meal. They'd made a nice living. So had the hawks.

The thought of the ostriches made Hud smile. They had escaped once, wreaked havoc on the nearby cottages, eating geraniums, pecking at anyone who approached them, then chasing the pampered little barking dogs. The birds had finally been rounded up by a couple of horsemen who looked as if they had ridden straight out of a cowboy movie. Everyone had feared the lion would get out sooner or later, and it wasn't long after the great ostrich escape that the little zoo had been closed down. The price of an ice-cream cone doubled overnight.

Hud stopped as the road began to slope down. Moran eased up next to him. "My dad used to bring us here. How about yours?"

He shook his head. "I used to live over there." He pointed to the first house on the other side of the ravine. It was empty, too; in a little better shape than the Dip, but not much.

"At the Emporium?" Moran said.

Hud had never called it the Emporium. None of the locals did. It was just "the shop"; always had been, always would be, the way he saw it. "It was my grandfather's place. My grandmother, Gee, kept it going after he died."

"I think I still have a T-shirt I bought there."

"We sold a lot of things over the years. Souvenirs, T-shirts, blow-up floaties for the kids. That was one of my jobs. Blow up the inflatable ducks, sea serpents, giant fish, then hang them out on the line to draw attention. That junk fed us for a lot of years."

"Must have been cool to live next to the Dip."

"Sometimes in the middle of the night, I think I can still hear the lion roar," Hud said, then plodded down to the abandoned building.

~~~~~~~

"Tell me about her."

"My mother?"

"Yes, your mother. You rarely talked about your time with her."

"I was eight when she disappeared. It was a long time ago. She's nothing more than a ghost in my memory now."

"Describe her in one word."

"Beautiful."

~~~~~~~

The mist had turned to rain, and an angry wind whistled down from the north with a ferocity usually reserved for the winter months. A gray soup surrounded Hud and Moran as they eased up to the Dip. The sign, a large ice-cream cone bordered in neon, looked like food for some kind of invisible rust-eating insect. It swung wildly and threatened to fall to the ground with a direct burst of the cold air.

"Come on," Hud said to Moran, as he holstered his .45 and took out the little flashlight he carried. The sudden beam cut through the dim light about as well as a butter knife cut through a tough steak, but it was enough to see a few feet ahead of them.

The smell of ancient feces, of the presence of animals, immediately assaulted Hud's nose as he pushed into the first cage. No amount of moisture could tamp down the smell of death.

Moran stopped at the door. "Was this the lion's cage?"

Hud shook his head. "Ostriches. The lion's cage is the farthest one back. Or it was. There was a den made of chunks of limestone, but I wanted to check here first." His voice was low, and he flashed the light on a collection of old tires, crates, and barrels that looked like they had been sitting there since the place had been first built. He pulled back when he was certain that the boy was not there.

"I think this is a wild goose chase," Moran said.

"You have any better ideas?"

Rain dripped down her stoic face. "Wait for a positive ID. You're trusting an old woman who might not know what she's talking about."

"That could take a little while. She was certain it was the girl."

Moran shrugged. Hud pushed by her and headed toward the vacant lion's cage. He stopped about ten feet from it, froze as if he had just walked into an invisible wall, and couldn't go another step farther.

"What's the matter?" Moran stopped next to him, her Glock aimed straight at the cage.

He looked over at the young deputy, whose face was soaked with rain. "I was sure that my mother was here after she disappeared, that Fred Myerson had cut her up and fed her to the lion after he was done with her."

"Why would you think that?"

"Because he always looked at her like she was an ice-cream cone. All of the men did."

"She was a looker?"

"She was."

"But she wasn't here? It wasn't true?"

"I don't know; it could be true. We never found a trace of her. My grandmother thought she ran off and started a new life. Simple as that. Just up and left us one day. It was easier for her to think that. Rejection of the brutal terror that I dreamed of, saw everywhere around me. It wasn't hard for her to believe that my mother would do that, that she was irresponsible. It was easier than believing she was dead."

"How old were you?"

"Eight. I was eight." The rain drenched his face. His skull felt wet, soaked, like it would collapse any second.

"But you never believed that she ran off, that she just left you?"

"Would you?"

Moran didn't say anything, just stared at Hud, her face hard to read. He wasn't sure if he saw compassion or disbelief. Either way, it didn't matter. "I could always feel her here," he said. "It was the last place we had a good time; we shared an ice-cream cone, laughed about the ostriches together."

"And that's why you left? Went to Detroit?"

Hud walked through the invisible wall, to the back of the property. The cage was overgrown with briars and a thicket of wild raspberry. "You're good at questions, Moran, there's no doubt about that," he said, looking for a way inside the lion's cage.

$$\sim\!\sim\!\sim\!\sim\!\sim$$

Hud's trained vision paid off. A few low branches of the bramble were freshly broken, their inner flesh white and pure—the snapped ends of the plants glowed like distant Christmas lights. When he looked closer, Hud saw a worn pathway leading into the cage, one that might have been traversed over and over again by a troop of raccoons or opossums. Or it could have been a boy. A scared little boy.

"I'm going in," Hud said.

Moran nodded. "I'll keep an eye out."

In a matter of seconds, Hud was inside a tunnel, crawling to the one place he could never go as a boy, could never check for himself to satisfy his constant need to know the truth of what had happened to his mother. "Hello," he called out. "Are you in here? Don't be afraid. I'm here to help you." He stopped and listened.

A siren wailed in the distance, the wind pushed into every crook and crevice it could find, howling as it went, but under those sounds Hud was certain he heard footsteps scooting away from him.

He shined the light deep into the manmade lion's den, suddenly afraid that he might come face-to-face with the beast—or find a pile of human bones. The light reflected off a pair of eyes, but they were not the eyes of an animal. They belonged to a frightened little boy. The boy was trapped, running back and forth in the depth of the cage, looking for a way to escape the man coming after him.

"I won't hurt you, I promise," Hud said, as he eased toward the boy.

The child screamed like he had been slapped, then stopped and looked directly into the light. The boy's head looked odd, bigger than it should have been, and it took Hud a long second to figure out what he was seeing. It was a man's hat, green and worn, with a state emblem embroidered on it. Just like a CO would wear.

Hud had called out to Moran to radio the crime scene to keep Sherman from leaving. The call had come too late. Somehow, the CO had managed to slip away unnoticed.

<center>~~~~~~~~~</center>

The office was cold, but Hud didn't mind. The walls were still bare, and the dust bunnies were safe in their places. The smell was gone, though. Maintenance had found a dead mouse in the ductwork and sprayed some kind of pine scent to kill the odor. It was a pleasant smell, and it reminded Hud of the stuff his grandmother used to mop the floors with.

"Good job," Burke said, standing in the doorway.

"We don't know anything yet," Hud said from his desk.

"You have a suspect and an ID for the girl."

"It's not a positive ID."

"It will be, and you know it."

Hud shrugged. "Next of kin still needs to get a look at her. The grandmother's coming up from Texas." Burke started to say something, but Hud cut him off before he could utter a syllable. "I'm not taking the kid to the morgue, so don't even suggest it."

"You want a positive ID?"

"I want to be able to live with myself," Hud said.

"Your call."

"I appreciate it."

"That could've turned out a lot different." Burke tapped the door frame with his fingers. "How'd you know to look for the kid at the Dip?"

Hud sighed. "It's where I'd go every time I got a chance. My mom would stand on the front porch and say, 'Don't go any farther than where I can see you,' but I always did. I'd sneak down there every chance I got. You know that; you were usually leading the way or hanging around when I got there."

"You going back there? It'd be good to have you as a neighbor again." They had teased the lion together as boys. Burke had grown up in the cottage across the street from his grandmother's souvenir shop.

"To the house? No, I don't think so. I'll clean it up, sell it. Too much work needs done, too many memories to paint over. It needs new memories, and so do I."

"I'm glad you came back."

"Thanks." Hud was surprised by the genuineness of Burke's declaration.

"You're not so sure, are you?"

Hud shrugged, then turned back to his computer, away from Burke. "Moran's got good instincts," he said. "You should consider her for a shield the next time a spot comes up."

"You need a partner?"

"Not really. But backup's nice to have on a rainy day."

"If you say so."

"I do."

"I'll call you when the search warrant for Sherman's house comes in," Burke said. "I've got eyes on the house. So far, it's quiet. No sign of him. His wife's a little upset."

"I imagine she is."

"All right. Good job. We'll catch this creep. It's just a matter of time." Burke walked away, his footsteps echoing down the hall at a steady pace.

Hud looked around to make sure the chief was gone, that he was alone, then turned back to the flickering computer screen and clicked on the file that held all of the available information about his mother's disappearance. A dialog box immediately popped up: Access Denied.

CHAPTER FIVE

The Demmie Lake Hotel sat inches from the shore and threatened to crumble into the shallow water if someone didn't prop it up soon. It was a simple three-story wood-frame building that had been built in the early 1920s. Like most of the area hotels and road-houses from that time, the Demmie had the unseemly history of having been a speakeasy during Prohibition. Everyone said Al Capone had slept and gambled there, but there was no actual proof of that. Just like there had been no proof that John Dillinger had ever robbed the local bank after his escape from the Crown Point jail. Those old rumors and stories appealed to the tourists and curiosity seekers, so there had never been any reason for the long string of owners of the Demmie or the local historians to deny the tales. Anything for a buck, anything to help bring in business and survive the season, whether it was true or not. Hud knew the huckster game. He'd lived the feast-and-famine roller coaster of the tourist season all of his early life. He was surprised someone hadn't spotted a monster in the lake by now.

There were twelve rooms to let in the creaky old hotel. Most all of them were on the second floor, with the office, restaurant, and bar below, and an open ballroom on the third floor, which was mostly used for storage these days. The restaurant was more of a small diner than a proper sit-down eatery, and it didn't look like the plastic red-and-white checkered tablecloths, or anything else for that matter, had changed since Hud had been there as a boy. He'd liked the pancakes then. His grandmother always burnt them at home.

The diner opened before sunrise to appeal to eager fishermen, and closed just after lunch, bypassing the lag of business once the heat of the day took over and drove those same fishermen back to their rental cottages for an afternoon nap. Dinner was served at Johnny Long's Supper Club next door, another lakeside institution that had somehow weathered the years and the recent economic downturn. These days, onion rings, lake-perch sandwiches, and big-as-your-head tenderloins could be ordered from the grill in the hotel bar anytime—up until an hour before closing, which was three a.m. sharp. The bar drew a different, less formal crowd than the Supper Club. Most nights, the thump of the jukebox, and the smell of grease, lulled Hud to sleep in his room at the hotel.

A set of unstable steps led up to the individual rooms on the outside of the hotel, accessible by a narrow wood plank walkway that skirted three sides of the Demmie. Views of the lake were available from every room except the ones that faced the front of the building—those were the cheap ones, accessible only by a narrow staircase on the first floor.

The walkway looked like it had been there since the Al Capone days. Hud tried not to consider how shaky the planks were underneath his feet. He was just glad to be home. If it could be called that. His room was small, held a queen-size bed, a nicked up dresser with an old TV on it, and a bathroom a little bigger than the clothes closet. He could barely turn around in the standup shower, and the plumbing looked and acted as if it was original. Hot water was hard to come by at certain times of the day.

Rent for the room was paid week-to-week, and sporadic, unpredictable maid service came with the deal, along with a just-as-sporadic Wi-Fi Internet connection. The room on the second floor of the Demmie was all he'd needed, at least until he figured out what he was going to do with his grandmother's house.

Night had fallen, and the room was dark. Out of habit, Hud stopped and flipped on the overhead light before stepping fully inside. He'd walked confidently into a dark room once, relying on his memory, on his instincts, and had come face-to-face with someone looking to settle a score. A young Detroit thug hadn't taken kindly to being arrested for selling heroin, and he'd tracked Hud down after bailing out, intent on exacting revenge. Hud had collected a broken nose and a greater understanding of caution and paybacks out of that encounter; he'd been young, cocky, new to the badge. That injury was a far cry from the bullet wounds he carried now. The scars were still pink and itchy, a reminder that his mortality and his past mistakes were never far away.

The room looked just like he'd left it. The bed was rumpled and unmade, the top dresser drawer stood open, and his bath towel lay on the floor outside the bathroom door where he'd dropped it. He'd been running late for work, and the last thing Hud had been concerned with was tidying up after himself. Burke had no tolerance for tardiness—he found it disrespectful. Hud understood that and didn't want to draw the chief's wrath any sooner than necessary. He really wanted to remain on his new-hire honeymoon for as long as possible, but being on time had always been a problem for him, so it was just a matter of time before the shit hit the fan.

Hud could have chided himself for being overly cautious. This wasn't Detroit and no one held a grudge against him or had a reason to come after him, at least that he knew of, but old habits were hard to break. Just because this was his boyhood home didn't mean he knew where he was at.

~~~~~~~

"Gee wore flowery housedresses most of the time. She was a big woman. My height plus a hundred pounds. There was usually a cigarette dangling out of her mouth, and she had this hard, raspy Lauren Bacall voice that could stop a rabid dog in its tracks. But that's how I want to remember her. The pictures of her when she was young were different. My mother got her looks from Gee. As a girl, Gee was statuesque, could've been a movie star if she'd taken off for California instead of marrying my grandfather. But after bearing five kids—only three lived—life kind of took over. Changed her. She didn't take shit from anybody. But that was pretty obvious."

"It was just you two after your mother . . . ?"

". . . Disappeared."

"Okay, disappeared."

"Yes, it was just us. If there was a man in her life, I didn't know about it. I wouldn't have noticed anyway. I was lost in my own confusion, grief, and little-boy rage. She focused on me, wanted me to turn out all right. I was Gee's soft spot."

"Are you still lost?"

"I'm sitting here, aren't I?"

~~~~~~~~~~

The bar was nearly empty. Two people, one woman and one man, sat at a table in the corner, just beyond the pool table, huddled over their drinks, keeping to themselves. Neither of them looked immediately familiar, though it would have been hard to tell from where Hud stood. The corner was full of thick shadows, and he wasn't interested in another encounter like he'd had with Harriet Danvers.

A low and mournful George Jones ballad played from a radio behind the bar. The jukebox opposite it stood silently waiting, like everything else, for the next tourist season to begin. The music machine, a Wurlitzer still loaded with old 45 rpm records, flashed all of its red, blue, and yellow lights relentlessly, beckoning anyone with a quarter, but there were no takers. The pair in the corner obviously liked the happy hour beer and free music.

The smell of grease was distant from lack of use, further announcing the slowness of the off-season. Clyde Evans looked up from behind the bar when Hud walked in. Clyde was the bartender, chief bottle-washer, grill cook, and the only server, at least through the week and sometimes on the weekends, especially in the depth of January and all the way through to Memorial Day. Then there were at least three girls working the floor.

Everybody called Clyde "Tilt" because he was as tall and lithe as a willow tree, and he'd been a world-class slalom waterski champion in the 1960s. Tilt could lean to within an inch of the water and skim it with his elbow, shooting a rooster tail of water fifteen feet to the side like it was child's play. Rows of dusty trophies sat on a shelf behind the bar, along with a collection of black-and-white pictures of Tilt's glory days: speedboats, bathing beauties, and a hale and hearty young man ready to take on the world. Out of habit, Hud scanned the photographs for a glimpse of his mother. He didn't see her, but in the dim light it would be difficult to pick her out at that distance.

Tilt had been bartender at the Demmie Grill for nearly as long as anyone could remember—his championship days were long past him, but he still got out on a ski every chance he could, which had served him well. He was tanned and fit, though his skin was leathery from the long days under the sun, and his pure white hair and mustache always shone as if a spotlight was aimed directly on them. A faded blue tattoo on his right forearm hinted at his navy service during the Vietnam War, but that period of his life was never spoken about. Tilt demurred if someone brought it up. But the thing that most intrigued Hud about Tilt was the steel trap he had for a mind. Tilt Evans never forgot a face or a name, was a strong opponent on any trivia game, and was as reliable a person at remembering important dates and obscure events around the lake as could be found. Bartenders like Tilt came in handy, and Hud had made it his business to ingratiate himself with Tilt as quickly as he could.

Hud sat down at the end of the bar and looked up at the blank TV that sat opposite the trophy shelf. A big mirror sat in between the two shelves, giving Hud full view of the door, of anyone coming in or going out. He was glad the TV was off.

"I figured you'd be in sooner or later," Tilt said, wiping the top of the bar in front of Hud with a clean white towel. Tilt wore a blue-striped Oxford shirt, with the long sleeves rolled halfway up his forearms, khaki shorts, even though it was October, and a pair of well-worn L.L. Bean boat shoes. "It's been all over the news all day."

"I suppose it has."

"Murder's big news around here."

"Bad for business, I suppose."

"Would be in the high season. If there's any luck in this at all, it's October not July."

"I suppose so." Hud reached for his pocket, then stopped halfway. The Demmie was a no-smoking bar. State law said you had to stand eight feet from the outside entrance of a place where food was served to smoke a cigarette legally. It was a silly law, as far as Hud was concerned, but it was the world he lived in. He sighed and let the thought of smoking a cigarette fall away for the moment. When he looked up, he caught a knowing look from Tilt. "I guess I'll need to quit one of these days," he said.

"They'll just come after something else." Tilt kept on wiping the bar, eyeing Hud as if he was still in the process of sizing up his mood, how the day had affected him.

"You're right about that." A smile flickered across Hud's face, then disappeared. He used to go buy cigarettes down at the Dip for his mother when he was a kid. That couldn't happen now. A lot of things couldn't happen now.

Almost as if by magic, a tumbler with two fingers of Wild Turkey appeared in front of him. Tilt was a quick study, but Hud made it easy. He only ordered one drink, never strayed from the Turkey.

"Thanks," Hud said. "But I better have a cup of coffee if you have any brewing. My day's not over."

"Oh?" Tilt answered curiously, waiting for a second longer than he normally would.

Hud offered no explanation. He offered Tilt the best glacier stare that he could muster.

"All right, then" Tilt said, moving away toward the coffeemaker.

Movement caught Hud's eye, drew his attention away from Tilt, to the mirror. He watched a blonde woman stand up from the table in the corner and look his way, then followed her every step as she made her way to the restroom. Even though he hadn't seen her in twenty years, there was no mistaking who she was. Goldie Flowers. The princess of the lake, daughter of the coroner, heir to one of the wealthiest families in the county. At least she had been once upon a time. Maybe that had changed, too. Hud didn't know. He hadn't kept up. He regretted waving off the Wild Turkey.

The Jones ballad ended and the music was replaced by a string of commercials, with a promise of the news to come. Tilt traded the whiskey for coffee, but Hud didn't notice. Goldie had exited the lady's room and was walking directly toward him, ignoring her friend in the corner.

"I thought that was you, Hud Matthews," she said, coming to a stop a foot from Hud. Her jasmine perfume and red lipstick had both been freshened up, but there was no erasing the years that had accumulated on her face since he'd last seen her. Even in the dim light, Goldie's attempt to hide her crow's feet with the best dime-store makeup she could find had failed. The wrinkles were ditches full of flesh-colored mud; her skin still held onto her summer tan, making the flaws more distant but still noticeable. Her once-luminous blonde hair was cut short, highlighted to cover the dawning gray, and her eyes looked clouded, not bright and hopeful like they once had. Her body had held up well, though that could have been an illusion too. All of her curves were still in the right places, even with a thin sweater and a skirt that came to her mid-thigh. Her shapely legs looked to go on forever, and Hud resisted the urge to remember her in a bikini, worshiping the sun. Her sweater was a V neck, and Hud's eyes lingered on the sight of her healthy cleavage a second longer than he should have. She was less than perfect now, which made her as beautiful as she ever had been, if not more.

"Good to see you, Goldie." Hud glanced down briefly, saw the fresh white band on her tanned ring finger where a wedding ring had recently rested. Some histories were easy to read.

"This is last place I expected to see you today," she said softly, staring into Hud's eyes.

"Just taking a break." Hud broke her gaze, looked past her to the man at the table. He was watching them intently. Hud wasn't interested in the man. Thankfully, he didn't look familiar. He hoped he wouldn't be a problem.

Goldie continued to ignore her friend. "I was just going to step outside for a breath of fresh air and a cigarette. Care to join me?"

"What about your friend?"

"Who said he was my friend?"

A smile flickered across Hud's face. He couldn't have fought it off he'd wanted to. "I was just thinking I could use a smoke." He got up, letting her lead, and left the steaming cup of coffee behind him. He'd settle his tab with Tilt later.

CHAPTER SIX

The air was cool, but not too cold to be outside, and the rain had weakened into a thin, familiar mist. Goldie disappeared into the darkness, around the corner from the entrance of the bar, leaving only a hint of jasmine in her wake.

The parking lot to Johnny Long's Supper Club stood empty, but all of the lights were still on, flashing aimlessly, like the old Wurlitzer inside the bar, to an uninterested and preoccupied world. A slight wind pushed off the lake, rustling the oak leaves in the trees, the ones that hung on through the winter, stubborn about their release, the timing of their fall. The rest of the trees had already shed their bounty. The ground was covered with red maple, yellow birch, and brown sycamore leaves as big as a pie tin. Wet leaves made the ground slippery as ice; Hud nearly lost his balance in pursuit of Goldie, then righted himself and took more deliberate, cautious steps.

A flash of light illuminated Goldie's face as she brought a flame to the cigarette perched between her lips. She was pressed against the clapboard wall of the hotel. Waves lapped up to the rock seawall five feet away. "How long's it been since you left?" she asked after distinguishing the flame and exhaling smoke.

"Twenty years, give or take." Hud leaned against the wall so he was shoulder to shoulder with Goldie. He had lost his urge for a cigarette. The smell of hers was enough. All he'd ever wanted was to be alone with her. He was surprised she knew who he was. "I couldn't wait to get away from this place."

"And now you're back," she said, with a half-smile in her voice.

Neither of them looked at the other, just stared out into the blackness of the moonless night. The water and the sky had joined; it was hard to see where one left off and the other began. The only light came from the hot end of Goldie's cigarette and the flashing signs in the background. The neon buzz accompanied Vacancy as it reflected in the water to the left of Hud.

"I said I'd never come back," Hud said. And it was true. He'd said it over and over again as a kid.

"And then Gee up and died. Never say never, right?"

A wave of discomfort washed over Hud. "I'm sorry. I mean about her arrangements. It was what she asked for."

"I have no interest in the family business. Too depressing. Makes no difference to me that you used another funeral home. Daddy might care, but not me." Her eyes narrowed, and she drew on the cigarette tightly, inhaled the smoke as deep as it would go.

"I didn't know."

"I'm sure you didn't." She exhaled a thin stream of smoke from her nostrils. Her words vanished as soon as they appeared. Goldie turned and looked at Hud, then flipped the cigarette as high as she could toward the lake. The tiny hot orange orb looked like a falling star, diving from the sky, offering a brief moment of light, of hope.

Hud looked away, followed the streaming flight path, and blinked just before it hit the water in a sizzle. He saw the outline of the decaying Ferris wheel across the lake and felt remorse for not seeing its demise. When he turned back to Goldie, she was inches from his face. She smelled of smoke and expensive perfume and something else—something unexpected—she smelled of need and want.

The day had been long and trying. He wasn't immune to seeing a dead body, a young woman shot in the back of the head. The death affected him, like they all had, but he hadn't faced it. He'd tried not to. Until now.

He leaned in and kissed Goldie Flowers long and hard, pressed her up against the wall. He wanted to feel young again, alive in a way he hadn't felt in a long time. To his growing pleasure, she didn't object, responded to his kiss in kind. It was a moment he'd dreamed of a million times as a thirteen-year-old boy, fantasized about, ached for at every sight of her. He explored her body with his hands, unstopped, just like he had with his eyes as she'd made her way from the table to the restroom. His right hand careened downward to the hem of her skirt and beneath, not hesitating, expecting the touch of silk, but came into direct contact with warm, welcoming flesh. She wore no panties. Goldie gasped at his touch, nibbled his ear, encouraged him to go farther, all the while pulling his zipper down, releasing his hard, pent-up desire almost immediately. There was no turning back. Just as he entered her, his cell phone rang.

"Don't stop," Goldie begged. "Jesus, don't stop."

It was a special ring. It was Burke's ring. The theme song to the old TV show *Dragnet*. The search warrant for Sherman's house must be in. Hud stopped but couldn't bring himself to pull away from Goldie, to give up, leave her. He was panting, his heart was racing, all the while he considered the consequences of not answering his phone, ignoring his new boss. "I have to."

Goldie grabbed each of his ass cheeks and pulled him closer to her, deeper into her. "You have to finish this."

Hud could barely restrain himself. He gasped as Goldie wrapped herself around him as tightly as she could. "I can't," Hud said. "I have to go. Goddamn it, I have to go."

~~~~~~~~~

The Shermans' house sat at the end of the lane on the backwaters of the lake. It was a world away from the tourist cottages and the murder scene on the opposite shore. All of the surrounding houses belonged to full-timers as far as Hud could tell. Even at night, they looked more like homes than places to party for a few days.

The backwater was shallow, weedy, and full of cattails and water lilies in the summer. It throbbed with migrating ducks in the spring and fall—making the spot less than desirable for pleasure seekers and sun worshippers. A thick woods populated the farthest end of the marsh. It was state-owned land; a nature preserve named after a dead war hero that Hud couldn't remember. Duck stamps were handed out by lottery in the county, but Hud had never hunted ducks in the backwaters—he'd been more interested in fishing than hunting as a boy. He'd learned how to tell a bufflehead from a merganser because of his time spent in the shallow end.

The CO's house was a simple cedar-sided, pre-War bungalow. All of the windows blazed with light and gleamed with the discipline of a twice-a-year application of elbow grease and pride. Two ricks of wood sat neatly piled alongside the garage, ready for the coming winter. A silhouette of a stove pipe protruded from the roof at the back of the house, and Hud figured Sherman used the wood to heat the house as much as possible.

A good sized dog barked in the distance as Hud stepped out of the Crown Vic. The mist was thick, the air even colder now since he'd left Goldie behind. He stopped, did a full turn to get his bearings, and took in the sight of the house again. The dog didn't belong to the CO, or if it did it was a long way from home. Hud was glad of that. He was in no mood to deal with an overprotective guard dog, a big German Shepherd from the sound of the bark.

The lane that led up to the house bothered him. It was one way in and one way out. The only other escape route was over the lake or into the preserve. Even at this time of year, the land there was sink-to-your-ankles soft and full of critters and slithery things that would do anything to protect themselves. Hud shivered at the thought.

He was certain that Sherman had at least one personal boat, as well as the state patrol boat, and he likely knew the lake as well as, or better than, anyone else. Night added to the disadvantage, but there were plenty of spotlights to go around to search outside the house. It was beyond, searching the preserve if the need arose, that concerned him.

Hud hadn't been out on the water in a boat since his return. It would take him more than a minute to figure out where he was if he had to go out on the lake. His memory of the coves, of the landmarks of his youth, were out of reach, locked in a place he had never thought he would have to rely on ever again. He realized that it had been a mistake, not taking some time familiarizing himself with his old haunts, his old life, before returning to work. His navigation skills were rusty.

He shrugged off the regret and headed over to the county cruiser sitting in front of the house. The drizzle hadn't let up. It was like a cloud hung over the world, encasing everything in sight in its grey dampness.

"Detective," Bob Varner said, as he rolled down the driver's side window, making no effort to get out of the car. "Fancy meeting you here." Varner had been the deputy who had arrived first at the murder scene earlier in the day. He was a little older than Hud, but they had not been friends as kids. The deputy wouldn't have been easy to forget. Most assholes weren't.

Varner stared up at Hud with the same distant animosity he'd shown at their prior meeting. Hud decided right then and there that the man's attitude had nothing to do with him, and, if it did, then the pecking order disdain wasn't his problem.

Hud smelled a recently extinguished cigarette from two feet away from the cruiser and ignored it the best he could. "You seen anything?"

Varner shook his head. "Been quiet since we told the wife that a search warrant was coming. No one's been by, no one's left. I take it that's why you're here."

Hud nodded. "Burke's on his way."

"That's why I'm here."

Garbled voices on the radio chatted back and forth, the volume low but unmistakable. Standard talk, nothing worth Hud's attention. He'd left his walkie-talkie in his vehicle. "How was the wife?"

"A tad bit confused and upset," Varner said. "Who wouldn't be?"

"It was genuine?"

"You don't know Kaye Sherman, do you?"

"Not that I know of. I've been gone for a long time."

"I heard that, too." The radio drew Varner's attention and he looked away from Hud. "Burke just turned onto the lane. Looks like it's show time."

"I can hardly wait," Hud said, looking down the road, still uncomfortable about the only other way out.

~~~~~~~~

"You really thought the man that owned the Dip fed your mother to the lion?"

"I was a kid. It made sense."

"But you gave up on that idea."

"Sure, if you say so."

"You still think that's possible?"

"I don't know what I think. But I know this: a healthy, happy woman just up and disappeared, and the whole world was pretty quick to come to the conclusion that she had run off just because of her reputation."

"She liked men."

"Get it right."

"She liked married men."

"Yes. They were easier, I guess. They didn't want to live happily ever after. They just wanted her, and I think she was all right with that, that that's what she wanted, too. No attachments, no heartbreak. She'd had enough of those kinds of troubles to last a lifetime. You try losing the person you love in a fiery car crash."

"Gee told you that?"

"Gee told me everything once I got old enough to understand. Or, at least, I thought she did. One of the last things my mother told her was that she was in love and that it was going to change everything. And she was right. It did. Everything changed."

CHAPTER SEVEN

Burke pulled up behind Varner's cruiser in his own Crown Vic. Even in the dark of night and inclement weather, it was obvious that the chief's car was brand new. Modes of transportation were synonymous with rank, no matter the department. Hud glanced over to his own battered Crown Vic, just to reaffirm his own status. Best to know where you were on the totem pole going in.

Burke wasn't alone, which made things a little more interesting. He had another detective with him, one of Hud's counterparts, Tina Sloane. Her presence didn't surprise Hud at all. The scope of the case had grown by the second. It had been clear to Hud once Sherman disappeared from the crime scene and became an immediate suspect that the investigation wasn't going to be a one-man show. Burke would've been a fool to throw the reins to Hud with complete authority, given Hud's lack of time in the department. Once the media sniffed their way in, everybody wanted their face time, no matter how small the TV market or the size of the readership of the newspaper asking the questions. Hud had seen the competiveness inside a department blossom before, and he didn't expect it to be any different in a small county than it was in the big city.

Tina Sloane had been a detective for five years. She was a no-nonsense woman, who always wore plain pant suits, usually in black, gray, or tan, and had short brown hair that complimented her soft oval face and brown eyes. Beauty wasn't Sloane's thing, not like it was for Goldie, but it was there, purposely obscured, undeniable in the genuineness of her face and the shape of her body, regardless of what she did to hide it. Hud hadn't been around Sloane enough to know anything of substance about her, only the basics. She was native to the area, had been born and raised in the county seat twenty miles to the south, so she had attended a different high school than him and Burke, and her deceased father had been a small-town cop. It was easy to see that law enforcement ran in her veins all the way down to the durable, comfortable shoes she wore. Other than that, the slate was blank. Hud had no opinion of Detective Sloan, of how good a cop she was. Not yet, anyway, but he figured that was about to change.

"You smell like the inside of a tavern," Burke said to Hud, coming to a stop at the hood of Varner's cruiser. Sloane stood shoulder-to-shoulder with the chief, her face blank and unreadable. Every cell in her being looked to be on alert, stiff with attention, but she didn't seem to be angry or to need to prove herself to anyone, including Burke. She was in observation mode, just like Hud.

Hud shrugged. "I took a time-out at the hotel bar. Ordered a coffee."

"If you say so," Burke said.

"I do."

"You should pick a better place to spend your time. That place has changed since you've been away."

"Thanks for the advice. I'll keep that in mind."

"You're on duty until I say you're not," Burke said. The German shepherd barked in the distance, closer. The warning bounced off the surface of the lake behind Sherman's house and lingered a long second before fading.

"If you say so," Hud answered, not breaking eye contact with Burke.

The air suddenly turned thick with silence. Mist quickly covered Burke's windbreaker jacket, and he was the first to look away, but not before biting the corner of his lip and glancing at Sloane. They had a silent language. Hud made note of what he saw. Added it to his own list of curiosities and suspicions. Beyond that, he was sure he had a lecture on obedience coming. It wouldn't be the first time that had ever happened, but it would be the first "official" one from Burke.

"Tell me what you've got," Burke said to Hud.

"Just got here. Varner says no one has come in or out. Mrs. Sherman is obviously confused and upset. I'm sure she's going to be thrilled to have us come into her house like she's a criminal."

"She might be," Burke said.

"Never say never," Hud replied.

"Let's go." Burke pulled away, leading the two detectives to the door. Varner stayed behind, in the cruiser; the rear guard, waiting, as always, for orders on what to do next.

~~~~~~~~~~

"What about you?"

"What do you mean?"

"Do you avoid attachments?"

"I'm not sure what that has to do with anything."

"Humor me."

"If I have to."

"I would appreciate an answer, but you know you don't have to give me one."

"I was married once, early on. It lasted a year. She didn't like being married to a cop. I was gone a lot. The job takes its toll. People need their releases. She didn't like my choices. Simple as that."

"And that's all there was to it?"

"Isn't that enough?"

"Nothing since?"

"I really don't see how this matters."

~~~~~~~~~~

The three of them walked up to the door in a solemn line, Burke leading, Sloane following, and Hud bringing up the rear. Burke knocked gently on the front door next to a fall wreath made of plastic red maple leaves. Hud stood behind Sloane with his hand at his side, two fingers from the .45. He caught the scent of her bath soap: simple and pure, nothing flowery. She was consistent. He liked that about her.

No one answered the door, and no detectable sounds came from inside the house. No radio, no TV, no barking dog. A guy like Sherman always had some kind of bouncing hunting dog.

Burke looked at Hud. "You sure Kaye didn't leave?" There was no mistaking the frustration in his voice.

"I'm just telling you what the deputy told me," Hud answered.

"And you trusted that?" Burke seemed immediately comfortable in his doubt about Varner's capabilities, which wasn't a surprise in such a small department that was mostly overused and underappreciated.

Hud knew the best thing he could do was keep his mouth shut. The line Burke was taking was obvious. The chief was pissed because of the time Hud had taken at the hotel. He'd really blow his stack if he knew about Goldie.

Burke knocked on the door again, only this time harder, with authority. It no longer mattered if there was a personal relationship between Burke and the Shermans; there was a warrant to serve. "Mrs. Sherman?" he demanded, just short of a yell.

The door creaked open, and Burke stiffened. They all did. Burke spun to his side, grabbed his gun, a black Glock 9mm, and glanced at Sloane. "Cover the back door. You come with me, Matthews." He had dropped his voice to a whisper. It was Matthews here, not Hud. This had just turned serious.

Sloane nodded, produced her own Glock, pushed past Hud, and disappeared into the dark, misty night. Burke said nothing more, just eased the door open gently, and slid inside. "Stay close," Burke ordered.

Hud had wondered why Burke had sent Sloane out on her own to cover the back, and not him, until that moment, when the first order came, and then he understood: Burke didn't trust him, hadn't seen him in action. It was an understandable reaction, but it still rubbed Hud the wrong way.

Every hair on Hud's body stood at attention as he followed Burke inside the Shermans' house. The light was almost blinding. There wasn't a lamp, sconce, or overhead light that wasn't turned on. A furnace fan hummed in the distance, and it sounded as though there was water running, a faucet left on somewhere close. Other than that, everything looked normal, tidy, no sign of any kind of disturbance. The floor was so clean you could eat off it.

The interior of the house reflected the exterior: simple, austere, rustic. A ten-point buck's head hung over the fireplace, its glassy eyes focused and unnerving. The furniture looked worn and comfortable: thick green corduroy with knitted afghan blankets thrown over the back of the sofa and chairs. Twenty-year-old pictures of three perfect blonde-haired children adorned the walls, along with a cheap print of an outdoor painting framed in barn siding. A clay pot full of potpourri, dried flower petals and herbs, scented the room with a faraway woodsy smell. There was no sign of anyone at home.

Burke edged his way to the entrance to the kitchen, drawn there, like Hud, by the sound of the running water. One step inside the small shadowy room was like walking from one season to the next in the blink of an eye. Everything changed. The light, dimmed and soft, the overheads off, the texture of the air, a sudden drop of temperature, and most noticeably the smell. Gone was the sweet aroma of the front room, orchestrated to provide comfort and a sense of well-being. It had been replaced by a more repugnant and unfortunately familiar smell. The first hint of blood and death touched Hud's nose.

Burke stopped. "Shit."

Hud pushed up next to him and saw the reason for the exclamation, knew before he had to witness it. A middle-aged woman lay on the floor just in front of the sink, her eyes fixed distantly past Hud; blood pooled under her head, fresh enough to still have a shine to it. The back door stood wide open, and Sloane's concerned face suddenly appeared.

CHAPTER EIGHT

"How long was it before you realized that she was never coming back?"

"A trip away overnight wasn't out of the question for her, but it was unusual. Gee usually knew where she was and when she'd be back. It was a day or two before the real panic set in, before Gee set off the alarms that something was wrong. I felt it deep in my stomach, but I didn't know what to do about it."

"They had an agreement?"

"I don't know that I would call it that. Gee was hard on her because of me. I think she wanted her to settle down, find a respectable man, find me a father-figure, get on with her life. Gee worried about that, made her disapproval clear, but she was good at knowing how far to go with her opinions, especially with my mother. They tried to keep their fights away from me, but I could always tell when the water was choppy."

"What about your mother?"

"What about her?"

"Was she concerned about you having a father-figure?"

"I don't know."

"How could you not know that?"

"She never talked about it. It was like our life was as normal as everyone else's. It was the three of us and that was enough. Just Gee, her, and me. We had the souvenir shop to feed us, plenty of things to keep us busy, and we lived in a wonderfully beautiful place, according to her, especially between Labor Day and Memorial Day."

"When all the vacationers were gone?"

"Yes."

"What about you? Was it enough? You know, with just the three of you?"

"What do you think? Every boy who doesn't have one longs for his father. She'd given me hope that things were going to change, and then she was gone. I had nothing but Gee to hang onto."

The moment Burke found a pulse Sloane dropped down and started performing CPR on the woman. Hud had thought she was dead, that Sloane's lifesaving attempt was a hopeless task, but there was no question he would've done the same thing. Maybe not with such fervor, but he would have tried to save her nonetheless.

He stood and watched, impressed by Sloane's work ethic, all the while taking in the scope of the kitchen, silently cataloging everything he saw. At first glance, the running faucet was the only thing out of place in the kitchen. There was no weapon on the counter or floor; no knives or tenderizing mallets, thick with blood, lying in plain sight. Nothing. It looked like Kaye Sherman, and it was still an assumption that the woman on the floor *was* Kaye Sherman, had walked into the kitchen, slipped, fallen, and hit her head on the counter. Which could have been the case under normal circumstances, but Kaye Sherman's husband had disappeared and was a person of interest in an ongoing murder investigation. There were three detectives in her house to serve a search warrant, and, sooner rather than later, the media was going to show up and start hounding her. Normal was hardly the case at the moment.

Hud's eyes trailed to the back door. It was standing wide open. Not quite a murder weapon, but perhaps an escape route, an indication that someone else might have been in the house. Or, maybe it was nothing more than a matter of coincidence—that normal circumstance that always lurked as a possibility. Maybe Kaye Sherman really had come in from outside and slipped and banged her head right before the police showed up. It was a plausible scenario but an unlikely one. Hud had learned a long time ago to never trust his first assumption. Proof was required on all fronts. Even if it meant not trusting himself, what he thought he saw or didn't see. He looked across the kitchen again for a weapon, for any sign of a struggle.

Burke continued to bark orders into a handheld that had appeared from underneath his overcoat. He looked at Hud after calling for an ambulance and said, "Go take a look outside."

Hud nodded, but a cookbook caught his eye. It lay on the lip of an old hutch as though it had been taken out and not put back in. It was a big book, *The Joy of Cooking*, and he had to wonder if the weight of it could knock someone out. The short answer was yes, maybe from behind, in a surprise move. That would work, to grab the first thing available if you were inside a house you weren't supposed to be in and the owner came in unexpectedly. *But why not have a weapon, a gun?* Hud asked himself. *Maybe they did. Maybe they didn't want to make any noise. Maybe they were looking for something.*

Sloane continued to count off her chest compressions. "One, two, three . . ." It sounded as if she was playing an accordion without any music coming out of it.

"You have a flashlight with you, don't you?" Burke said to Hud, pulling him out of his thoughts.

"Sure," he said.

"Go on, take a look, see what you can find."

"All right." Hud felt trapped inside a bubble and wasn't anxious to leave, even though he was being dismissed. He was sure he was overlooking something, but he knew by Burke's look that lingering much longer was out of the question, or at least a stupid thing to do.

Without any further hesitation, Hud walked slowly to the kitchen door, eyes on the floor, then looked up the jamb and at the ceiling, inspecting everything as he went. Each move was methodical, planned, as he inched closer to the darkness of night. He saw nothing to stop him and continued on as he was ordered. Sloane's attempt to raise the dead faded behind him and was replaced by the onslaught of wind and mist. This was not the welcome home that he had been hoping for.

~~~~~~~~~

Hud's flashlight beam cut sharply across the backyard, providing him a clear path to the lake. There were no unusual sounds, not even a siren, yet. The call had just gone out. It would take the ambulance ten or fifteen minutes to arrive this far out. The barking dog had gone silent, and there was no traffic noise, nothing but the dulled presence of nature settling into the deep isolation of a misty night. He felt like he was walking inside a black ball spun of wet cotton.

The first place Hud headed to was the pier, a freshly painted white wood-slat walkway that extended twenty feet out into the lake. His windbreaker and face were instantly soaked. He was glad he didn't wear glasses. He'd need windshield wipers.

Sherman's state CO boat was tied up to the end of the pier. It was a modified bass boat with a 250 horsepower Mercury motor on the back. The fiberglass hull was cut low to the water at the bow, and wide at the stern. The boat was built for speed without the intention of pleasure; it had been converted to be a police vehicle for the water.

The sides of the pier were empty. If Sherman had a personal boat, it was either out on the water or stored for winter. It seemed a little early for a guy like Sherman to put his boat into storage. Hud aimed the flashlight downward to the water and saw nothing in the shallow blackness, then scanned the lake looking for a sign of movement, lights, anything sitting or moving on the water. He saw nothing, not even a duck. But that didn't mean the lake was vacant of any boats. Not in this weather. Somebody could have been sitting on the edge of darkness watching him, spying on the crime scene with binoculars. He hadn't felt a pair of eyes on him, but that didn't mean they weren't there.

Sherman, of course, would be the main suspect in the assault on the woman inside, but there had to be other considerations. They just hadn't presented themselves.

The boat didn't look like it had been touched. If there was one thing that stood out to Hud, it was the fact that the boat was open to the weather, uncovered. That seemed unlikely, too. It was obvious that Sherman took care of things. He would put a tarp over the boat on a night like this. Unless he didn't have time, or he had been interrupted. Hud swung the flashlight beam slowly across the boat again, making sure there wasn't any place for a man to hide. It was empty.

He looked at the water again and suddenly felt vulnerable. It was too dark to see a clear reflection of himself, even on the surface of the water. For years he'd looked for any sign of his mother in the lake, everywhere he went as far as that went, but always in the water. It had been easy for him to imagine that she'd had an accident and drowned; one of the many scenarios that he had come up with that would have explained her disappearance. He'd wished she would wash up on the shore, beaten and battered by the waves, nipped at by the turtles, bloated by time, anything that he could have touched and mourned. It would have been better than the nothingness that had followed him all of his life.

The mystery of the water had always been a draw to Hud, but now, after so many years away from it, he was unsure in its presence. He couldn't rely on his old confidence, his old memories. That had been clear from the moment he had returned home, but he hadn't realized that the uncertainty would stay, grow. He had thought he would be the same as when he left and known what he had known as a boy, but almost every skill had been lost or was so buried that he didn't know how to retrieve it. He had never thought he would be afraid of the water.

"Things have a way of disappearing around here, in that lake. It's deeper than people think it is," Harriet Danvers voice suddenly whispered in his head. It had felt like she had been trying to tell him something—or at least that she knew things. She had been right about the dead girl, had sent them to rescue the boy at the Dip. He was going to have to talk to her again.

A dog barked, and the echo of it over the lake drew Hud's attention away from the water. He turned back to the house, to face the bright glow of the interior, and blinked to refocus his vision. A rush of wind and a blur of movement suddenly approached out of the corner of his eye, but Hud was too slow to react, to realize that it was the first sign of an assault. The night screamed with a slap. He recognized the shape of an oar and bit his lip as the heavy wood slammed against the side of his face. Stinging pain exploded on the right side of his head. Wood against skin, force against bone, accompanied by the surprise taste of blood. The force of the blow buckled Hud to his knees, turned his neck, left him incapable of protecting himself.

He had thought he had been alert enough to see a surprise attack coming, but he had been wrong. A second blow to the stomach, a kick or a punch—he wasn't sure which—didn't allow him to scream for help or order the attacker to stop. Blood mixed with the bile of failure and shame, and Hud wondered, as he fell to the ground in a heap, if this was going to be his last mortal memory: *You failed to see it coming. You failed again.*

There were no dreams in the sudden darkness, just the helpless feeling of floating to the bottom of a black hole. There was nothing he could do to save himself.

CHAPTER NINE

Flashing red lights pierced the back of Hud's eyelids. He was lying flat on his back, face up on a stretcher. It felt like he was buried under a blanket of cement. He couldn't move: not his toes, not his fingers. Nothing. He feared he was paralyzed, permanently injured, until he realized that he was awake, still alive, just coming out of a daze. A familiar pain in the side of his head told him that he had survived. He had been hit like that before; unaware. But not by an oar. All he could think was that his life might have been a whole lot easier if he had become a baker or a janitor instead of a cop.

Hud sighed, swallowed the best he could, then blinked his eyes open. The first thing he saw was Burke staring down at him. The disappointment on the chief's face was impossible to misinterpret.

~~~~~~~

"Life went on?"

"It had to. I was in third grade. It was winter. If I remember right, we had a lot of snow that year. And ice. There was a lot of ice. There was no time for fun, no ice fishing, no skating or sledding. Even if there had been, Gee was in no mood to let me out of her sight. She didn't smile for a year, and rarely after."

"The police came, of course."

"Burke's dad. He was sheriff then. Paid an obligatory call to the shop once he figured out he was going to have to calm Gee down, that she was going to keep raising hell until he did something, acknowledged that something was wrong."

"She didn't call the newspaper?"

"Sure she did, but there wasn't much of a paper around here then. Everybody got the Daily Press, but that was mostly for the box *scores in the summer. People are on vacation, they don't give a shit about the news when they're here. They want to go skiing, fishing, lie in the sun, forget the world and its problems exist. Besides, the* Press *was thirty miles away. We were in our own little world out here."*

"Things have changed."

"I suppose they have. Now you can get the New York Times *on your phone."*

"What did Gee do once she figured out the police weren't going to do anything?"

"She did what she always did. Took it into her own hands. She had no choice but to go looking for my mother herself."

"And you went with her."

"Every chance I got."

〰〰〰〰〰〰

Hud knew he had been lucky to get away with a mild concussion and a black eye. The ER doctor had dosed him with morphine and prescribed some pain meds. The doctor was a young guy, not long out of med school. He'd recommended that Hud take a week off the job, and talk to the worker's comp people. "Sure, I'll do that," Hud had said. The doctor had exited the triage bay unconvinced, and that was just fine with Hud. If he claimed workers comp every time he got a scratch on the job he'd never get anything done.

A battery of x-rays and an MRI cleared him of any broken bones or any serious brain damage. He would add the scar tissue to his collection.

Hud could stand, but he was hardly capable of making his own way back to the hotel. Burke had sent a deputy to drive him home. He had been relieved to see Moran push into the ER. She stood at the opposite end of the bed staring at Hud, still in her uniform and looking less like a kickboxer and more like a woman exhausted from a hard day's work, ready to go home. Her blonde hair, pulled back tight with ambition that morning, had begun to fray at the edges, protesting at being confined, anxious to be released. Her skin was paler than it had been when he had seen her earlier, as if her enthusiasm for life and police work had been drained from her by what she had witnessed throughout the day. Hud knew the look, the feeling, especially from the beginning of his career, when he hadn't been accustomed to murder investigations. There was a price to pay for trying to make sense out of chaos, for digesting the smell of blood and evil, for being a witness to the ultimate nastiness that one human being could inflict on another. He could still taste death on the tip of his own tongue, and he was sure Moran could, too. She was a rookie exposed to madness. She didn't know that it was contagious.

"You're sure you're up to walking out on your own?" she asked.

Hud shrugged. "Not much more damage I can do if I go face down."

"Says you."

"Says me." He stabilized himself by grabbing the cold metal rail of the hospital bed. His knees were wobbly, and Moran looked like she was seven miles away. She'd never make it to him if he withered to the floor. It had always been like that. Even Gee couldn't catch him when he fell.

The interior of Moran's cruiser was clean and as organized as it could possibly be. Electronics cluttered the dash: a mounted laptop, three radios, a GPS screen, and other gadgets that were turned off or asleep. There was nothing to do about that kind of mess, but the seats and the floor were free of bags and wrappers, and there was no lingering smell of cigarette smoke or doughnuts. He figured Moran for a health-food freak anyway. Maybe a vegan or one of those New Age non-meat-eaters. She was lean; he wondered how long that would last, how long before the spread of time affected her body, from spending so much time in the driver's seat of a county cruiser.

"I could have got home on my own," he said, settling into the passenger seat.

"Sure you could have. You're stoned."

"Like that's ever stopped me before."

"Nice." Moran put the cruiser in gear and navigated it out of the parking lot. "Where to?"

"The Demmie."

"Oh, yeah, that's right. You're not staying at the shop."

Hud said nothing, just stared past the beam of the headlights, into the darkness ahead. "What time is it?"

"Almost three."

The hospital disappeared behind them, and a row of fast food restaurants lined both sides of the road. Their signs were off and the lights dark. Even if he was hungry—which he wasn't—there wouldn't have been a place to stop to eat. It didn't take long for civilization to fade away into a rural stretch of road.

"You've had a long day," Hud said. Moran's features had softened in the dashboard lights, and even though she was at least ten years younger than he was, he suddenly felt comfortable in her presence. It might have been the morphine, but he doubted that. He'd liked her directness from the start.

Moran flicked her head to him, reacting to the change in his tone. "It's been a long day for us all. Nothing like this happens around here."

"There's always been crime here."

"Not like this. Stupid stuff. Winter burglaries mostly, from what I remember. A boat theft every once in a while. That's why there's three detectives. Break-ins are so common, especially in the winter, there isn't time for anything else. Sloane's never caught a murder. Lancet, either. You're not going to be popular with them."

"I've never had a seat at the cool kids' table." Hud had heard the rub in her voice again, heard her desire to rise up in the ranks. Sloane wasn't going anywhere, and he knew Burke well enough to know that he wasn't going to promote another woman to detective. One woman on the squad was enough to keep the wolves at bay. It didn't matter if Moran was qualified or not. He hadn't met Pete Lancet yet. Didn't know him from the past, but he'd heard good things about him from Burke. "I suppose you're right," he added.

"Of course I'm right."

Hud smiled and relaxed even more. His mind started to wander, and he realized that he knew nothing about Moran, Sloane, or even Burke for that matter. He was sitting at *their* table, and he was the newbie. The emotional landscape was familiar, just like the physical landscape, but he didn't know it. Not like he should. He'd never been very good at starting over. With the pain distancing itself and the swelling in his face growing more noticeable, Hud began to wonder if he had made a mistake by coming home. Not that he'd really had any choice.

The road curved, and Moran took it a little faster than she should have, sending Hud's shoulder into the door. He grimaced, bit his lip, and tried not to show any discomfort, even though the smack against metal hurt like hell.

"Oh, sorry," Moran said.

"The Demmie's up on the right about two miles." The pain lingered, hung on like it wanted to spread and conquer him. He should've had Moran stop and fill the prescriptions the doctor had given him, but he wanted to crash in his own bed as soon as he could.

"Yeah, I know," Moran said.

"Of course you do."

Moran flashed Hud a smile, then returned her attention back to the road. "You like being a cop don't you?"

Before Hud could answer, his cell phone buzzed with a familiar alert tone. It was Burke, and he had sent a text. Hud struggled to get to the phone and struggled even harder to read the text:

Autopsy at 0800 sharp. Don't be late.

"Great," Hud whispered.

"Something wrong?"

"No, it's just Burke. The autopsy is at eight o'clock in the morning."

"And he wants you there?"

"Looks that way."

"Figures."

Moran wheeled the cruiser into the hotel parking lot. There were a few cars in the lot. One that Hud recognized as Tilt's. He thought for a second about going into the bar for a late one, or to see if the grill was still hot, but decided against it. His skin felt like glass, like he would shatter at the sound of loud music. It was best to forgo any human contact at this point.

"You need help to your room?" Moran asked.

Hud studied her face for a second, thought about the possibilities, then let the idea drop before he went to a place that he wasn't up to. A flash of memory from earlier in the day flittered through his mind, and he had to wonder if his reunion with Goldie Flowers had been real or was just a drug-induced fantasy. He hoped it had really happened. "I'll be fine," he said.

"All right, I'll wait until you're in the room before I leave."

Hud shrugged and reached for the door handle, but stopped. "What happened back at the Shermans'? How's the woman?"

"DOA."

"Damn it, I was afraid you were going to say that."

CHAPTER TEN

There were places that Hud had always longed to visit, but once he got there he wished he were somewhere else. The morgue was one of those places. He had imagined himself countless times as an eight-year-old boy walking into the cold, sterile room to identify his mother after she had been found, a victim of murder or some freak accident; a lightning strike on the lake, an attack by the lion at the Dip, or maybe the ostrich had pecked her to death—something, anything. The adult in him knew that he longed for closure. Why else would he want to go to the morgue voluntarily? He had been told that he longed for closure over and over again. Most recently in Detroit by the droning psycho-something woman who had finally determined that he was still fit for police work after being shot. He wondered if he would have to go through that crap again, then thought, *I just want to know the truth*. It was the one thing that pushed him forward, urged him to get out of bed, face whatever pain he had to, and do his job.

He stood in the open doorway staring at a sheet-covered body lying prone on a stainless steel examining table. His nose had already been invaded by the antiseptic hospital smell that permeated the building, but there was another layer to the aroma in the basement. Mustiness mixed with death and cleaning fluids. For a second, he thought he was going to puke.

The smell, along with his little-boy desires, had stopped Hud in his tracks. It was like he had run headlong into a wall. Maybe it was nothing more than a morphine hangover, or the queasiness in his stomach from his coffee and four-Advil breakfast, or maybe it was something more than that. It was that handshake with death after being smacked upside the head the night before.

He certainly wasn't at his best, even though he needed to be.

"Detective Matthews," a familiar voice called out, distantly, from down the hall behind him.

Hud looked over his shoulder to see Bill Flowers and another man he didn't know heading his way.

"You're late," Flowers said. He held a manila folder in one hand, a steaming cup of coffee in the other, and his jaw was set so hard that Hud thought the bone might pop out of its socket.

Hud looked at his bare wrist to see what time it was. He relied on his cell phone these days. His watch had been a casualty of the Detroit incident. He shrugged. There was no use checking the phone to see how late he really was. If Flowers said he was tardy, then that was obviously the way it was going to be, no matter what any clock said. Burke was going to be thrilled when he read the autopsy report. *Detective Matthews was late for the procedure . . .*

Hud turned and faced the two men as they came to a stop before him. His reactions were slow, tempered by the lingering pain that the Advil couldn't touch, the haziness of the drug fog, and the lack of sleep. He extended his hand, even though the coroner's were full. An "are you serious?" look crossed Flowers's face. Hud nodded, then quickly pivoted to the man he didn't know.

"Hey, there, pardner, it's about time we met." The man grabbed Hud's hand and shook it furiously. His hand was as cold as a January morning and as big as an omelet skillet.

"Oh, you're Pete Lancet aren't you?" Hud said, taking in the man as fully as he could.

"The one and only."

There was no mistaking Lancet for anything but a cop. He wore a heavily starched white Oxford shirt and a thin black tie, while a 9mm Sig Sauer sat holstered comfortably on his hip, and a shiny silver detective's badge hung on his belt. He was a head taller than Hud, his thick black hair slicked back with some kind of oily pomade, and a bushy but well-trimmed mustache. His body was lean, and, as if his height alone wasn't enough, he wore a pair of custom-made cowboy boots with two-

and-a-half-inch heels. The boots looked like they were cut from yellow snakeskin instead of leather, and they glowed spectacularly below his sharply creased black slacks.

Another smell invaded Hud's nose. Lancet wore a cologne so thick it had completely obliterated all of the other smells. It brought Hud close to puking again. This fragrance was worse than all of them combined. It was a spicy, manly scent, probably one of those cheap dime-store brands advertised by a pair of busty blonde beauties on TV. Hud closed off his nose the best he could. He could hardly breathe.

"Boy, that's some shiner," Lancet said, leaning in to Hud. "Sloane said you took a good one for the team, but I didn't expect that."

The left half of Hud's face was black and blue, and his eye was bright red. A blood vessel had popped from the impact. If there'd been a carnival in town, he could have auditioned for the freak show.

"You sure you're up to this?" Lancet went on.

"I'll be fine."

"Sure you will." With that, Lancet smacked Hud between the shoulder blades with the open palm of his hand. "We're gonna be good together. You wait and see," he said, spinning around, heading into the morgue with a little more purpose and glee than was necessary this early in the morning.

Flowers looked at Hud with disdain and shoved the folder at him. "You need to bring yourself up to speed." he said, then quickly followed after Lancet.

Hud was left to himself in the empty basement corridor with pain radiating down his back and more questions swirling in his head than he knew what to do with.

〜〜〜〜〜〜

"I always looked for her. In a crowd. In the lake when I was fishing. I looked for her everywhere I went. Always."

"And that's why you became a cop, went into police work?"

"I didn't mean to."

"It just happened?"

"Burke and I were friends. His dad was a looming presence, even when he wasn't around. Which was most of the time. But when he was, I felt safe, like nothing bad could happen when he was in the house. I liked feeling that. It was rare. If your mother can disappear without a trace, anything can happen, can't it?"

"Burke's dad calmed you, even after?"

"He changed. Grew more distant. I think he was uncomfortable around me. I didn't know that then. Couldn't know it then. But that's what I think now. He couldn't solve my problem. He couldn't bring her back—or even find her for that matter."

"Did he talk to you about it?"

"He never mentioned my mother again. Not after he quit coming by to see Gee."

"You think he knew something?"

"He was always on my list."

"So, you wanted to do that for other people when you grew up? What Burke's dad did for you when you were a kid? Make them feel safe?"

"Sure, if you say so."

"Or did you do it for yourself?"

"I really have to go take a piss. Do you mind?"

~~~~~~~~~

Harriet Danvers had been right. The victim had been that Pam girl. The brief at the top of the report read:

Victim has been identified as Pamela Lynn Sizemore, age twenty-six, Caucasian female, unmarried, divorced two times, mother of one eight-year-old boy, Timmy. Currently unemployed. Last place of employment was Cottage Maids, a local cleaning service. Death from a single gunshot wound to the back of the head requires validation. No other visible wounds. Two ex-husbands, Roy Vaughn and Tim Sizemore have been placed on the interview list, but not located. Last seen alive outside the back door at Johnny Long's Supper Club by a busboy, Jordan Rogers, five hours before she was discovered dead on the lakeshore by CO Leo Sherman.

Hud nodded and glanced away from the report, from Burke's signature. He wasn't sure how it had been determined that the dead girl was Pam Sizemore. Burke hadn't alerted him that she'd been ID'd—but then Hud had been out of the loop for a few hours. Still, it seemed a text would have been appropriate. The lack of communication wasn't important—at the moment—but it would be at some point.

The feeling that Hud was lead on this case was falling farther and farther away. He had to wonder if it had really been his in the first place.

The revving of the bone saw drew Hud's attention away from the report, from his position in the department. Any more details about Pam Sizemore's short life would have to wait. So would his ego. The file for both was thin.

The case was still building twenty-four hours after the discovery of the body, and, as far as Hud knew, the primary suspect, CO Sherman, was still at large. The desirable forty-hour window where everything was fresh and possible ticked away without regard to justice—or the truth, for that matter. There was still a lot of work to do, and he wished like hell that he had a clear head. If he ever needed one, now was the time.

The buzz and whirl of the Stryker saw echoed past Hud as he walked into the morgue to witness the autopsy. Flowers had on a thick, black vinyl apron and wore goggles, as he went about cutting off the back of Pam Sizemore's skull. Detective Lancet wore the same gear. They both wore clear plastic gloves. A similar outfit was piled on an empty examining table beyond the two men. Hud made his way to it, not taking his eyes off the victim as he passed.

He had lost any rookie discomfort in attending an autopsy a long time ago. The sight of dead people didn't bother him. The stark nakedness of the girl had no effect on him, either. He was there to witness, to assist if asked, and to find answers that would help deliver justice in a court of law, and nothing else. Still, the sight of the girl's body troubled him.

There was no question that Pam Sizemore was a drug user of some kind. Whether it was meth, heroin, or something else would soon be determined, along with how much and how recent the use was. Her body was emaciated to the point that she almost looked like a concentration camp victim. Her extremities were thin as broomsticks, her chest flat, and her skin was as pale as the whites of her eyes. Any healthy blood vessels had retreated long ago. Even the three tattoos that Hud could see, two butterflies above her pubic bone and one heart broken into two pieces on her right shoulder, seemed lifeless and faded. Her right arm was pinpricked, along with all of her toes. The addiction had been an extensive one. Hud figured the girl had a record to go along with the suffering her body expressed. If a bullet hadn't killed her, an overdose was coming soon.

He put on the protective garb quickly and made his way to the table, across from Lancet, as far away from the man's pungent cologne as possible. Flowers didn't acknowledge his presence, just kept on sawing.

The autopsy went quickly, according to plan. In the end, the coroner's speculation about Pam Sizemore's cause of death was proven correct. At least the preliminary cause of death. Toxicology hadn't come back yet. But Bill Flowers was certain that she had been felled by a single bullet and nothing more. He was also confident that the weapon had been a 30-aught-6, a typical and prolific rifle used locally for deer hunting. The cartridge hadn't been found. A couple of deputies would be sent to scout for it. But Flowers had bet his reputation that he'd be right about that, too. Lancet took him up on it out of fun. Hud watched, listened, and felt a stir of discomfort about the two men's relationship. It was parochial, born of the closeness of the area and the intersection of the jobs, but all the while far more friendlier than it should have been.

The biggest find, though, was that Pam Sizemore hadn't been running for pleasure—which was no surprise to Hud. She had been running from something, from someone. She was afraid, fleeing, in a hurry, which explained her lack of proper clothing for the weather. There was skin underneath her fingernails suggesting she'd been in an altercation of some kind shortly before her death. It had been sent off for testing. There were no other marks on her body. No bruises, no scratches, which seemed a little odd, but not unheard of, if she was fighting off an attack of some type.

Bill Flowers was reasonably pleased with himself at the validation, which also didn't come as a surprise to Hud.

~~~~~~~~~~

The noonday sun burned Hud's eyes when he exited the hospital. Lancet remained behind, while Flowers walked out with him.

"You'll be back in the morning for the Sherman autopsy," the coroner said. It wasn't a request.

"You're certain it's Kaye Sherman?" Hud stopped, squinted past the sun, and fought off a throb of pain that radiated behind his forehead, threatening to shatter any bone that got in its way. He took a few deep breaths and closed his eyes for a brief second and hoped Flowers didn't pick up on his discomfort, his weakness.

"I've known the Shermans a long time. I've buried more of Kaye's relatives than I can count. Leo's, too, as far as that goes. It's Kaye Sherman, there's no doubt about that. I'd know Kaye Sherman from a hundred yards away. You know I'm right."

Hud opened his eyes and wished he had his sunglasses with him. "Not until I see it on paper, I don't. I didn't know either one of them."

"I forget that you've been away for so long."

Hud flickered a smile, then pushed it away. The biggest surprise of his return so far had been an unexpected reunion, or more to the point, a fulfilment of an age-old fantasy. "I saw Goldie last night."

Flowers stiffened and turned away from Hud. "That's not my problem."

The rift he'd detected from Goldie must have been real. *Good to know.* Hud decided not to pursue anything else about the coroner's personal business, at least for the moment. He noted it, blinked the sun away again, then stared out to the parking lot. His eyes fell on a car in a reserved spot. It was a black Cadillac, shining like it had been spit polished. He knew it was Bill Flowers's car without even asking. "That your Cadillac?"

Flowers turned back to Hud. "Of course it is. I've driven Cadillacs since I was old enough to get behind the wheel of a car."

"Black ones?"

"It's the business I'm in."

A shiver ran up Hud's spine as the flash of an old, but very well-worn memory crashed into his headache. Something shattered, but it wasn't bone. Just briefly, in a faraway fog, he saw a black car pulling away from the souvenir shop with his mother inside. It was the last time he had seen her. The pain was so intense he thought his brain was going to explode.

"You know everybody around here, don't you?" Hud said. He couldn't control the change in his tone, the harshness in it. A funny taste engulfed his mouth.

"Not like I used to. Things have changed. But there's still a core of the old crowd here."

Hud nodded. "Do you remember my mother?"

Flowers's gasp was noticeable. It was a big suck of air, like he had been punched in the gut. Hud was certain that the old man's face paled.

"Don't be late in the morning," the coroner managed to say, then took a big step forward that looked more like the start of a run than a walk.

"You didn't answer my question," Hud said, calling out after him.

Flowers hurried to the Cadillac, didn't turn around, didn't acknowledge the demand, just got into his shiny black Cadillac and sped away, leaving Hud standing there feeling like he was about to relive something that he didn't want to but had no choice about.

CHAPTER ELEVEN

The dreariness of the day before had disappeared. It was nothing more than another gray, misty memory. Half the day had passed before Hud even noticed that there was hardly a cloud in the brilliant blue sky. The sun was bright overhead, and the air looked like it was sparkling, like it had been washed thoroughly, completely rinsed of any dirt and ugliness. Clarity was the gift of the day, but it was lost on Hud.

He sat in his battered Crown Vic, still in the hospital parking lot, staring out the open window, letting the cool, comfortable autumn breeze rinse the smell of the morgue out of his nose. His face still hurt, but the pain had been numbed slightly by the Advil he'd taken earlier. He was resisting filling the prescription for Vicodin. The gunshot wounds had proven to him that he liked those pain pills too much. Being numb had its benefits.

There was nothing Hud could do to extricate the vision of what he'd just witnessed other than let it pile on top of the rest of the bloody, naked memories of autopsies he had attended since putting on the badge. There was a special cavern in his soul, accessible by a well-worn path, where all of his experiences as a cop came to rest. Beyond that, the worst things that had happened in his life were stored in a darker, deeper place that had been locked and ignored a long time ago. Until now. The gate had been pried open by Gee's death and all of the decisions that had followed. Mainly, the one to stay on, not return to Detroit. It had been easy once Burke had offered him the detective's job. *"Try it out,"* he'd said. *"It'd be good to have you home where you belong."*

There was no real view from where Hud sat. The lake was miles away, and this hospital sat on the northern edge of town, three miles from the building that housed the county sheriff's offices. It was a narrow five-story building, with multiple sections and wings that had been added on over the years, all in conflicting architectural styles. None of the local buildings had the old art deco flair like those in Detroit. Even crumbling and in disrepair, they had more style than the hospital. Funny the things you noticed when you weren't there any longer. It surprised Hud that he felt nostalgic about Detroit. He'd been lucky to get out of there alive. His snitch had been made. The only way out was to kill Hud. They both had guns, and one of them ended up dead. That was the story, and he was sticking to it.

The police radio was on. Moran was back on the job. Varner, too. Both of them were at the Pam Sizemore crime scene searching for the 30-aught-6 cartridge. He'd stop by. Give them a hand, look for himself, even though he doubted anything would be found. But first, there was somewhere else he wanted to make a stop at.

Hud reached down and pulled a cigarette from a freshly opened pack. He lit it casually, like he'd done it a million times before. The smoke burned all the way down his throat and into his lungs. He coughed like it was his first time, and it nearly was. Smoking was an old habit that had come back to him almost as soon as he'd returned home.

~~~~~~~~~~

The little yellow clapboard house sat three streets back from the lake. Most of the surrounding cottages had already been winterized, shut up and left to the elements of the coming cold season. October was the first month of noticeable silence in vacationland. Other than a few full-timers, it was rare to see a boat out on the water. If there was, it was mostly diehard fishermen, since the lake was turning over, the water temperature changing from warm to cold, driving most of the active game fish deeper to the bottom and into a state of stasis. The fish fed and moved only when they had to. Crappie and perch were the exception, especially in winter. If the lake froze solid enough, there would be a brief second tourist season that catered to ice fishing. But that was a ways off; January, at least. For now, the lake was smooth, vacant of any activity.

Hud parked the Crown Vic, checked the address again to make sure he was in the right place, and popped a breath mint into his mouth.

The silhouette of a woman appeared behind the screen door as Hud made his way up the walk. Marigolds and petunias withered in a neglected border, leaves littered the yard, and paint was starting to peel just above the door. An old speedboat sat in the driveway on blocks. The casing was gone off the thirty-year-old motor. It looked like a project that had ended in frustration, lack of funds, or interest; Hud really didn't care which. He knew the struggle to survive when he saw it.

He stopped just before the stoop and the woman became clearer to him. She was older, early sixties, a little overweight, wrapped in a purple terrycloth bathrobe even though it was nearly noon. Her thin gray hair hadn't seen a comb in at least a day, and her eyes were tired and suspicious.

"I ain't got no time for company," she said through the screen. It was ripped in several places, offering easy entry to any insect curious enough to go inside.

Hud flashed his badge, then slid it back into his pocket. "I'm not here to sell you anything."

"Burke's already been here. I've answered all of the questions I have to."

It suddenly felt like there was a pebble in his shoe; a brief moment of discomfort at the news of Burke's visit. "I'd like to talk to the boy, if I could."

"Lookin' like that?"

Hud's discomfort was immediately replaced by a rare feeling of self-consciousness. He skimmed the side of his face unconsciously with his fingers, and felt like a failure all over again.

"You'll scare the boy to death," the woman continued.

"What's your name?" he said. He really wanted to say, "I'm not a monster," but he held his tongue.

"I told you, I done answered all the questions I had to. What's *your* name?" the woman demanded.

"Matthews. Hud Matthews."

"Oh," she peered closer at him, trying to look under the bruises for a face she recognized. "I heard you was back."

Hud looked a little closer. "Do I know you?"

"I was in and out of Gee's store over the years. Kids liked that nickel candy you used to sell. Pixie Stixs, Milk Duds, and such. Always told them that stuff'd rot their teeth, but they never paid me no mind. Made me walk up there once a day if they could scrounge up some pennies. I sure was sorry to hear that your grandmother passed. God rest her soul. Are you gonna keep the shop open?"

"I don't think so."

"That's a shame, but I guess I ain't surprised. Everything around here has dried up and closed. Not like it used to be, that's for sure. I can't imagine there not bein' no Emporium, though. You sure you won't reconsider?"

"I'm not sure I have the time, ma'am, but I appreciate the support. The shop got me and Gee through a lot. She made a decent living from it. But its time has passed, I guess." Hud couldn't place the woman. It was hard to keep track of all of the people who came and went at the shop regularly, unless they were somebody like Goldie Flowers.

The woman didn't say anything else for a long minute. A cloud of gnats, hardy enough to survive a weak October frost, whisked by Hud's face. He pushed the mass out of the way, surprised by their presence. Lake creatures had a lifecycle all their own. Sometimes, he wondered if there wasn't magic in the water instead of the darkness and mystery that always seemed to lurk just underneath the surface.

"That boy's been through a lot," the woman finally said.

"I know he has," Hud replied.

She nodded and opened the door. "If it was anybody but you, Hud Matthews, I'd be sendin' them on their way. I 'spect you know a thing or two about bein' a little boy and losin' your momma that most men don't."

Hud didn't say a word, just walked in the door unsure of what he'd find, or what he was going to say to the boy. All he knew was that he had to talk to him, make sure for himself that the boy was in good hands and safe.

~~~~~~~~

"Why did you go to Detroit?"

"I had family there. My Aunt Bernadette, Gee's oldest, and her husband had moved up there, so I had a place to stay while I went to school."

"In Ann Arbor?"

"Yes."

"How was that?"

"It was school."

"Did you ever come back home?"

"Only when I had to."

"You didn't miss Gee?"

"Of course, I did. I missed her every day. How could I not?"

"But you stayed away."

"I needed to get on with my life. I needed to stop looking for my mother."

"Did you?"

"Here I am."

~~~~~~~~

The house smelled of cigarettes and bacon grease. It was familiar, reminded Hud of Gee, of walking into the back of the shop where they lived. He stopped just inside the door. "I'm sorry," he said softly, "I didn't catch your name?"

"I didn't figure you recognized me," the woman said. Her face hardened. All her wrinkles seemed to fill in and disappear in a quick puff of air.

The TV was on, but the sound was down. Something buzzed in the distance, like a fluorescent bulb that was about to burn out. A full ashtray and a Diet Coke can sat on a TV tray next to a worn maroon recliner.

"I've been gone a long time," Hud said. "I'm sorry."

"Linda Dupree is my name now. It was Wayland, and then Sizemore for a brief time when you was a boy."

Sizemore made sense, and Wayland sounded familiar. Hud had gone to high school with a couple of kids with that last name, but he still couldn't place the woman's face. He nodded, then said, "How are you related to the boy?"

"I'm not really. Tim's always been the name on the birth certificate, but all one has to do is look at that kid and know he's no Sizemore, that he's not really his father. Got blue eyes and an odd-shaped nose. Gentle kid, too, all things considered. All our kids are mean as mongooses."

"So, you're kind of his grandmother?"

"Lord, no. Tim's my nephew. Look, between you and me, I know Pam named that boy Timmy after Tim just to hook him in to giving him a decent last name. Wasn't none of my business who the real father was, so I just kept my mouth shut. It didn't seem to matter 'til now, did it?"

"I'm sorry."

"Easy mistake to make; no worry." She blew a stray strand of brittle gray hair from her forehead.

"Why's the boy here?"

"Nowhere else for him to go. Simple as that. Pam ain't had people around here for a long time. Between you and me, I'm surprised it hadn't come to this long before now, the way she carried on. Tim never paid no money to her for support or such, or even acted like the boy was his too much. But he loved Pam at one time, so he didn't object to the legalities of it all, I guess. That was their business, not mine. I got troubles of my own. Anyway, I wasn't about to let any boy I knowed get lost in the government system. He knows me, been here once or twice, which don't make me much more than a stranger, but at least he's seen my face before."

Hud flinched, reacting to the sting of judgment about the dead girl's reputation, but tried not to show it. "I suppose you told Burke all of this and where he could find Tim?"

"I did, but I figured this mess was just startin' since that boy was here now. And I was right about that, too, wasn't I?"

"Probably so. Burke say anything about putting a deputy out front?"

"Why in the hell would he go and do that?"

"The boy might have seen something he shouldn't have. I figured you knew the risk you were taking."

Linda Dupree shook her head, and the color drained from her face. "He didn't say a word about that."

"All right, I'll talk to Burke about it."

"You don't think somebody would try to hurt that boy do you?"

"I hope not. Seems to me he's been through a lot the way it is. Can I talk to him?"

"Sure, sure, he's in my room. It's this way," Linda said, then turned and headed down a narrow hallway.

Hud lingered for a second, looked out the screen door to the vacant road with concern, then followed after the woman and the scent of cigarette smoke she'd left in her wake.

CHAPTER TWELVE

Memories of his own childhood danced just underneath Hud's skin. The tips of his fingers tingled, his chest ached, and his face felt as if it was on fire. He clamped his lips together so the boy wouldn't see his pain. Everything around him was lost in a swirl of gray light. The air was still, dank, and musty, with a hint of a woman's perfume just out of reach. Creaky floors threatened to collapse underneath his feet, encouraging his fear of falling, unaided into the darkness, that had pursued him since he had returned home. Somehow, even this far away, he could still taste the autopsy on the tip of his tongue.

The curtains were three-quarters drawn in the bedroom, and the boy laid in the middle of an unmade bed, curled up in the fetal position, staring off into space. A whole wall of disinterested family pictures stared down at him.

"Timmy, there's a man here to see you," Linda said.

Hud had almost forgotten that she was there, in front of him. He couldn't take his eyes off the boy. If his chest hadn't been moving, it would have been easy to mistake him for dead.

Timmy was small for his age. He was tall enough in a normal way, but his extremities were thin and fragile, just like his mother's. When Hud had seen Pam Sizemore naked, laid out, ready to be filleted, he had been convinced that she had abused her body with drugs and the lifestyle that came with them, but now he wasn't so sure. The boy almost looked like he had rickets or some debilitating disease with thirty-two letters in it that he'd never heard of. No one had suggested such a thing to him, that Timmy was sick or sickly, and there wasn't anything in the file. Maybe no one knew. That was possible. Somehow, Hud had missed seeing the frailty when he'd pulled the boy out of the fake lion's den at the Dip.

The boy didn't flinch, didn't acknowledge Hud's presence. He just kept his vision trained on some distant, nonexistent object or place. "Can he make momma better?" he finally said. It was almost a girl's voice, sounded exceptionally high. Hud hoped it would change when puberty hit, or life was going to be even tougher for Timmy Sizemore than it already was.

Linda Dupree looked at Hud sadly. Her tongue was all tangled up in her loose, yellowed false teeth, and she was unable to answer the boy. The corner of her right eye glistened with a tear.

"I'll just sit with him for a while, if that's all right?" Hud said to Linda, his voice low and gentle. He touched her arm, didn't let it linger. *Leave us alone. I've got this.*

"That'd be all right," she said. "I gotta get us some supper anyways. You holler if you need me, you hear, honey?" she said to the boy.

Hud nodded. "We'll be fine."

"I'm trustin' you," Linda Dupree insisted.

He nodded again. "I'll do my best not to upset him."

"I know you will," she said, backing away into the hallway, her eyes glassy, and her intention and route uncertain. She really didn't trust Hud. He knew that. Heard it in her voice. He didn't blame her. Trusting strangers in your house was something he could never manage for himself.

Hud eased into the bedroom like he was about to share space with a wild animal he didn't want to spook. "My name's Hud," he whispered, stopping halfway between the door and the bed.

"Momma said never to trust a cop," Timmy said.

Most mothers told their kids to never talk to strangers, Hud thought, but didn't say.

"You're another one, aren't you?" the boy went.

"Why's that?"

"What?"

"Why'd she tell you that?"

Timmy sat up and stared Hud directly in the eye. "Just because they wear a badge it don't mean they're the good guys." He blew a long strand of brittle blonde hair from the middle of his face. The boy needed a haircut, not so much because of the length, but because it needed to be pruned, encouraged, like a neglected bush in front of the house. There was nothing healthy about the boy. Even his eyes were dull and curiously dry. Hud hated to think it, but maybe the boy would get the help and sustenance he needed at Linda Dupree's house. Maybe he was better off with his mother dead, even murdered like she was. Maybe he had a chance at a decent life now. It was raw hope. Selfish hope. And Hud knew it. The boy was fucked. Most likely had been from the moment he'd been born.

"Well, I suppose your mom was right about that," Hud said. "You don't have to talk to me if you don't want to. I'll just sit here with you for a while if that's all right?"

Hud understood the distrust that had been bred by the boy's mother. He'd known bad cops and mean cops, along with weak cops who carried a gun and wore a badge to give themselves courage, who used the position to boost their ego, found reasons to search out the weakest ones and tower over them. Those kinds of cops were more common than not, but he wasn't quite sure they had been what Pam Sizemore had meant. He didn't know what her relationship with cops was, but something had set her off enough to warn her kid about the bad guys. In his own way, Leo Sherman had been a cop, a man charged with keeping the peace and law enforcement. He wore a badge. Maybe that's what she'd meant, that she'd had reason not to trust the CO long before she fled in fear and took a bullet to the back of the head.

"You don't have to trust me," Hud said after a long stretch of silence. "But all I want to do is help you."

The boy shrugged. "I want to go home. I just want to go home."

"I don't think that's possible."

"Ever?"

"Probably not."

"I don't like it here."

"I'm sure you don't."

"You can't make her better can you?"

Hud shook his head. "I wish I could. I wish I could tell you that this is all going to be okay, that you'll get everything back the way it was, but I can't tell you that. I can't lie to you. I won't lie to you."

"What's going to happen to me?"

"I don't know. But you're lucky."

"How's that?"

"You've got a lot of people that are looking out for you, who just want you to be safe and happy."

"I'll never be happy again," the boy said. "Never. Not until she comes back home."

"She's never coming back," Hud said.

Timmy Sizemore stared at him, and a sudden flash of understanding crossed his eyes. It was a mix of pain and horror, a look and feeling Hud knew too well.

"It's just you and me now," Gee had said ... But it was Hud's own words that rang in his ears, not Gee's. They weren't hateful or mean. Just as honest as they could be. Too honest. "I'm sorry," he offered. But it was too late.

Timmy Sizemore collapsed on the bed and let out a wail so loud that it threatened to shatter the windows of the small bedroom and every small bedroom beyond it. The pitch of it hurt Hud's head, reminded him of his own wound, and reignited his desire for another dose of morphine.

Hud couldn't offer anything more to the boy than he already had. He couldn't reach out to him and offer a comforting touch. He didn't say another word. He just backed away from the bed and walked as slowly out of the room as he had entered it.

He passed Linda Dupree in the hall. They slowed, but neither stopped, had the ability to. "What'd you do to him?" she demanded.

"I told him the truth."

~~~~~~~~~

The road curved around the lake, with cottages on one side and the shore on the other. The sun was starting to angle downward to the west, casting harsh yellow light onto the few feathery clouds that dotted the endless blue sky. A flock of ducks floated on the surface of the still water, and a great blue heron hunted ankle deep in the shallows, each move as calculated as its next breath. Hud slowed in hopes of seeing it strike but knew that if he stopped the Crown Vic the prehistoric looking bird would light into the air, its opportunity for a meal taken away by a man's desire to see a kill, to see nature working in its glory, the way it was intended. Hud knew the heron only killed so it could live. Unlike the human who had killed Pam Sizemore. He didn't know what the motive for the crime was, and he was no closer to finding that out than he had been when he first started. But he knew this: the kill hadn't been for survival or pleasure. It had been for something else. Greed. Betrayal. Passion gone wrong. A drug deal gone bad. A secret threatened to be revealed. Something human. Something immoral. Something the great blue heron could not even begin to comprehend.

Hud looked in the rearview mirror just in time to see the bird thrust its long beak into the water. But he had to glance away to stay on the road. He didn't see if the heron stabbed its prey successfully or not.

~~~~~~~~~

"Do you ever wake up in the middle of the night?"

"What kind of a question is that?"

"A yes or no one."

"You want more than that. You came back to this one."

"So it's a yes?"

"I didn't say that."

"Will you answer me?"

"No, I don't think I have to. We all have things that keep us awake at night."

~~~~~~~~~

Burke was waiting for Hud at the door. "In my office," he growled.

Hud looked past the chief into the well-lit conference room.

Lancet and Sloane had their backs to him, staring at the board of clues. The overhead fluorescent lights hurt his eyes, and Burke's tone, while not shrill, made Hud feel as though an icepick was being shoved into his eardrums. He said nothing, just did as he was told and followed Burke into his office like a dutiful dog. Whatever Lancet and Sloane were puzzling over would have to wait.

"What's up?" he said.

Burke pushed the door shut, then angled past Hud. He stopped at the front side of his desk so the two of them were facing each other. "What are you up to?"

Hud sighed, rolled his eyes to the ceiling. "I wasn't that late," he offered, defending his tardiness to the autopsy, trying to defuse Burke.

"What're you talking about?" Burke's pockmarked face was drawn tight, dancing just on the edge of anger. It was clear that the pressure of the murder was getting to him.

"I figured Bill Flowers told you I was late for the Sizemore autopsy." Hud tried not to react to the obvious anger that had accompanied him into the room. Burke was always angry about something, and he'd expected this confrontation sooner or later.

"Oh, I talked to Flowers all right. He called and raised hell with me about you, but not your bullshit tardiness. You promised me that this wasn't about *her*." Burke stepped forward so he was inches from Hud's nose.

Hud could smell the onions on Burke's breath from his lunchtime burger.

"Now it's my turn," Hud said. "What the hell are you talking about?"

"Her," Burke said, "your mother. You told me coming back here wasn't about her. But before I could turn my back, you're querying the computer, trying to access her file, then you're asking Bill Flowers questions. You lied to me, and I don't like it one bit. The last thing anyone needs around here is you going around stirring up more shit while there's a killer on the loose."

Now that he knew what Burke was really pissed about, the air between them changed. Hud had known Burke would be upset about his search for his mother. He had known, too, that he would get caught poking around about his mother sooner or later, and he hadn't cared. Not really. He couldn't help himself. "I didn't lie to you," he said.

"Then why in the hell did you come back here?"

"I didn't have anywhere else to go, goddamn it. I didn't have anywhere else to go."

CHAPTER THIRTEEN

The late afternoon light was pure gold, cascading through red oak and yellow birch leaves, dappling the ground in warm, earthy tones and hues that promised to be as short-lived as the sunshine. The smooth surface of the lake looked like the top of a bowl of soup, transforming it into something comforting and serene instead of the foreboding and bottomless blackness it had offered the night before. A slight breeze pushed cold, moist air off the water, hinting that the wind would get stronger in the coming weeks. Dry leaves vibrated with anticipation, spreading autumn's song to anyone who would listen.

The change of seasons and the coming of night promised a brief moment of beauty, but Hud was in no mood to digest scenery or spend time in awe of it. He was certain that he had overlooked something important on his first visit to the original crime scene. He just didn't know what.

He stood at the shore, just outside the yellow tape, staring at the ground where Pam Sizemore had taken her last breath. Bill Flowers had been absolutely sure that she had not been moved there, and Hud agreed with that conclusion, had seen no evidence to suggest otherwise. But it was an odd place for her to die.

What where you doing, Pam? Out and about on a rainy day wearing jogging shorts, a T-shirt, and no shoes? Was he chasing you? You left Timmy. Was he alone? Did you leave your little boy alone, Pam?

"I thought I'd find you here," Moran said, walking down the slope that led to the lake.

Hud looked up directly into the deputy's face, recognized the voice first, then struggled to remember her first name. Luckily, it came to him quickly: Joanne. The kickboxer. She moved easily and comfortably toward him, unaffected by the physical or emotional gravity of the land and the duty that she was in the midst of.

"Why was she here?" Hud asked out loud as Moran eased up to him.

~~~~~~~~~

"You know we have to talk about the incident in Detroit."
"The shooting is well documented."
"It is."
"Then you know all you need to know. A snitch turned on me. Not uncommon. Not unheard of. He'd been made. Killing was me was his redemption. I was double-crossed, lured into a situation that I wasn't prepared for."
"And you were carried out on a stretcher."
"I got lucky."
"The snitch took it a little worse."
"I was faced with a tough choice."
"To kill a man or not to kill a man?"
"Yes."
"It was your first time?"
"Yes."
"Do you regret it?"
"I don't know how to answer that question."
"Humor me."
"I'm just glad to be here."

~~~~~~~~~

Moran looked at Hud curiously, then cast a glance over the golden surface of the lake. "You have a theory?" she said.

"The obvious one," Hud said.

"That she was being chased. Hunted."

"Exactly."

"But you're not sure about that?"

"No. There were no deep footprints in the mud. It was raining that day. She would have left a full impression if she had been running for her life, you know? But there was nothing to suggest that. There were hardly any footprints at all. It was like she was dropped there, or taking a casual stroll, which is why I initially disagreed with Flowers's assumption that she hadn't been moved."

Moran nodded. "I looked at the pictures. You're right. There were no deep footprints. She wasn't running."

Hud studied the deputy's face, searching for the ambition he had first seen there. It was gone. Any anger at his sudden appearance as a detective had been replaced with need, determination, and curiosity. He was starting to like her even more. "There were other pictures that weren't on the board in the office."

"I saw enough," Moran said. She shifted her weight uncomfortably, looked at the ground for a brief second, then back at Hud.

"You have a theory of your own?"

"Not my place," she said.

"Yes it is. The victim, or victims in this case, deserve every consideration there is. You have a voice, a badge, skin in the game."

"Burke doesn't like deputies poking around where they don't belong."

Hud flinched, knew she was right. "He's not here. Tell me what's on your mind."

Moran looked him in the eye. Her tight jaw relaxed, and relief flitted through her blue eyes. "You've been gone from here a while. Things have changed around here," she said.

"It almost feels like I was never here. Everything and everyone I knew is gone, or changed in a way that I don't recognize."

"I get that," Moran said. "But some things haven't changed at all. There's a lot of people who aren't in tune with the modern world. They want things to be like they used to be. They don't want to acknowledge anything has changed at all."

"This *is* vacationland," Hud answered. "Some of those cottages look the same as they did sixty years ago. Inside and out. That's what people want when they rent them for a week. They want the memories they had as kids for their kids. Change is resisted for that very reason.

And then there's the fact that some people don't have the money to change. I've never seen this place as run-down as it is now."

"It's more than that. Burke's a Luddite. You have to know that. He walks around like it's the 1970s. We're lucky to have decent radios in our cruisers. Have any of you guys looked at the vic's social media pages?"

A weak tremor throbbed in the side of Hud's face. He felt pale and hungry. "No," he said. "I haven't. Sloane and Lancet haven't said a word about it, or posted anything on the board from it." Hud stared at Moran in a fresh light, looked at her from head to toe and imagined her dressed in plain clothes with a detective badge on her belt. It was easy to see. "Something tells me you have."

"Yes, I have, actually."

"Can you show me?"

"Sure," Moran said, as she pulled a cell phone out of her back pocket, and headed back to the car.

~~~~~~~~~

There was no way that Hud could not be aware of the wave of technology that had washed over the world since he was a boy. He had been born into a world of mainframe computers and phone booths on every other corner. Cable television was in its infancy. But by the time he was a teenager, cell phones and the rumbling of the Internet had burst into the mainstream as an affordable and necessary utility. He had seen the effects of technology on law enforcement over the years, welcomed it, actually. Unlike Burke, Hud was no Luddite, but he wasn't an early adopter, either. He saw no reason to have a Facebook page or spend any time on Twitter. Just as with the office computer, he knew how to navigate social media to get almost everything he needed, but he didn't have the skills to hack a file that had restricted access. He was going to work on that when he found the time. He wasn't surprised that Moran had skills and talents that he hadn't considered. *You might be more useful than I thought.*

"Her last entry on Twitter was posted about three hours before the call came in," Moran said.

She offered her phone to Hud. He didn't hesitate. The entry was simple: *Last call*.

"What do you think that means?"

Moran shrugged. "The rest of her posts are sporadic. Two, three weeks in between them. Some are pictures of the lake, of Timmy, of her out partying over the summer. But she never looked happy. There was nothing there to indicate that she was involved in drugs, was afraid, nothing. I looked."

"But the trailer was being used to cook meth," Hud said. "And she looked sick."

"She did, even the older pictures. I think she had a condition of some kind."

"I agree. Timmy is thin and frail just like her. They both looked malnourished, starved, and maybe they were. We don't know enough about their lives to know that yet."

"Unless she was sending out messages in code, I can't find a thing that suggests she was selling drugs except the very last one, and even then it's not certain that she wrote it, or that posts haven't been deleted. I'm just going on what I can see. That Tweet might not even be about anything we think it is."

Hud sighed, looked down at the phone one last time, then handed it back to Moran. "Anybody can see this, can't they?"

"Yes. But Burke needs to look deeper. Get a warrant. Look at everything. Facebook, Pinterest. Everything she did on the Internet. She might have left us some bread crumbs. We might have a motive for her death, for what's going on."

"I'll push him on that if he hasn't started down that path already."

"I bet he hasn't."

"He doesn't tell me everything."

"That doesn't surprise me." Moran stuffed the phone into her shirt pocket, then looked away from Hud, out the half open driver's side window. "I hate it that it gets dark so soon these days. We need more light. We need more time to find Leo Sherman."

Hud had barely acknowledged the shortening of the days. The last few were a blur. He followed Moran's gaze and watched as the golden light slowly retreated beyond the horizon, leaving grayness in its wake. "You don't think he killed her?"

"I've known Leo for a long time. This just doesn't fit his profile. He's a good man. Hard working. Loves his life. You'd know that if you ever spent five minutes with him when he was off duty. As far as he was concerned, he lived in paradise. I don't get it. If I was going to pick a man who'd fall prey to drugs or the money made by selling or making them, Leo Sherman would be the last person I would think of. The last person. Period. He hated what has happened here. He longed for the old days just like the rest of us. He escaped to the past on the water."

"Maybe you didn't know him as well as you thought you did," Hud said. "Everybody has secrets, a dark side just waiting to be pushed out. People break. And you don't know what that thing that breaks them will be. It could have been anything. Sex. Drugs. Money. You know that. You see desperation every day. I know I do."

"Maybe. But he is a *good* man. I don't want to believe it, I guess. That he could have fallen on hard times without asking for help," Moran said.

"I haven't seen that there's much help to be had around here."

"There's not."

Hud was about to reach out to her, say something, tell Moran that she'd done a good job, but he heard a distant sound that stopped any words from coming out of his mouth. In less than the blink of an eye, the windshield shattered. It was like a rock had been thrown at it from out of nowhere. But it wasn't a rock. It was a bullet. Someone had taken a shot at them.

"Get down!" Hud yelled. "Get down!"

CHAPTER FOURTEEN

For the second time in two nights the cottage lane was lit up like a carnival of flashing lights. Long fingers of reds, blues, and yellows reached into the early darkness, leaving shadows and uncertainty just beyond their grasp. Several men in county and state police uniforms milled about. A pair of ambulances sat at the crest of the hill, overlooking the lake. One ambulance sat with its back door open, its engine still running. Hud sat on a gurney inside and stared out into the gathering crowd.

"This is going to hurt," said a skinny male EMT in his mid-twenties, as he leaned in to pull a tiny shard of glass from Hud's lip.

Hud didn't flinch, didn't acknowledge the EMT. He was numb inside and out.

He focused on the blurry faces just beyond the brightness of the ambulance, looking for a familiar face, expecting to see the same nervous Social Security crowd as the day before, but Harriet Danvers and her cohorts were nowhere to be seen, and that concerned him. She'd seemed like the kind of woman who wouldn't have missed a reason to gawk, especially another incident most likely linked to "that Pam girl."

Hud recoiled as the EMT drew back with a glittery little diamond-like sliver perched in the grasp of a pair of tweezers. Blood trickled across Hud's bottom lip. Salt and the flavor of life and death. He made no effort to wipe it away. The bottom of his face felt like it had been stung by a squadron of wasps.

"I don't see any more glass in your face, but I really think you need to go in to the ER and get yourself checked out," the EMT said. He had a slight lisp and seemed self-conscious about it. He was a few years out of school and had the look of an adrenaline junky, but he was hard to take too seriously.

"I'll pass," Hud answered. "They might think I have a real problem if I keep showing up every day."

The EMT looked at him curiously.

"I was there yesterday," Hud explained, with a tap to the side of his bruised face.

"Oh."

"Can I go?"

"Sure, if you're up to it."

"I'm fine," Hud said, as he hoisted himself off the gurney and stepped down from the ambulance. The ground immediately threatened to swallow him up, and he had to reach to grab the side of the cold metal door to stabilize himself.

"You're sure you're all right?" the EMT said.

Hud ignored him, took a deep breath, and found his center of gravity. He wasn't sure where he was going; he just knew he had to get away from the ambulance, from the EMT, who smelled like sterile soap and had a bad case of coffee breath.

The other ambulance had its door closed. It had its engine running, too. Moran was inside. At least, she had been the last time Hud had seen her. Her face had been all bloody, peppered like his with pieces of the windshield, but she hadn't been hit, either.

There had been one shot. No more. But neither of them had moved until backup arrived. Luckily, Varner had just been up the road. They were both lucky—or the shooter was a bad shot. Something told Hud that wasn't the case. They were being warned off or scared off. Neither strategy would work. At least not with Hud.

Heavy footsteps kicking through soggy leaves approached Hud from behind. He glanced over his shoulder to see Burke heading toward him. *Great. He's on a mission.*

Hud stopped. Waited dutifully. "I figured you'd show up sooner or later."

Burke's ruddy face glowed in the flashing lights. The red and yellows hide the agitation brewing under the chief's skin. "Every time I turn around I'm cleaning up a mess you've made."

"I didn't do anything."

"The hell you didn't."

"I was just sitting here with Moran and we got shot at. How can that be my fault?"

"Watch yourself, Matthews."

"It's a valid question."

"Jesus, I'm starting to think bringing you into the department was the biggest mistake that I've ever made. First I get an uncomfortable phone call from Bill Flowers, then this woman, Linda Dupree, calls the office and says you terrorized the Sizemore kid. She went on forever complaining about you."

"Terrorized? That's a load of shit, Burke. All I did was ask the kid some questions, and answered some for him. I would never do anything to upset that boy for the fun of it."

"I didn't say you did. Linda Dupree said she couldn't calm him down thanks to you. Did you did tell him his mother was dead?"

"Yes, I told him she wasn't coming back."

"Like that's the easiest thing for the kid to hear."

"Somebody had to tell him."

"It didn't need to be you, goddamn it." Burke stepped closer to Hud. "You need to leave your personal baggage out of this. Out of everything, you hear me? I warned you about old business from the start. You promised me that you'd leave it alone," he said. "And stay the fuck away from that kid. He doesn't need to hear your shit."

"I can't help it. What'd you expect, that I was cured of my past? None of us are, Burke. You of all people should know that. You see it every day. I'm no exception. I can't help it if my mother disappeared when I was a kid. It had a price, an effect. How in the hell could it not?"

"Then it *was* a mistake."

"I can't say that," Hud said. "I'm glad to be home, to have this job, but I'll be damned if I can help it that I walked into the flat side of an oar one night, then got shot at on the next. You have an active investigation going on, and it has nothing to do with me other than I'm the one who was in the line of fire because I'm out here doing my goddamn job."

"Seems to me you're a target," Burke said.

"Maybe I am. Maybe any detective would be. If it's Sherman doing this, he doesn't know me. He's just trying to keep me from finding out the truth, or from finding him."

"And if it's not Sherman?"

"Why would you say that?"

"Because we don't know shit. For all I know, Leo Sherman is at the top of the world hanging out with the Eskimos and hunting polar bears."

Hud shrugged. "Maybe."

Burke glared at Hud, exhaled deeply, then looked past him at the closed-door ambulance. "How's the deputy?"

"I don't know. She was talking, not hit by a bullet, just glass, bloody as hell. I hope she'll be all right."

"Me, too. That's the last thing I need right now." Burke paused, focused his attention back on Hud. "I think you ought to go home. Call it a day. Take a few days off. You need some time to get yourself back up to speed. It's been a rough couple of days."

"This is the worst time for me to take time off. This thing is just starting to heat up. You need every man on this that you have."

"Don't tell me what I need." Burke's nose flared, and, without knowing that he was doing it, Hud stepped back. It was then that he saw Lancet and Sloane milling about just on the edge of the light, watching, listening to everything being said between the two of them. He didn't like it, especially when Sloane made eye contact with him, then looked away just as quick as she had made it.

"You know what I mean, Burke. I've got more experience in my right hand with a thing like this than those two will ever have. That's why I'm here," Hud said. "Isn't it?"

Burke held his ground, looked like he was about to snap in half as he restrained himself, aware, just like Hud, that there were eyes on him. "It's not a request, Detective Matthews. It's an order. I don't think you'll do any of us any good in the state you're in now. Get some sleep. Take it easy. I'll call you if something comes up that I think you need to know; if we need you."

"I don't have a choice?"

The closed ambulance revved its engine, drawing everyone's attention. The unseen driver hit the siren in three short blips, then put the truck in gear. The strobe bar on the roof flashed quicker, whiter, brighter. Without any further warning, the ambulance lurched forward on the gravel lane and began to drive away. For a brief second, Hud's concern fell away from himself and back to Moran. He really hoped she was going to be okay.

"No, you don't have a choice," Burke said, once he was able to hear himself speak. "Go home, Hud."

Hud drew in a deep breath, ready to protest more, but the stern look on Burke's face warned him off saying another word. He had to swallow his words, his pride, and walk away. This was a fight he couldn't win. He knew it as sure as he knew he was breathing.

~~~~~~~

"You could have gone back on the force in Detroit, not lost your seniority, your retirement."

"I could have, and I did until Gee died."

"How long was that."

"Six weeks, maybe seven officially. I wasn't marking a calendar."

"How was that?"

"How was what?"

"Going back after you'd been shot and the IA investigation had cleared you for duty."

"Fine, I guess."

"You weren't nervous, a little gun shy?"

"Would you be?"

"Maybe. Hard to say. The incident you were involved in wasn't simple."

"We've established that."

"You didn't have a twitch? You just got right back up on the horse *and went back at it? Your snitch network was destroyed, exposed, and you'd taken a hit. How'd the other detectives treat you?"*

"You want to know if I played well with the others?"

"Something like that."

"I'm surprised you have to ask."

~~~~~~~~~

Hud set the gym bag down next to the bar. "I'll have one for the road," he said.

Tilt Evans had his back to him, polishing a highball glass with a bleached white towel. He stopped in his tracks when he turned around. "Damn, son, you look like hell."

"Good to see you, too."

"I heard you took it a little tough."

"My day got worse."

"You need a drink?"

"I'm a little overdue."

"The usual?"

Hud nodded, swallowed in anticipation of the first sip of Wild Turkey. "Tell the morning clerk that I'll be back for the rest of my things tomorrow."

"You're leaving the Demmie?" Tilt finished pouring two fingers worth of whiskey into the glass, then nudged it toward Hud.

"I think it's time to go home," Hud said.

"If you say so," Tilt said, standing back with crossed arms.

"You don't think that's a good idea?"

"Not my business, is it?"

"Not really." Hud took a sip of the Turkey and longed for a cigarette. That would have to wait until he was outside, in his car. The amber liquid burned the back of his throat and offered a familiar hint of warmth that told him he'd found the pain reliever that he had been looking for. "Got a question for you, if you don't mind?"

"You've always been full of questions."

"Thank you for your support." Hud tipped the glass Tilt's way and took another sip. He let the burn fade away before he spoke again. "Did that Sizemore girl ever come in here?"

Tilt shrugged. "I wondered when you'd get around to that. Sometimes, sure. But she mostly hit Johnny Long's. She worked there on and off in the summers. She'd come over with some of the other waitresses and busboys after they closed up. I haven't seen her for a month or so, if I recall. One of your partners came in earlier asking the same thing."

"I don't have any partners yet."

"Too soon?"

"Sure, call it however you want. Which one was it?"

"The cowboy."

"That doesn't surprise me. Johnny Long's was the last place Pam Sizemore was seen alive. He probably went there first."

"You would."

"No, I'd come here first. I wouldn't want to spook whoever it was she went to see."

"You asking me that?"

"I am," Hud said, taking another sip, not taking his eyes off of Tilt.

"Couldn't tell you for sure. Like I said, she always came in with a small crowd. Most of them are gone now that the season is over with." Tilt paused, ran his leathery hand through his thick white hair, then stared up at the ceiling for a long second. When he looked back at Hud, it was as if a light had turned on in his faded blue eyes. "There was one kid that's from around here that still might be working there. Jordan Rogers is his name, I think. Yeah, that's it. Jordan Rogers. He worked down at the marina before it closed up, then started at Johnny Long's when he couldn't find nothin' else. Maybe you ought to talk to him."

"Thanks, Tilt, that's helpful. I will talk to him. Did you tell Detective Lancet that?"

Tilt shook his head. "He didn't ask. Seemed to be more interested in you than what was going on over at Johnny Long's."

"Is that so?"

"It is, but I didn't offer him much because there wasn't much to tell him. He's an odd one, the cowboy."

"That's good to know," Hud said, as a jolt of unsettled nerves pulsed up his spine. "What about the CO? Sherman? Did he ever come in here?"

Tilt shook his head. "Nope. Not once that I can recall. He was a by-the-book kind of guy. At least, he appeared to be. You were more likely to see him out on the lake in his boat alone than here or any of the other bars around."

"All right, thanks, you've been really helpful, Tilt." Hud started to turn to leave.

"There was somebody else in here looking for you," Tilt called out quietly.

Hud stopped and faced the man. "Who?"

"Goldie. Goldie Flowers. She said she'd give you a call when I asked her if she wanted to leave a message."

CHAPTER FIFTEEN

Soft morning light filtered into the bedroom, rousing Hud from a deep, fitful sleep. Once he opened his eyes, he wasn't fully convinced that he hadn't traded one nightmare for another.

His memory of driving from the hotel to the shop was dim, distant. He'd been on the edge of too much whiskey and on the threshold of pain that promised to stay with him no matter what he did. Hud had still resisted filling the prescription for pain killers, had relied on the benign over-the-counter medicines and his own personal grit to give him a little bit of relief. He liked the numbing effects of whiskey nearly as much as he did pain pills. Except the next day, when the aftereffects were usually worse than the cure. There was always a price to pay. He had enough addictions to manage.

Somehow, he'd fumbled the key into the locked door and navigated through the darkness to his childhood bed. It was a well-worn path, one that he'd taken a million times, and he could always count on Gee, living or dead, to keep things the same as they ever were. If he'd encountered an obstacle, he hadn't known it. Memory had guided him to safety and taunted him now that he had his eyes open.

Just like the rest of the house, Gee hadn't changed his bedroom since the day he'd left for college in Ann Arbor. Everything was still in its place; the movie poster over the bed, the case of science fiction paperbacks on the far wall, and, he was sure, the *Playboy* magazines stuffed in between the mattress and box springs. She had known they were there, and knew boys would be boys. There was no stopping what came naturally as far as Gee was concerned.

A thin layer of dust covered everything. All the old CDs, the bed posts, even the flimsy curtains that looked like they had been a feeding ground for a squadron of moths. Gee's last days had been weak, house-work the least of her concerns. Up until then, everything got a weekly cleaning. It was as if she were expecting Hud and his mother to walk in the door at any second and pick up their lives where they had left off. Unspoken hope had been an addiction for Gee, even though her face and gestures suggested bitterness and pessimism. If only that had been her only addiction. *It was the damn cigarettes and grief that killed her . . .*

Hud sat up in the small twin-sized bed, rubbed the sleep out of his eyes, and confronted the pain of the past couple of days. It felt like he had been run over by a raging bull and then rolled in a hornet's nest to top things off; his face felt like it was on fire. He hated to admit it, but Burke had been right in forcing him to take a few days off. He could barely think straight, much less go after a killer.

Coming back to Gee's house, on the other hand, had been his own idea. He wasn't comfortable in the bed, in the house, wasn't sure that he ever would be, but he felt he desperately needed familiar surround-ings. Not only to rest, but to recuperate and to see clearly, to see what lay before him and behind him. He needed a stable platform, and he longed to trust something, anything. He knew avoiding the inevitable was never going to solve anything, but he had resisted spending one night in the house for fear of the same thing. There was as much here that would hurt him as there was at the Demmie Hotel. But maybe from here he could see the big picture, find his way around.

Making it to the bathroom was a chore. His stomach was queasy along with everything else. After forcing himself to stand up and walk, Hud found his way to the shower and stood under the weak stream of hot water for what seemed like an hour. Afterward, he headed to the kitchen and fumbled around to make himself a pot of coffee. The kitchen had been Gee's domain. Even Hud had been treated like a guest, waited on no matter the meal or the snack.

Like most of the surrounding cottages, Gee's house had been built in the early 1920s, before the start of the Great Depression, as a summer getaway. It had been converted into a souvenir shop in the early 1950s, with a ten-by-twenty addition tacked onto the front by his grandfather. Over the years, the house had aged, the foundation settled, but the shop remained on a newer crawl space, so there was a six-inch step down into the house. A thick red velvet curtain acted as a door and separated the house from the shop. Just like everything else since Gee had died, Hud had avoided going into the shop, too. With the exception of making sure the Closed sign hung securely in the shop's front window.

He poured himself a cup of coffee and sat down at the Formica-topped dinette table. It was the same spot he had sat in every morning, eating his breakfast cereal, before going off to school. There were two other chairs. One was worn from use and had been Gee's, and the other, reserved for his mother, still looked new, untarnished. Hud sighed and looked deep into his cup of coffee. He had no desire to have a conversation with ghosts, which was one of the main reasons he had chosen to stay at the Demmie instead of coming back here.

There were no answers in the coffee cup, and no avoiding the ghosts, either. Memories of his mother danced just out of reach. She had been nearly lost from his sight in a haze of time, perched on the edge of a hangover, untouchable. Hud strained to hear her voice, but he was deaf to it now after so many years. He longed to hear her say his name, call him in for supper, anything. He wouldn't care if she were screaming at him—which she never did—just so he could feel the vibrations of her voice in his eardrums and in his heart.

His mother was a tall shapely woman, always in a summer dress, it seemed, white or yellow, her skin tanned and healthy from ample time out in the sun, sitting on the beach, reading or slathered in baby oil and iodine, baking to a darker brown. She always wore a smile, and her fresh lipstick covered her red lips. Ray Ban sunglasses shaded her eyes from the sun, and she never had a hair out of place. "You have to keep up with yourself," she'd told Hud more than once. It was a permanent image; one Hud couldn't have altered if he tried—which he didn't. His memory of her as happy and perfect was what sustained him, even though he knew it was nothing but a fantasy, only partially the truth. She had darker seasons. Not just summer. Alcohol came to claim its price from her the next day just as it did for Hud. Both of them suffered horrible hangovers.

The ghost of Gee, on the other hand, was all gloomy and decrepit, bent over in a cough or trying catch a breath of air. Green oxygen containers still stood stacked in the living room next to the couch. Lung cancer had taken her in the end. Years of smoking cigarettes had caught up with her, and, though she had been a big woman for as long as Hud could remember, the old, shrunken woman that had lain in the casket had hardly looked like Gee at all. Hud tried his best to conjure the younger more vibrant memory of Gee, but he couldn't. All that he could see in his mind now was the more recent one. The sick one, the frightened one being eaten up from the inside out. The one that screamed that death was inevitable, that there was no stopping it for anyone. *Hadn't Gee suffered enough?*

Hud had tried to quit smoking because of her, and he'd nearly succeeded until he'd taken the county detective job. The thought of a cigarette provoked him to tap the breast pocket of his bathrobe, but it was empty, propelling him to stand, to walk away from the ghosts at the kitchen table.

Hud reluctantly made his way to the red velvet curtain that separated the shop from the house. It still smelled of cigarettes and bacon grease. He closed his eyes, grasped the warm ceramic handle of the coffee cup as if it would keep him from falling over or give him the strength he felt he was missing, and then pushed through the curtain.

It was like walking into a museum. The shelves were lined with perfectly folded T-shirts, most of which said: "Demmie Lake—A Little Piece of Heaven." Some of them bore rainbows over a lake, while others had nothing on them other than three sailboats in front of half a red sun. The T-shirts had always been the cash cow of the shop—that and refilling the propane tanks for campers and gas grills. Filling the tanks had been Hud's summer job once he was old enough. He hated the smell of it to this day: raw eggs mixed with something dead. Summers weren't as long for him as they were for the rest of the kids. Gee always had something for him to do around the shop. She had, of course, wanted him to take it over when she couldn't run it anymore, but that hadn't been the case. Hud wanted nothing to do with the hard work of summer. He wanted to be as far away from the lake as possible.

He'd never felt like Gee approved of him becoming a cop, or had been proud of him at all. Every time he went to see her, she would always ask when he was coming back to where he belonged. The trips to see her grew sparser, until, in the end, he had stayed away almost a year.

The rest of the shelves in the shop bore coffee cups, ash trays, miniature cups and saucers, all with the same logo as the T-shirts. Gee bought them in bulk from a merchandise salesman who came around in the early fall, selling the next season's wares to her. There was a fun section, one that held whoopee cushions, fake vomit, and dog turds for the practical jokers. There was also an adult section behind the counter: girlie magazines, books with dirty jokes, and squirt guns shaped like penises; anything for a buck. How could Gee keep such things from a curious boy? She didn't have the energy or the inclination.

The front of the counter held rows of penny candy, or at least they had used to cost a penny a piece. Now it was a dime or a quarter. There was no escaping the smell of stale bubble gum. And, of course, floaties hung from the ceiling—multicolored rings with dragon heads, mermaids, and horses, which were best sellers. They were deflated and faded like ghosts of past summers, of forgotten childhoods and lost days.

Gee sold some fishing gear, bobbers, sinkers, and line, but she had never had any desire to compete with the local bait shops. She wasn't having insects or worms in her house. The smell of such creatures was more than she could take, or so she said.

Hud wasn't looking for treasures or keepsakes. His eyes went straight for the shelf under the cash register and found exactly what he knew he would: Gee's cigarettes. She'd been a devoted smoker to the very end.

He set the coffee cup down on the counter, hesitated for a second, then grabbed up the pack of Chesterfields and proceeded to light a cigarette. The smoke burned all the way down his throat. Just like everything in the shop, the cigarettes were old and stale. Hud coughed and eased the discomfort with a long swig of coffee. He should have put some whiskey in it. Hair of the dog. He hadn't thought of it, and, besides, he didn't know if there was any alcohol in the house or not.

There was nothing for him to do in the shop. He wanted to get out of there as soon as possible. The ghosts had followed him. Including the memory of himself, of all of his summers before and after his mother had disappeared. He wished he could forget them, forget the boy he was, but that was impossible. There was no escaping the past.

A sound drew his attention to the front door. A car pulled into the lot and came to a stop, just as so many customers had in the past. Only this was no customer. The car was familiar. It was a county car, a Crown Vic just like he drove. Only it was not Burke behind the wheel. It was Detective Sloane.

～～～～～～

"You know there was doubt about your account of the incident?"
"You read all of the report. I'm impressed."
"It doesn't bother you that they didn't believe you?"
"They obviously did in the end, didn't they?"
"If you say so."
"The fact that I'm here speaks for itself."
"Will you recount your movements that day from beginning to end for me?"
"No."
"Why not?"
"The fog of time is powerful. You know that. It's all there. I stand by my testimony."
"You'd be a fool not to, wouldn't you?"
"Yes, wouldn't I?"

～～～～～～

Hud made his way to the door, unconcerned that he only wore a bathrobe. He opened it, with his coffee and cigarette in one hand, and stood on the threshold barring Sloane immediate entry into the shop. "Come to check on me," he said, not believing a word of it.

"Something like that."

Hud looked around her to make sure there wasn't anyone else in the car or another cop car in sight.

"I'm alone," Sloane said. She looked him up and down, from head to toe. "Rough night?"

"Something like that," Hud said. "You want to tell me what this is about? I don't think you stopped by to check on my personal welfare."

"We need to talk. Do you mind?" She nodded, motioned inside, then glanced over her shoulder, looking down the road for a long second. She wasn't sure she was alone, either.

"No, sure," Hud said. "Come on in. But the place is a mess. I wasn't expecting company."

CHAPTER SIXTEEN

The two of them sat at the kitchen table doing their best to ignore the discomfort in the air. The faucet dripped steadily, and someone ran a chain saw off in the distance, getting their woodpile ready for the coming winter.

"Good coffee," Sloane said. She was dressed in a plain gray pantsuit, typical for her, from what Hud had seen. He wondered what she looked like with her hair down and her curves pressed tight into a nice pair of jeans. Even with a raging headache, he couldn't help himself from trying to find the beauty she had tried so hard to hide.

Tina Sloane had perplexed him from the moment they'd met. She put a lot of effort into being taken seriously. Too much as far as Hud was concerned. He wondered what she was afraid of, what she was hiding, and, of course, why in the hell she was sitting at his kitchen table first thing in the morning.

"So'd Burke send you?" Hud finally said.

Sloane shook her head. "He'd be pissed if he knew I was here." She looked around the kitchen, taking everything in. She was curious, observant, cataloging everything she saw. Hud knew the look. There was no judgment on her face. "I always wondered what was behind that curtain," she said.

"You came here as a kid?" Hud felt the urge to light another one of Gee's Chesterfields but restrained himself. He searched Sloane's face for a hint of familiarity but couldn't find it. Thousands of kids had walked through the front door of the shop over the years. It was impossible to put a face to the past, but he couldn't help trying. There was a wistfulness in Sloane's voice, a hint of loss that Hud recognized without any urging.

"My dad would come over from time to time, go fishing with some of his friends."

"His cop friends," Hud said. It wasn't a question.

She nodded, her eyes lost in a private memory. "We lived in town, but twenty miles away might as well have been a million on most days. It wasn't vacationland on my street growing up."

"You think it was easy where I grew up?"

"Never said that." Sloane took a sip of coffee, peered over the brim of the cup the entire time, never taking her eyes off of Hud.

"I suppose it was tough being a cop's kid," he said.

"You saw that with Burke. It wasn't easy for him, either."

"His dad was a hard-ass. Makes him look like a puffball, even now. But I was a kid then, like you. He seemed like he was ten feet tall, carried the world on his shoulders. I don't think I ever saw Burke's dad crack a smile."

"Me, either."

"Cop friends. You've known Burke for a long time." Hud stared at Sloane's face again, closer. It frustrated him that he didn't know who she was. "How come I don't know you?"

She shrugged. "We didn't come over a lot, and when we did, I usually wasn't let out of my mother's sight for long. She was determined that I'd be a prim and proper girl, even though I wanted to be out in the boat fishing with the boys. We drank tea and ate cookies with Mrs. Burke while everybody else was having a good time. Hard to get dirty in a dress. I suppose I could have used the ribbons in my hair for fishing lures. My dad would sneak me away and teach me to shoot, how to handle a gun. I wanted to be just like him from the time I could remember."

"So you're one of Burke's old pals, too. Some of the deputies have a chip on their shoulder about the chief's crew. That it's made up of all old friends; that that's the only way to get a position around here."

"Cronyism. Yeah, I've heard that, too. I just try to ignore it. We've known each other for a long time. So what? It's really a small town here, especially after the season's over. It's green eyes and envy, that's all."

"Gee used to say that. There were a lot of green eyes coming and going around here."

Sloane set the coffee cup down with a long sigh. "I'm sorry. I didn't come here to tell you my troubles. I don't know what came over me."

"It's this place," Hud said. "It still smells like bubble gum and happier times. That's what we sold. False happiness and plastic memories. That thing you take home with you and look back on fondly. It doesn't matter that it was made in China, cost pennies to make, and was sold for a nice little profit. The drag of time doesn't help, just makes it more appealing. Maybe the lake is the one place you thought you had the happiest day of your life. You'll remember it when you see a T-Shirt or a floatie like you had as a girl, which I would have guessed would never have been the princess one for you. You must have been a huge disappointment to your mother."

"You could say that. I think she sits in terror every day, waiting for me to come home to tell her I'm a lesbian—which I'm not, by the way. I'm just more like my dad. Practical, less interested in flare, and more interested in the job than what I see in the mirror or what anybody else thinks."

"What are you doing here, Sloane? What's so important that you're willing to piss off Burke to tell me?"

She trembled—distantly. Hud only saw it because he was staring at her, watching every fiber of her being for a sign of something, anything, that would explain her presence. She made him uncomfortable.

"I think you should be careful, that's all. I just think you should be careful."

"It's a little late for that. I've been ambushed with a boat oar and shot at in the last two days. My face is peppered with little pieces of glass that the wiry little EMT assured me would work themselves out over time, and Burke has put me on the sidelines of the first case I caught since coming on the squad, and I should be careful? Speaking of glass, how's that deputy, Moran? The ambulance drove off with her last night."

"She checked out fine from what I heard, was cleared for duty."

"Good. Now, what exactly is it that I should be afraid of? Leo Sherman?"

"I don't know what to think," Sloane said with resignation. "I've known Leo for a long time. He loved his job, his wife, where he lived. It doesn't add up." She paused and stared at Hud for a long second. Her soulful brown eyes felt like a trap, and he had to look away from her quickly. "If he wanted you dead, he would have killed you the first time."

"Maybe he didn't have time. Burke was there pretty quick from the way he tells it."

"Maybe. But he wouldn't have missed the second time. Sherman was as good a shot as there was and a skilled deer hunter. We wouldn't be sitting here talking if Leo Sherman had pulled that trigger. I'm sure of it."

"Then who's taking shots at me?"

"I don't know. I wish I did. And I wish I knew where Sherman was. It's like he's vanished into thin air."

Hud sighed. "That seems to happen around here."

"Oh, I'm sorry. I didn't mean to bring up anything."

"Burke told you about my mother?"

"He mentioned it." Sloane paused and drew back. "You should be wary of him."

"Who?"

"Burke. You should be careful of Burke."

Hud leaned back in his chair and dug into the pocket of his robe for the pack of cigarettes. "You mind?" he said, as he struggled a Chesterfield out of the pack.

"Suit yourself. Your house, your lungs."

Hud proceeded to light the cigarette, took a deep drag, then exhaled away from Sloane. "I've known Paul Burke most all of my life. He's more bark than bite. Always has been. If you were around as a kid, then you know that to be true. You're like your old man, and so is Burke. He's always been kind of a bully, but he doesn't scare me. Never has."

"That's the problem. Burke's stepped into his father's shoes. He idolized his father. You know that," Sloane said.

"You would know. Seems like you're two peas in a pod, now that I know you a little better."

"More than I want to be."

What's that supposed to mean? Hud wondered but didn't ask. Her voice cracked, suggesting an exposed nerve had been touched. "What's Burke's dad have to do with me, with what's going on now? He's been dead for years," Hud said.

"As long as Burke wears his badge, his father's legacy is still alive. Burke will do anything to protect what he thinks of him. That's what I wanted to talk to you about. He's been on edge ever since you came back. This murder case has him wound up tight as a drum. One more hit and I think he'll snap. Just be careful. That's all I'm telling you. This place has changed. Burke's changed. Everything is one push away from falling apart. Look around; it doesn't take much to see that."

Hud tapped the cigarette on the edge of the ashtray. "I'm still not sure what you're telling me."

"Just do what he tells you to do, that's all. Do your job, don't rile him. Ease your way back into his good graces."

"I didn't know that I was out of them. He hired me."

"So he could keep an eye on you," Sloane seethed. It was almost like she wanted to call him an idiot, but she'd restrained herself, bit her lip, and grabbed the edge of the table. After a long second, she stood up from the table abruptly. "I have to go. Really, I shouldn't be here." She started to walk away, but stopped halfway to the red curtain and turned back to Hud. "Forget that I was here, please. Don't mention it to anyone, especially Burke. You can't tell Burke I was here." There was fear on her face and in her voice. Her comfortable complexion had suddenly bleached white.

Before Hud could say anything, tell her that her presence wouldn't be known to anyone, Sloane spun around, pushed through the curtain in a rush, and disappeared.

～～～～～～

The sky was clear of clouds, a mild topaz blue that reflected down on the lake, making the whole world look calm and serene. A flock of sandhill cranes circled high above the water, their chorus of melodic calls filling the air. The big gray birds sounded like the French horn section of an orchestra. It wasn't long before a distant flock of Canadian geese filled in the absence of any other sound, and the presence of the birds became a full performance. Red and yellow leaves fluttered to the ground. There was hardly a breeze, and the sun felt warm on Hud's face. Gee had called days like this Indian summer, but all that mattered to Hud was that he didn't need a jacket. It was nice to feel free, be alone in the world. Even in its decaying state, Detroit was always noisy, with a throng of people coming and going somewhere.

Sloane's visit had unsettled Hud. That and the closed up air inside the house. It smelled of death and loss in there, and it was too much for him, one of the things he had purposely avoided. He still expected Gee to bust out of her room, a cigarette dangling from her mouth, dressed in a clean purple flower-print muumuu, her hair freshly colored black and piled up two stories atop her head, barking orders for the coming day. But that didn't happen. There was no one there to tell Hud what to do at home. Maybe that was part of his problem.

He'd dressed for the day, opened all of the windows to air out the house, then made his way outside to smoke a cigarette. He was already back up to his pack a day habit. His .45 was stuffed comfortably in the small of his back, and he was keenly aware of everything around him. Or tried to be. Spotting a sniper with a scoped rifle would have been impossible, and it would most likely be too late if he did see one. Still, he wasn't going to walk around like nothing had happened the day before.

He puffed on the cigarette thoughtfully as he gazed at the shop. The outside was in as bad a shape as the inside was. The sign at the entrance was faded, almost a ghost of its original self. Another winter and it would be. A Closed banner was pasted across the road sign, and another one stood in the door. Even though it was past the season, people still pulled into the parking lot and came up and peered in the dirty windows. A sash hung cockeyed, and, like the rest of the building, it was severely in need of a coat of paint. At one time, there were plywood cutouts of boats and T-shirts nailed to the shutters, but they had fallen to the ground or been stolen. With the settling foundation and the sagging roof, the place really looked like it was ready for the bulldozer.

Hud turned away from the shop and stared down the ravine at the Dip, which was in similar disrepair, and longed to see something that wasn't so depressing. He had no desire to revisit the ice cream shop. Pulling Timmy Sizemore out of the lion's cage had been enough of a reunion.

He walked away, allowing his feet to take him down a familiar path, one that wound past the back of the shop, beyond the two-car garage, and ended up at the shore of the lake. But to get there he would have to go through a small resort—seven cottages, each about the same size as the garage, that were, at one time, painted bright green to go along with an Irish motif. The place was called the Shamrocks. To full-timers, the resort was called the Shams, mainly because it was the most expensive resort on the lake and didn't even offer inside bathrooms. Every little cottage had an outhouse, and all of the vacationers shared a shower room, set at the back of the office. People gladly paid whatever the rent was in the summer, just glad to have a place to stay. But that was a long time ago. It was in the off-season that the Shams had earned its most notorious reputation, but those days were long gone, forgotten by most people.

Hud knew the cottages would be in as bad a shape as everything else around the lakes. He was right, of course, and didn't linger to consider what was left of the Shams. A big red Condemned sign was posted next to the road. He kept walking; he'd spent enough time poking around the place to last a lifetime. The cottages didn't look as if they'd housed a vacationer in ten years. Another victim of decline, another memory eroded by time, weather, and neglect.

Hud walked steadily down the hill, keeping an ear out for any sign of human presence. There was no one to be seen. The cranes had flown on, but the geese still winged their way from one end of the lake to the other. The trail was lined with tall pine trees and deciduous trees that had lost nearly all of their leaves. Woodpeckers worked out of sight, and nuthatches and chickadees bandied about in search of a seed or two for a quick meal. Hud walked and smoked, taking it all in, never losing the feel of the .45. He had walked that trail a million times as a kid, usually carrying a fishing pole and pail of worms for bait.

Hud slowed when he came around the next bend. He was almost to the lake. The house he was staring at sat on the lakefront, just at a point, giving it one of the best views on the entire body of water. Unlike everything else in the area, the house looked exactly like it had when he was a kid. It was freshly painted, a spotless white that almost seemed to glow in the bright sunlight. All of the windows shone like diamonds, and the shutters were painted a deep blue. A fishing boat sat covered next to the garage, and he could see the water of the lake just beyond, smooth, calm, and dotted with ducks and geese.

Hud stopped at the driveway just as the back door of the house opened. A woman stepped outside, not elderly-looking or decrepit, just an older, more mature version of the woman that he remembered so well. "I was wondering when you'd get around to coming by to say hello," Paul Burke's mother said with a hard, direct glare.

〜〜〜〜〜

"Did you want to die?"

"You know, I'm starting not to like how you ask questions. I thought you were pretty good up 'til now."

"I won't apologize for that. You walked into a tense situation alone, didn't call for backup, didn't let anyone know your intentions. It's an obvious question. You had to know the risks."

"I was involved in an investigation. It was a meeting with my snitch."

"Off the record. It was an off-the-record meeting."

"It's in the report. I'm not answering that."

"Okay. You're hostile. You refuse to cooperate. Is that really how you want this to go? I've been extremely patient . . ."

"I don't see how the Detroit incident is relevant. I've already said that."

"Do you refuse to cooperate?"

"I'm still sitting here aren't I?"

"Can we continue?"

"Yes. If we can get past this."

"We will. I just have a few more questions that I need answers to before we go on."

CHAPTER SEVENTEEN

Helen Burke walked with the precision of a drill instructor, even when she was on a stroll. Her short gray hair looked soft and cared for, washed, cut, and set twice weekly at the local beauty parlor if she still adhered to her former routine. Her hair was a fitting contrast to her deep, hard-as-steel blue eyes. She wore a light jacket, just a little heavier than a windbreaker, that looked like it had never been worn. Her jeans were creased, recently ironed and starched, and her tennis shoes bore no marks or wear. They glowed white. If Hud had to guess, Helen Burke polished or bleached her shoes regularly, just like everything else that came within her reach.

"The place looks the same," Hud said, as they walked the lane that edged the lakeshore, water on one side, vacant cottages on the other. Some were rentals, while others were seasonal regulars who had already winterized and gotten on with their life elsewhere, waiting for spring to roll around again so they could visit the lake every weekend again. At least, that was how it used to be.

Helen walked along steadily, looking straight ahead, almost ignoring Hud. "It's my sanctuary. Always has been. But you know that, don't you?"

"Sure, I suppose so." He twitched at her tone, not quite sure what it meant. The chief got as much of his no-nonsense personality from his mother as he had from his late father. Maybe more.

"Times have changed," Helen went on. "The lake has changed. It's dirtier than I ever remember. We all get older, I suppose." She stopped walking, and Hud followed suit, automatically allowing her control of the moment. There was no use fighting it. "I was sorry to see Gee go," she said. "It's the end of an era. Especially with that new, big buy-everything-you-need store just outside the entrance on the south end of the lake. It's the one economic bright spot in this miserable place, I guess. But all of those fast food restaurants popping up around it are just awful. There's hardly anywhere to get a good meal around here. Even Johnny Long's isn't what it used to be. Do they even have supper clubs in the outside world anymore?" Most full-timers were keenly aware that they lived in an isolated world, and Helen more than most.

"Fast food and those big stores are what people want," Hud said. "Little mom-and-pop shops like ours can't compete, and nobody wants to shop around anymore. Not even in vacationland. They want everything under one roof."

"It's a shame. What're you going to do with it? Tear it down?"

"The shop? I haven't given it much thought. Clean it up, sell it, I suppose. I don't want to live there, but I hadn't thought about tearing it down. I don't think I could do that. But I don't want to stay there."

"It's that hard?"

"Hard enough. I've changed, too. No sense in living in a past that I can't change."

"You really expect me to believe that?" Helen Burke said.

Hud stiffened, tapped his chest for a cigarette, then decided against it. Helen had been a smoker once, too, and then become a fierce opponent of it once her husband died of lung cancer—just like Gee. "You can believe what you want."

"It's not that simple, and you know it, Hud. You've been asking questions. I still hear things, even though I'm not out and about like I used to be."

"That's my job."

"When it comes to that girl and Kaye Sherman, it is. It sure is. That business needs to be put to rest as soon as possible. We're all lucky it's not the middle of the season. It'd be the straw that breaks the camel's back around here. We don't need any more bad press. But that's not what I'm talking about and you know it. Don't go playing coy with me Hud Matthews. I've always been able to tell when you've been up to something and now's no different. I don't care how old you are or what your job is. I know what a cop does. I married one and raised one."

She paused, looked closer at Hud's face. "You look like hell, by the way. Maybe you'd be better off selling T-shirts again. Police work doesn't look like it suits you very well."

Hud resisted the urge to touch his face and test the swelling. He could feel how it looked from the inside out. "I'm not up to anything other than getting on with my life and taking care of the things I need to." It was Hud's turn to pause. "Did you know Kaye Sherman well?"

"You're assuming that I knew her at all."

"I know you knew her. You always made it your business to know all of the full-timers."

"Part of my unofficial duties."

"Sure, if you say so. Did you know her well?"

"Our circles overlapped from time to time. I can tell you this: Kaye Sherman was a good, honest woman. Kind hearted as the day is long. And her Leo was a decent man, too. At least I always thought he was, but I have no idea what he was doing with that Pam girl."

That Pam girl . . . touched a nerve. "Do you know Harriet Danvers?"

"The old woman?"

"Yes."

"Only one that I know of. Our circles never cross, I can promise you that. I heard she was the one that called in the murder."

"Seems to me you know a lot for not being out and about much."

"I can see why someone shot you."

Hud didn't know if Helen was kidding or not. It was always hard to tell with her. She was always serious—except when she wasn't.

Helen smiled quickly. "Sorry, you've always been a bit of a smartass, Hud."

"Gee taught me well." Hud stared at Helen Burke longer than he should have, and he knew he couldn't stop the thought that was forming in his mind. "The circles seem to be the same now, only with a few more people missing."

Helen stiffened, sneered, then looked away to the lake. "Time marches on Hud. You aren't the only one who has lost somebody."

"Suck it up, right? Get on with my life. Keep a stiff upper lip . . ."

"Don't you get that fresh with me, Hud Matthews. I've never tolerated such behavior from you or anybody else, and I'm not about to start now."

"You have somewhere to go," Hud said. It was almost a whisper. "You can put flowers on a grave, mark the anniversary. There's a place you can go to talk to your husband if you're so inclined. I don't have any of that. Just questions that nobody could, or would, answer for me. I have old faded pictures and a bedroom with a lock on the door. It quit smelling like her in there ages ago. I used to sneak in and try to conjure her up in my mind anyway I could. Now even that's mostly gone. It's just a museum now. I can barely picture her in my mind, and when I do, she looks like an old black and white picture, not a real person."

Helen Burke's hand came up from her side so fast it was as if she was about to pull a gun on Hud. She pointed her index finger straight at his face, a few inches from his nose. "You listen to me and you listen good. Nobody around here had anything to do with your mother disappearing. Did you ever consider that she just up and left? Abandoned you and Gee for a better life? Did you ever consider that? You didn't know your mother like I did. She always wanted something more, something better. But you don't know that. All you know is what Gee filled your head with and the fantasies that you made up yourself. Face it, Hud, she's gone. It's the past. You're right. Just leave it alone. For your sake, and everybody else's."

"I was just a boy," Hud said, the whisper softer, farther away.

Helen dropped her finger and shook her head. "I'm sorry. You're right, you were. But you're not anymore. You're a grown man." And then she spun and stormed off back toward her house, leaving Hud standing alone with the warm sun trying to soothe his face as the sadness grew deep in his gut.

~~~~~~

"You were aware of the IA investigation into you before the shooting?"

"I suspected."

"But you weren't sure?"

"That's what I just said."

"You weren't afraid that your snitch was going to turn on you?"

"I've answered that question before. The only way I had motive to kill him was if I had something to hide. I had nothing. Nothing. I shot him in self-defense. I didn't plan on going there to kill Leroy. End of story."

"You're consistent."

"I have no reason to lie about Detroit. I took my shots. I've healed."

"Physically."

"What are you suggesting?"

"There were lingering concerns. Anything could send you over the edge. Like losing a loved one. That's all. But you know that, too."

~~~~~~~

Hud couldn't help but wonder what circles Harriet Danvers *did* travel in. The last thing he wanted to do after being scolded by Helen Burke was go back to the shop and revisit the emptiness that he couldn't escape, so he figured the best thing he could do was go find out for himself.

He drove toward the first crime scene, hesitant only because of being shot there, and not because he was disobeying orders from Burke by working the case when he was supposed to be taking some time off. Harriet Danvers lived close by.

It was ridiculous to expect that he was just going to lie around. That wasn't his style, and Paul Burke knew that as well as anyone else.

Hud eyed the landscape with interest as he drove away from the shop, trying to reconcile it with his memories of the past. The style of the cottages looked the same, all boxy bungalows. Very few of them had garages but instead had boathouses on the lake and fish-cleaning shacks not far beyond that. A lot of them had names on them like the Hideaway or Tiny's Retreat, painted on plaques that hung by the front door. None of them looked familiar, though they should've. He'd driven the lakeshore road a thousand times, if not more. Everything looked smaller, distant, rundown in a fading, crumbling kind of way that Hud didn't remember. It was like the lake and the earth were trying to reclaim the land from the humans, wearing down the structures with rain, wind, and vining ivy that threatened to take over the world. Left to the elements, some of the cottages didn't look like they would last out the year.

The police radio was on, quiet mostly, until he heard the dispatcher call for a deputy. Moran answered. Hud was relieved to hear her voice, that she had come back to work as quickly as he had, though her capacity was obviously official and his wasn't. Someone had reported a boat stolen from the Demmie Lake Boat Company, and Moran was closest. Hud looked around, figured out where he was in comparison to the marina, and brought the car to a stop. He was heading the wrong way.

If his thinking was right, he could get there at about the same time as Moran. He didn't call in, didn't let anyone know he was on the way, just put the car into reverse, spun it around, and headed to the marina as quickly as he could.

CHAPTER EIGHTEEN

The county cruiser was empty, sitting by the front door of the boat company with its strobes on when Hud arrived. There was no one milling about. He parked on the side of the lane, just at the edge of a row of tall pine trees. He could see the building clearly, along with anyone who came and went from it, but it would be hard for anyone to see him unless they were looking. He rolled down the window so he could smoke and listen. He wasn't about to horn in on Moran. Not yet.

The Demmie Lake Boat Company was a small marina set back from the lake in a cove that was only accessible by a narrow manmade channel. A dense wood surrounded the cove, and a series of well-worn foot trails cut through it. A few bare fishing spots dotted the shoreline in between bunches of cattails, protected from the hot sun in the summer by the canopy of tall walnut and oak trees. Thickets and a host of itch-inducing plants made everything else difficult to get to for humans, but plenty of wildlife—deer, raccoons, possums, and a huge variety of songbirds—had no trouble at all navigating the woods.

Hud had fished a lot of those spots as a boy, hit them all when the bluegill were spawning next to the shore in the spring, then later, in the more difficult parts of summer, he had retreated into the woods to smoke cigarettes he had stolen from Gee. He had fond memories of watching people come and go from the boat company, while he was hidden from their view. It had been good practice for enduring stakeouts, though he hadn't known it at the time.

Six docks jutted out into the water, with twelve bays for boats, most of which were empty because of the time of the season. A few pontoons sat tied to posts, along with a few fishing boats that most likely belonged to diehard full-timers who took every chance they could get to be out on the lake. In the summer, there were more boats than there were spaces, and boats were parked and secured along the treeless sections of the shore. A smaller dock poked out just in front of the building with a gas pump on the end of the dock. It sat under an old rusty Sunoco sign, and there was a bell to ring if an attendant of some kind wasn't about. On a windy day you could hear the bell ring a mile away, especially when an impatient customer wasn't getting the kind of service he expected.

The Demmie Lake Boat Company's building itself was like most everything else in the area, old, rundown, but still standing. It was nothing more than a two-story barn that had been extended to triple its size over the years. The exterior bore horizontal slats, grayed by the weather and time, rotting away a little more every day. Inside was a wide open space filled with boats and motors for repair. Boats were also stored up on the second floor. A collection of lifts and pulleys were visible from just about everywhere in the building and always seemed to be in operation. The office and parts counter were no bigger than a tool shed, and the walls were lined with pictures of boats, barely clad big-busted women, and smiling middle-aged men holding trophy fish. The place always smelled of thick grease and dead worms.

Hud assumed Moran was inside interviewing the owner since that had been her last call over the radio. He didn't know who the owner was these days.

The place had been owned by a man named George Curlew when Hud was a boy. Curlew had been an old man back then, so he was probably dead by now. It was hard to tell whether Curlew's family had taken over the business; Hud couldn't remember if he'd had any sons or daughters. Not that any of that mattered. Curlew wasn't memorable other than for the fact that he'd had no use for trespassers who fished the bare spots in the cove. The short, squat, little man had run Hud off more than once, mostly when business was slow and he had nothing else to do. The boat company had been a little sanctuary for Hud, a place to get away, be by himself. He knew the place well and was glad that it hadn't changed much. He flashed on a sudden memory. He must have been thirteen or fourteen, had snuck away from the shop and was smoking a cigarette behind a glade of cattails. A big pontoon pushed up the channel, coming in for gas. There were three girls sunbathing on the open deck in the front, but Hud only had eyes for one. Goldie Flowers was stretched out in a yellow bikini, her skin tanned and supple, her curves highlighted by the overhead sun. She glowed like a teenage goddess. Just the thought of her back then aroused him all over again. He was going to have to find Goldie and finish what they had started.

Thankfully, Moran pushed out of the door, taking his mind away from the uncomfortable urge growing in his lap. She was followed by a tall, thin balding man who couldn't have been any relation to Paul Curlew. Moran stopped and waited for the man to put his Chicago Cubs baseball cap on, then followed him toward the farthest dock. Even from Hud's vantage point he could see two white Band-Aids on the deputy's face. Mementos of the glass from the shooting. The plastic strips stood out, and he couldn't help but wonder if her face would be permanently scarred. He hoped not.

The tall man pointed at an empty dock, and Moran nodded, took notes, probably writing down the slip number and location. She looked around and the man continued talking, but something suddenly drew their attention away from the dock. Hud followed their gaze to the back of the cove, where a smaller body of water lay behind it. In the summer it was covered with a blanket of thick green algae and choked with an abundance of lily pads. It was a great place to catch frogs and turtles but was mostly avoided because of the swarms of mosquitoes that chose the spot as their breeding grounds. With the leaves off the trees, though, the sun would have had the opportunity to beat down on the algae, and the cooler temperatures would have thinned the muck. It was entirely possible that the water was navigable—with the right boat.

The whir of a boat motor coming to life echoed across the still water and reached Hud's ears at about the same time that he saw movement beyond the trees. In another blink, just as his fingers grazed the door handle, he saw a johnboat speed out from the frog swamp and into the cove.

Moran's hand jumped to her gun, but the holster was snapped. She fumbled with it, trying not to take her eyes off the boat.

A man was piloting the flat-bottom fishing boat as fast as he could toward the channel that led out into the lake.

Hud pushed out of the car and hit the ground running. He focused on the driver of the boat as he drew his weapon, the .45. Even from a distance, there was no mistaking the man's identity. It was Leo Sherman, hands down, no question.

~~~~~~~~~~

"You waited almost ten minutes before calling for an ambulance."
"I was trying to save him."
"But you shot him."
"In self-defense. Why wouldn't I try and save him?"
"You weren't protecting yourself by letting him die?"
"I've already answered that."
"Okay, I suppose we can move on."
"You don't believe me?"
"Does it matter?"
"I think it might."
"Then no, I don't believe you. I don't believe a word you've said."

~~~~~~~~~~

Moran drew Leo Sherman in her sights. She was screaming at him to stop, but the clatter of the outboard motor drowned out her commands. The sound of the furious escape echoed across the cove, piercing an otherwise quiet and serene autumn day. Three mallard drakes erupted into the air, unconcerned about any hunters in the area.

Hud joined Moran cautiously, calling out for Sherman to stop, all the while staying as close to the trees as he could. Being shot at again was not on the top of his list of things he wanted to experience again any time soon.

Moran saw Hud approaching and tried to wave him off, but he

wasn't going to be deterred. He fired off a shot as soon as he was within range. The bullet hit the water just behind the boat in the center of the wake. It had been a warning shot.

"What the hell are you doing here?" Moran demanded, as Hud came to a stop next to her. Every muscle in her body was tight, and she had that hard, battle-ready face any good kickboxer needed before entering the ring.

He was glad to see she hadn't lost her edge, but he didn't answer. Sherman's boat was almost at the mouth of the channel, out of range. He fired off another shot. Somewhere close a covey of doves burst into the air, following the mallards. The shot missed, disappeared without leaving any evidence that it ever existed.

"Call for back-up," Hud ordered Moran, then turned to the tall man, who looked stricken and afraid, and said, "Do you have a boat ready to go?"

The man nodded, then pointed to a new model inboard/outboard speedboat tied up next to a pontoon three docks over. "Just getting ready to bring that one in and put it up."

"The keys in it?" Hud asked.

The look on Moran's face suggested that she didn't like taking orders very well. No surprise there. "Suspect sighted. Shots fired. 10-96."

The tall man shook his head, dug in his front pants pocket, and pulled out a set of keys. "Got 'em right here."

"Tell them I'm in pursuit," Hud said as he reached for the keys.

"The hell you are," Moran replied. "We are. I'm going with you."

"Suit yourself," Hud hollered over his shoulder. He was already halfway to the speedboat.

CHAPTER NINETEEN

The water was as smooth as Gee's glass-top coffee table, making Leo Sherman's wake easy to follow. It was like a trail had been suddenly cut into the water, widening by the second. Hud sped out of the boat company channel onto the body of Demmie Lake as if he wasn't worried about anything. And he wasn't. Not as long as he had Leo Sherman in his sights. He stood up behind the steering wheel of the speedboat—a sixteen foot fiberglass tri-hull with a 327 small block engine in it—instead of sitting down. This was no joyride.

The boat skimmed across the lake at forty miles per hour and probably topped out at sixty or seventy, though there'd be no need to go that fast. Leo Sherman's johnboat was no match for the speedboat, and he knew it.

"He's heading for the backwaters," Hud said, as he pressed the throttle, a T-shaped lever, forward. Wind from the speed whipped at his face, stinging his bruises and lacerations as he pursued his assumed suspect. The pain was negligible, but the air was cold, biting, almost bitter. It would have been better if the sun hadn't been beating down on them. His heart was beating a mile a minute, and his body was producing adrenaline in record quantities, reacting to the primal fight to flight situation. No matter the outcome, the thrill of the chase still appealed to Hud. Sometimes, he longed for it.

"Will he make it?" Moran asked. She stood shoulder to shoulder with him, holding onto the dash, her water legs not as stable as Hud's. Even though the water was smooth, the front of the boat jutted up at a thirty degree angle from the water, and the ride was bumpy as Hud jumped in and out of Sherman's wake, doing his best not to be an easy target. Even with that tactic, Hud was still gaining on the small fishing boat.

"We better hope not," Hud answered. "My bet is that Leo Sherman knows the backwaters better than anybody around here. He's lived on it and worked it most all of his professional life, from what I understand. He's probably been hiding out there the whole time."

"Burke had it searched. State police buzzed it with helicopters and heat-sensing radar. There was nothing human to be seen." Moran focused on the johnboat. She had a worried look on her face.

Hud tried not to notice. The last thing he wanted was to be in an intense situation with a person experiencing doubt of any kind. "I've got this."

"You're not even supposed to be here."

"I've always had a hard time sitting still." He wished he'd remembered his sunglasses. His eyes stung from the sun overhead and its reflection off the lake.

The wind whistled around Hud and Moran, but they didn't pay attention to it. Sherman curved the boat at a bend, twisted the throttle as far as it would go. Hud nodded, catching sight of the backwaters.

"Do you know it?" Moran asked.

Hud shook his head. "Not very well. This is the first time I've been out on the water since I've been home. I spent more time as a kid at the boat company than I did in the backwaters. I could walk there from the shop, but I needed a boat to get into the backwaters. I had one, but I didn't have a motor. Just oars. That was a long way to row just to be eaten by mosquitoes."

Moran tilted her head to the right. "Makes sense."

"How about you?" Hud said, never taking his eyes off the johnboat. They were still out of firing range. There was no stopping Sherman, at least at the moment.

"I can't swim, so I try to stay away from the water as much as I can."

That explained the discomfort Hud had sensed. He was relieved. "You should take lessons."

"Yeah, that's not going to happen." She glared at Hud and gripped the dash a little harder at the same time.

Hud knew better than to pursue the idea. It didn't matter anyway, other than for the fact that she had admitted a weakness to him. That was a surprise. Joanne Moran had been tough as nails and all business from the second they'd met. He was glad to see a human side to her. It had been starting to look as if she was nothing but cop from head to toe, and then she cracked a bit. He glanced over at her and saw the woman, the girl she had been, instead of the deputy she was trying to be. Everybody had their fears.

"He's going to go in as far as he can, then beach the boat," Hud said. "My guess is he's done it before. He has an escape plan." He pressed the accelerator lever forward a little more, and the 327 rumbled in agreement as the boat lurched forward a little faster. He liked the sound of the engine and the way the boat handled, but he resisted the urge to go full-out with Moran in the boat. He didn't want to scare the shit out of her, but being on the water in a good boat was a pleasure he had never forgotten.

"Like when he shot at us."

"If it was him."

"You question that?" Moran had to raise her voice over the growl of the engine so Hud could hear her. It was almost a shout.

"I question everything. Don't you?"

She looked away from him, back at the johnboat. "What are you going to do?"

"Go in as far as I can as fast as I can. Do the same thing he's going to do."

She shook her head. "Burke's not going to like paying for damages to a boat he didn't authorize using."

"You leave Burke to me. Besides, it won't matter if we catch Sherman, will it? All of his problems will be solved, and I'll make sure he gets all the credit. It'd be a win-win for everybody."

~~~~~~~

"How did you feel when you came home?"
"I had to attend to Gee's funeral. How do you think I felt?"
"You don't seem too grief-stricken."
"Me and Gee made our peace a long time ago. Once she under-

stood that staying away was the best thing for me, things changed.
She relaxed. Accepted my decision the best she could. Doesn't mean
she liked it, but I think she understood my need to create a life as far
away from here as possible."

"She never talked about your mother?"

"I didn't say that, did I?"

"What else was there to say?"

"She never quit looking for her. I told you that. Not until the day
she died, and then only because she had no choice."

"Then it was up to you?"

"Persistence is a family trait. We never give up on something we
believe in. Do you?"

~~~~~~

The backwater was almost completely bound up by a thick grove of
lily pads. The big round-topped browning water plants stretched out
a hundred yards from the shore and surrounded an occasional dead
cedar tree that stuck up out of the water like a gray, brittle skeletal
hand reaching for the sky. Logs with nowhere to go were stuck in the
vegetation, and in the summer they were loaded with turtles, mostly
red eared sliders and Midland painted turtles. Their dark shells were
nearly black, with beautiful patterned bellies underneath that had
always looked like roadmaps to Hud. It was disappointing seeing the
logs vacant. But there was hardly any wildlife to be seen at all. Just a
flush of mallards that burst into the air as Leo Sherman sped toward
the shore.

The lily pads didn't slow Sherman down. There was a thin trail cut
through them, used over the summer by fishermen, usually after large-
mouth that hugged the logs and tree trunks for cover and prey, and by
duck hunters in the fall, going back and forth from the blinds they'd
built in the swampy backwaters.

"You're really not going to slow down?" Moran said.

Hud shook his head again. "You'd better get down on your knees
and brace yourself."

Moran looked at him oddly. His command had been matter-of-fact, unconcerned. "Are you crazy?"

"You're not the first person to ask me that. You'd better do as I tell you, or you're going to get that swimming lesson, whether you want it or not." He stared straight ahead and watched Sherman beach the john-boat just like he'd thought he would. The last thing Hud was worried about at the moment was whether or not his own boat had come stocked with life preservers.

Moran didn't need to be told twice. She kneeled down, tucked herself into the passenger seat's leg space the best she could. It was a little fiberglass den that looked to be made for short people. "I hope you don't get us killed."

It was the last thing Hud heard before he slammed the throttle forward, demanding all of the power from the eight cylinders in the engine. The sudden rev sounded like the lion's roar at the Dip on a mid-summer's night: fierce, loud, and full of threatening intention.

Ice cold water drops spattered Hud's face, but didn't obscure his vision. Leo Sherman had beached the fishing boat at top speed, sending it sliding forward past the thick muck and onto a slice of sand. Sherman didn't wait until the boat came to a complete stop before he bailed out. It was more of a dive than anything else, as he rolled forward in front of the boat onto the soft ground. It was a graceful move, perfectly calculated, almost as if the CO had done it a million times before.

Hud had no intention of aping the man's gymnastic move, nor did he have the confidence in his boat that Sherman had with his own. For all he knew, they'd end up stuck in the mud long before they reached the johnboat.

Sherman jumped to his feet and immediately disappeared into the tall reeds as Hud's boat sped toward the shore. He had a fifty yard lead on Hud, and it was likely that the CO knew exactly where he was going.

It only took a long second to cut through the lily pads and plow through the muck with the big V-bottom boat. Hud pulled the throttle back and cut the engine. The ride was bumpy and loud, with the propeller underneath churning and moaning louder than the johnboat's little motor ever could. Hud smelled hot oil, and for a moment he feared the engine was going to blow up. At least they were on land. He glanced down at Moran quickly. She seemed fine as they rode out the plan.

The boat came to a stop just past Sherman's, pushing through a wall of reeds and landing in an algae-covered pond that looked shallow because of its size, although it was difficult to know for sure. There had been hits and bangs, like a hammer pounding through the fiberglass. The last thing he was concerned about was any damage to the boat.

Hud didn't hesitate. He jumped out of the boat, pulling his .45 out at the same time. Moran was on her own. She knew what to do.

He immediately sunk to his ankles in the mud and muck. It was black and stinky, like a thousand years of rot and death was being released with every hard step. He couldn't run until he reached the narrow strip of sand that Sherman had escaped on. As he reached it, he heard Moran jump out of the boat and squish into the mud just as he had.

The recent rains had left the ground softer than normal, so it was easy to see Sherman's tracks in the sand. Broken cattails, brown and fragile, also showed Hud the way. Once he was on the sand, Hud was able to run and listen at the same time, hoping to hear something, anything.

At first, he didn't hear a sound. The world was silent. Frogs had buried themselves in the ground for the winter, and the air was free of insects, dead or torpid since the cold snap. Any birds that had stayed for the cold season were afraid, frozen to become invisible statues, blending in so they were out of sight; a mesh of brown and gray earthy tones hid them perfectly. Even beyond the backwaters, there was no boat or car traffic noise to be heard, and for a moment Hud felt a tremor of fear, like he was walking into a trap. It was a feeling that he'd had before, and had been proven to have been right about. But he kept running. Sherman was in too big of a hurry to worry about covering his tracks.

And then he heard it. At first it sounded like a rush of wind, then a slap of two blades of grass together. Big grass, tall grass. *When you're trying to be quiet, you're louder than you think you are*, Hud thought. He stopped, eyed the tops of the reeds, hoping to see movement of some kind, but he didn't see a thing. He was too far away.

He had no choice but to go into the thick grass and mucky ground. He hoped Moran would follow him, cover the rear, but he wasn't taking the time to give the order. He had to take it on faith that she would know what to do.

Hud dove into the grass with his .45 up, his finger on the trigger, and his eyes and ears as open as they could be. He was in no mood to be smacked down by an oar again, or shot, for that matter, but it was a chance he was willing to take. It was a chance he had to take. He'd made the commitment when he'd shown himself to Moran at the boat company and commandeered the speedboat.

He pushed through the thick stand of reeds and cattails as quickly as he could and was surprised when he broke free of it sooner than he expected.

Leo Sherman was on the other side of the opening, on a slope covered in shorter grasses that led down to a pond. The pond edged up to the start of the barren hardwood forest. Sherman was struggling to get over a fallen tree. His face was wrenched in pain. His uniform was dirty from days of use and wear, and his cheeks were nicked and scratched, like he'd run as fast as he could through a thicket of some kind. It looked as if he had twisted his ankle.

"Stop!" Hud demanded, then drew the man's chest into his sight. "Police!"

Sherman didn't respond. His face went white with fear, then he dropped his head in resignation. He was tired, exhausted from being on the run. The fear vanished and was replaced with a look of relief. He stopped struggling, fleeing, accepting the inevitable conclusion that he had been caught. The jig was up, the game over.

Then a sudden, familiar sound came out of nowhere. A crack of thunder. An explosion. A sequence of firecrackers. But the sky was clear, and there was no one to be seen anywhere around. Not that Hud had had the opportunity to look around. The sound echoed past Hud. It had come from the north, in the opposite direction from where he and Moran had entered the backwaters.

The side of Leo Sherman's head exploded, sending shards of bone and huge chunks of his skull flying upward. A geyser of blood followed, raining to the wet ground just ahead of the man's body. The Conservation Officer hadn't known what hit him. Death had come instantly, out of nowhere, at the hand, once more, of an unknown and unseen shooter.

CHAPTER TWENTY

Hud dove to the ground before the report of the rifle shot completely echoed away. It felt as if something snapped inside him. Not a tendon or a bone, but something deeper, something in the recesses of his brain and maybe even deeper in his heart. Rage bubbled up inside him just like the black, cold water that oozed to the surface of the muck as soon as his full body weight had settled into a safe spot. Safe for the moment. Just like last time, Hud expected more shots to be fired.

He waited for silence to completely return, counted to ten, then opened his eyes, hoping that Moran had responded to the gunshot and dropped to the ground like he had. She was about twenty feet from him, prone on the swampy surface, half sunk in. "Are you all right?" Hud whispered. His anger subsided, but not completely.

Moran nodded. "I need to call for help."

"He's dead."

"For us. We're pinned down like sitting ducks."

Hud didn't respond; he was thinking, working his way through his anger, trying to figure a way out of the moment he was in. If this was the same shooter, then maybe they weren't targets this time. A pattern was starting to emerge.

There hadn't been any other cartridges found at the Pam Sizemore crime scene. Only one shot had been fired, and it had been a direct hit, taken her life. And there had only been one shot through the windshield of the county cruiser as Moran had started to show him the information she'd found on social media. If the shooter, killer, whatever, held true to their MO, then one shot was all it took to accomplish their goal. This time that goal was apparently killing Leo Sherman.

But how did the shooter know where Sherman would be? And where was the shooter perched? Hud wondered silently. Both were good questions. The first one needed investigating. The second one needed waiting out . . . for the moment, to see if he was right. It was entirely possible that once the shot had been fired, the target hit, then the shooter had an escape plan. It was broad daylight, and regardless of the time of year there were still people around. There was a chance at being seen, at getting caught. Though the backwaters were more secluded than other sites. There were a million places to hide. Sherman had been proof of that. Hud guessed he had planned on escaping back to his hiding place, his safe place. But there would never be any way to know now.

Emboldened by his deduction, Hud pushed himself to his knees. Both of his hands and the front of his body were covered with the cold, wet muck. He shivered as a slight breeze skipped off the lake and wrapped around him. It looked as if he had fallen face first into a pit of oil. The ground smelled worse than any gas station or engine ever could; rot and decay invaded all of his senses.

He wasn't stupid, though. Instead of standing up, he crawled to Sherman, just to make sure the man was dead. It was a short journey, but he took his time getting there. He was not entirely confident of his theory about the shooter, even though it made perfect sense to him. So, his ears were tuned for another gunshot. The shooter was obviously a good shot, a skilled marksman or a very good hunter or both, and Hud knew that every breath he took might be his last. This was not where he wanted to die.

The right side of Sherman's head was completely blown off. His brain was exposed to the world, a small gray blob covered in blood and sinew. A few flies had already descended out of nowhere to attend an unexpected feast. *Where did they come from? How can they still be alive after a frost? I hope I don't have to worry about snakes.*

Sherman's eyes were open, and he smelled rank, like he hadn't had a bath in days. Which was probably the case. The CO had been on the run since Hud had discovered Timmy Sizemore in the lion's den at the Dip. A lot had happened since then, including the death of Sherman's wife, Kaye.

Hud had to rethink everything from that moment until now. Leo

Sherman had been the primary suspect in both murders. It was possible that they had been looking for the wrong man all along.

He heard Moran rustling behind him. He glanced over his shoulder, saw her going for her radio but staying as low to the ground as she could. "Can you wait until I'm gone?" he said.

"Seriously?"

"I'll face Burke in my own time. I have a few things I want to check out first."

"You're just going to get up and walk out of this swamp with an active shooter still on the loose?"

"Sure, why not?"

"You are crazy."

Hud forced a smile, then let it fade as he watched Moran key her walkie-talkie.

"D-3 to base," she said, with a defiant look on her muddy face. "Be advised that assistance is needed at the current backwater location, one hundred yards in from the cove on the east side, longitude W 85, latitude N 45. Detective Matthews and I have taken shots. Repeat shots have been fired. The suspect is down." The look didn't disappear from Moran's face as she flashed Hud the screen of her smartphone, and the GPS on it. Modern technology never ceased to amaze him.

"D-3, this is Burke. Please restate your location."

She hesitated and looked to Hud for clarification. All she got was a glare in return. He stood up, stepped over Sherman's body, and pushed his way into the closest stand of cattails, his eyes on the ground in search of a game trail that led out of the swamp.

~~~~~~~~~~

"You went with Gee when she'd go out looking for your mother?"

"When I could."

"Where'd she go?"

"The usual places. By Johnny Long's, the Hotel, sometimes she'd check the Shamrocks, but not very often. She held that place in low esteem. In the off-season the little cottages were rented out by the hour, encouraging behavior and a type of business that she didn't approve of."

"Prostitution?"

"Most likely. The place was closed down by the time I got around to asking any questions, and not surprisingly nobody was talking. Gee was confident my mother would never have anything to do with that kind of trash. Her words, not mine."

"What about you?"

"I'm sorry, but what are you suggesting?"

"I'm not suggesting anything. I'm asking. You don't think your mother had anything to do with what Gee thought was going on at the Shams? Relax. I wouldn't desecrate the memory of your mother like that."

"Unless you had some kind of proof."

"I don't."

"All right. I suppose it's a fair question."

"So you have considered it?"

"Look, I was a kid. I didn't know what prostitution was then, and I certainly couldn't conceive of the idea that my mother might have been involved in something like that. We sold T-shirts and snow globes with summer scenes in them. It was innocent stuff that we sold to kids mostly, and the things adults needed for a perfect weekend. Whatever the nightlife was beyond that, what adults did for fun, was pretty much invisible to me."

"But you had to think about it when you got older, became a cop, that it might be a possibility?"

"No. I could never consider it. But I did look into the ownership of the Shams."

"And who owned it?"

"Hard to say. A real estate company based out of Chicago. But it didn't physically exist at the address it was supposed to be at, and I couldn't track down any of the officers listed in the corporation. It was like they didn't exist. It seemed like a shell game, a place to hide money, or something. I ran into dead ends at every turn. Somebody knew what they were doing. I think they hoped it would collapse on its own and sink into the ground."

"You never found out who the real owners were?"

"I gave up."

"That doesn't seem like something you'd do."

"A detective from Detroit can only do so much in Chicago."

The air was full of sirens. All of the sounds bounced off the lake, using it as an amplifier, but the blast and horns, along with all of the other expected wavering screams and howls, made it seem like World War III had just started. Hud tried to ignore the sirens, listening instead for anything that he needed to be concerned about. He wasn't totally confident that the shooter had hightailed it after the one and only shot, but he hoped he was right.

A game trail was easy to follow out of the swamp. At certain points, his shoes sunk up to his ankles. He was already wet and cold, so it didn't matter if he splashed water up on himself or not. He was numb, and certain that he wasn't ready to face Burke just yet. If he felt anything, it was remorse for leaving Moran to face the chief on her own. He wouldn't blame her if she never forgave him for running off.

About a hundred yards into the backwaters, the ground began to slope upward, and tall trees began to replace cattails. The trail became clearer, and so did the sounds from the road. Hud saw an ambulance buzz past in the distance, its lights pulsing, sirens throbbing with hope and reassurance, neither of which were needed. The coroner, Bill Flowers, was most assuredly close behind, or at least had been alerted to the latest murder.

Hud continued pushing forward, stopping behind a tree when the need arose. He zigged and zagged back to where he had come from in the beginning. There were some questions he wanted to ask the owner of the boat company, the tall man Moran had been talking to when he'd arrived. Like, *"Why didn't you look for the stolen boat in the small cove before you called the police. With the leaves off the trees, it would have been easy to see."*

It hadn't made an ounce of sense to Hud that Sherman was sitting there waiting to flee. There was more going on than what had initially appeared to be a simple case of theft. There had to be.

CHAPTER TWENTY-ONE

A rusty old Jeep sat behind the boat company. It had a tear in the canopy top and the rust looked like an angry red rash had attacked the metal, spreading without regard to anything in its path. It wasn't long before the tall man that Moran had been talking to hurried out the back door, his eyes focused on the Jeep and nothing else. The Open sign still sat in the window, and the man was in a big hurry.

Hud stepped out from behind one of the big pines that edged the road. "You got a second?" he said. His .45 rested at his side, firmly in his grip.

The man stopped a few feet from the driver's door. His face went pale. "Sure, I guess." He stared at the gun, trembling.

Hud flashed his badge at the man, let it linger at eye level long enough for him to determine that it was genuine, then stuck it in his back pocket. "I'm Detective Hud Matthews. I just need to ask you a few questions."

"I know who you are."

Hud squinted, looked at him closer. He still didn't recognize the man. "Do I know you?"

"Hard to say, 'less you ever had a boat worked on here. I was the head mechanic till Old Man Curlew died, then I bought the place outright from the estate, if you want to call it that. Charlie Sandburg's the name if'n you don't recall. I knew Gee from the local business owners' association in recent years. She was a good woman, that one. You have my condolences on her passing."

"Thank you," Hud said. He glanced at the man's hands. He had oversized knuckles and they were permanently stained a lighter shade of black from all of the oil and grease he'd handled in his lifetime as a mechanic. "The only boat I ever had had oars."

"Then I guess we wouldn't've crossed path then, would we?"

"Probably not." Hud sized up Sandburg all over again, then focused on the ignition key clutched firmly in the man's big right hand. "You in a hurry?"

"Got a part to run after." There was no hesitation, no flinch that suggested a reason to be questioned. It was a quick, believable answer.

"Nobody else here?"

"Nope." Sandburg shook his head and never broke eye contact with Hud. "I pare things down in the winter. I got a motor rebuild going on that'll keep me busy for a month, then I'll be sweepin' the floors and watchin' the barn owls get ready for spring. They got a nest up in the north corner that's been there since before I come along. Curlew said it was there before his day, too. Hard tellin' how many generations have came and went after all these years."

"Yeah, hard telling." Hud nodded, then said, "I want you to think about your answer to my next question carefully, but first you need to know that Leo Sherman's dead. He was shot in the head. Didn't feel a thing."

"You do that?"

"You think I'd be standing here if I had?"

Sandburg shrugged. "What do I know about how the law works?"

"You might want to think about it depending on how things turn out here." Hud paused, looked past Sandburg, then briefly around, calculating an escape route the man might take if he saw the need to run like Sherman had. "How come you didn't look in the small cove before you called the police about the stolen boat?"

Now the hesitation came. Charlie Sandburg looked at the top of his boots, a soiled pair of Doc Martens that looked like they'd been resoled more than once. "You know Leo Sherman?" he finally said.

"That's not the answer I was looking for."

"It should be. He's an innocent man."

"Was."

"The thought of such a thing makes me sad. Lost his wife, then his own life. For what?"

"Maybe you can tell me if you knew him that well?"

"I knew him."

"I need more than that . . ."

"He was the CO for a lot of years. What do you think? Of course I knew him pretty well. He stored his personal boat here along with the state's boat once the lake started to freeze. Didn't take them anywhere else. You get to know a man over the years by the way he takes care of things. They tell you stories at the counter waitin' for this or that. 'Specially the full-timers. Vacationers, they come and go, and more glory to them as long as their checks don't bounce. Snotty-nosed bastards want everything now and don't want to pay the goin' rate for a damn thing. You ought to know that. You lived off those folks all your life."

"When I was kid."

"Don't matter. You know what I mean. Leo was a rare breed, a real friend of nature. I never knowed of anything he killed that he didn't eat, and I think he felt bad about that. He fished mostly for the sport of it, catch and release. Even the rule breakers, the ones without a licenses, and such, if he could see a way clear of it. He had no heart for trouble, which makes all of this more of a tragedy than it should be. Yup, biggest tragedy I can ever recall 'round these parts. That enough of an answer for you to put that gun there away? It's makin' me a little nervous. I knew Leo Sherman as a good man, that's it."

"Everyone agrees with you. Did you know him well enough to let him hide out in your shop?" Hud made no effort to put away the .45. He didn't even acknowledge its presence.

"That'd be harborin' a criminal and obstructin' justice, wouldn't it?"

"I thought you didn't know much about how the law works?"

"I watch TV cop shows and read a Travis McGee novel every now and again, but I figure that's all made up stuff."

"Sure you do." Hud casually raised the .45 so it was level with the man's head. The end of the barrel was pointed at the bridge of Charlie Sandburg's nose.

The tall mechanic trembled. "Don't I get a lawyer?"

"We're just having a friendly conversation that no one knows ever existed. You give me a reason to arrest you, then I'll Mirandize you properly. But at the moment, what happens here is just between us. Who do you think is going to believe you once I can prove you hid Leo Sherman in your shop if you claim otherwise?"

"And I'm supposed to believe that I'll get my rights starin' down the ugly end of a gun?"

"Believe what you want. The only way this gun's going away is if you tell me the truth, what I want to know. Otherwise, we'll just have to see how far you're willing to take this charade you're playing."

Sandburg sighed, lowered his head, then nodded. "All right, I let him stay here."

Hud returned the nod. "I figured as much," he said, then lowered the gun back to his side. "Now, answer my original question. How come you called the police to report the boat stolen when you knew where it was."

"He was goin' to give himself up, claim his innocence. He couldn't stomach the thought of folks thinkin' that he killed Kaye, and it was gettin' harder and harder to hide. It was just a matter of time before someone came along and flushed him out. We both knew that. He didn't want to get me in trouble, too."

"Why'd he run?"

Charlie Sandburg stared Hud directly in the eye, and said, "'I don't know. Maybe he saw you. He was gonna give himself over to that deputy . . .'"

"I spooked him?" Hud took a deep breath, then looked upward for a long second. "Did he ever tell you who he thought the killer was? Why he ran in the first place?"

"He was tryin' to help that Sizemore girl. Don't know why, or how they was connected, but he had a soft spot for her. I guess he thought it'd look bad if he was known to be cavortin' with a known druggie, but I don't know that for sure. As far as who's behind the killin', well he never came right out and said it, but he thought there was a turf battle of some kind goin' on, and Pam Sizemore got herself caught in the middle of it somehows."

"A turf war with who?"

"Local people and an outfit from Chicago, but that's how it's always been 'round here, isn't it? Locals versus the big city folk. I wish they'd just leave us the hell alone," Charlie Sandburg said, sadly. "Can I go now?"

~~~~~~

"When was the last time you took a ride with Gee, looking for your mother?"

"I don't know, a few years back. I came home for one thing or another and she asked if I wanted to go for a ride, so we did."

"Where'd you go?"

"The usual places, then we stopped at the Ferris wheel. It was closed by then. Things had already fallen apart. It was a relic from the past collapsing into the lake like everything else. I think she thought her time was getting short, and she reminisced about her life here as a girl. Got her first kiss on the Ferris Wheel, if I recall. She had fond memories of how things were."

"She talk about your mother?"

"No. Didn't mention her."

"You expect me to believe that?"

"We've already established that you don't believe me, so why would I try to convince you otherwise?"

"To entertain yourself?"

"I don't have any place else to go, do I?"

"Noted."

"She apologized. Wished she could have been a better mother to me since I didn't have one in the important years. A father either, for that matter. I think she thought she failed me in one way or another."

"Because of how you turned out?"

"You'd have to ask her that."

~~~~~~

Hud had left the Crown Vic parked at the boat company. The first thing he did after climbing into the car was dig out a cigarette and light up. As he took the first long drag, he watched Charlie Sandburg drive off to wherever he was going. The old Jeep rattled up the gravel drive that led out to the main road and disappeared. There was no need to detain the man any longer. Burke could question him if he wanted to, but Hud was satisfied with the answers he'd gotten. Troubled, but satisfied. The idea that he might have spooked Sherman hit him deep in the gut. He was responsible for the man's death if that were the case. But still, how had the shooter known where Sherman was?

He looked up the empty road and saw nothing as another question for Charlie Sandburg formed in his mind: *Did you call anybody after Sherman fled? If so, who was it?*

Hud fumbled the cigarette as he reached for the ignition. How could he have not thought about that, asked the mechanic if he'd had contact with anyone. *You're slipping, Hud.*

He flipped the cigarette out the window, then started the car, expecting it to roar to life, but it choked and sputtered then died. He tried to start the engine again, but the cylinders wouldn't fire. The starter turned and turned but wouldn't catch. He jumped out of the car, intent on popping the hood, but something else caught his eye. The round door to the gas tank was standing wide open. He hadn't noticed it when he'd got in the car to leave. It only took a quick look, once he was close enough, to see that a thin pile of sand lined the lip of the gas cap. Someone had jammed up the engine by pouring sand into his gas tank. He wasn't going anywhere anytime soon.

That realization brought another immediate cause for concern: He was standing out in the wide open, unprotected, without a way to escape. He had his .45, his wits, and a police radio, and that was it.

Hud took a short breath, then jumped back into the Crown Vic. He half expected to hear the thunder of a gunshot follow him inside, but all he heard was the sound of a police siren off in the distance.

CHAPTER TWENTY-TWO

Hud had two choices, and neither was one that he favored. He could call for help over the radio and face Burke sooner than he wanted to, or hoof it back home, get Gee's car, and go from there. Burke was most likely busy with the murder scene, so Hud had time to avoid him. There was no use going back there—Moran could fend for herself. If he called for help, told dispatch he was stranded because someone put sand in his gas tank, then Burke would know where he was and start barking orders over the radio. He didn't want that, either. Which, of course, left his only alternative to leave the boat company on foot. It was a huge risk, but so was just sitting there and waiting for whatever happened next. Not the way he wanted to die. For all Hud knew, he was in the shooter's bead right now. If he was going to die, he wanted to be doing something, anything, not waiting around for death to come to him unannounced.

He had navigated the maze of trails behind the boat company before. But that had been when he was a kid. His secret paths had probably grown over, changed, were lost to time and memory. It frustrated him that the past was the only thing that could save him, get him home. He'd been trying to avoid that since he'd come back from Detroit, and, like almost everything else since then, he'd failed miserably. He longed for a swig of Wild Turkey and a jukebox blaring in the background, drowning out his thoughts and fears.

The sun had started to fall toward the western horizon, fertilizing shadows, adding a gray cast to everything behind it. Clouds were starting to roll in, and the breeze had transformed, just like the light, changing from comfortable and pleasant to a mad whisper that promised trouble was on the way. Hud had no idea whether it was a storm or not. He hadn't been paying attention to the sky. But now that he was, he knew by the looks of the clouds that he'd better get moving if he was going to make it home.

Wind suddenly swirled around Hud as he got slowly out of the car. If he'd held the .45 any tighter, the tips of his fingers would go numb, but he couldn't help himself. Every muscle in his body was tense, on alert. He was the mouse on the lookout for an owl.

It's no different now than it's ever been, he said to himself. The streets of Detroit were no fairy tale either. Still, Hud preferred to look his monsters in the eye. Gang bangers were cocky enough to walk right up to you. *Did the shooter put the sand in the gas tank?*

Hud scuttled away from the safety of the car, from the lifeline that shelter and the radio offered. He had no handheld, but he did have his cell phone on him. That was a mild comfort. He dodged in and out of the tall pine trees that dotted the landscape before they accumulated into a full forest. Once he reached the rear of the boat company, Hud stopped and took stock of his surroundings all over again. Alone. He still seemed to be alone. Except he couldn't shake the feeling that he was being watched, that there were a pair of eyes on him, waiting for him to make a wrong move, a final mistake.

～～～～～～

"You said your mother said everything was going to change, that she was in love."

"Yes, I said that."

"Did you ever find out who that was with?"

"Gee said my mother didn't tell her, and as far as I knew at the time, she really didn't seem to have a big circle of friends, you know, girlfriends to confide in, that kind of thing, so there was no one to go ask really."

"Why not?"

"I guess she was a loner."

"I'm not sure I totally buy that."

"Me, either, really. I guess the closest person she had to a friend was Helen Burke, but I think that's mainly because I was friends with

her son. I was in and out of Burke's house a lot when I was a kid. It was the first place she'd come to look for me if she needed me to come home. Sometimes, she would stay, and her and Helen would smoke cigarettes and drink iced tea or lemonade on the sun porch. My mother loved a good lemonade. Especially if it had a little vodka in it."

"How long have you and Burke been friends?"

"I think I've known him all of my life. One day he was just there, and always has been."

"But you were best friends as kids, right?"

"I wouldn't say that. I don't think I've ever said that."

~~~~~~~~~~

It was dark and shadowy inside the woods. The outside world disappeared, and Hud was instantly reminded how deep and thick the way home really was. If he hadn't had a good sense of direction, it would have been easy to get lost, at least until he figured out where the lake was, then he could trail the shore. Time in a big city had numbed Hud's comfort in the natural world.

The bright sunlight that had been so prevalent when he was out in the boat seemed like a distant memory; gloominess surrounded him like it had been sent on a mission to restrain him. Wind pushed all around Hud, coming from every direction, rattling the dried and brown weeds that had thrived on the ground during the summer, and what leaves remained on the trees. No birds spoke or sang, nor were there any to be seen. Hud was the only living creature willing to show himself in the forest. Everything else had been successful in their run for cover. Everything except him.

He hurried down a ravine, followed a well-worn trail, and hoped beyond hope that he would make it home before all hell broke loose, that the shooter wasn't following him—or waiting for him behind the next tree. He looked over his shoulder, felt his heart race as he picked up speed. The wind pushed at his back. The smell of rain invaded his nose. He hated feeling like the mouse, the bottom of the food chain. He wasn't used to it at all.

~~~~~~~~~~

The rain started to fall just as Hud reached the parking lot of the shop. He looked up to see clouds roiling overhead, an angry black and gray swirl that threatened to dump buckets of water instead of casual drops. By the time the rain hit his face, the wind had blown it sideways, and it was cold, felt like it was on that precarious borderline of freezing, making life even more miserable than it promised to be if he didn't hurry up and make it inside the shop. Ice was not a worry. The ground was too warm to allow it to form. Thunder rumbled behind him. The ground under his feet vibrated in a deeply concerning way. But the weather and its impending force were the least of his worries. There was a car in the lot that he didn't recognize and a person standing at the front door waiting for him, trying to stay dry under the extended eave that shielded the shop's entrance. Even in the grayness and dim light, it was easy to see that he had nothing to fear. While he didn't recognize the car, he did recognize the person. It was Goldie Flowers.

Hud hurried to her. Any fear that he had about being shot by the unseen shooter fell away, although it didn't entirely disappear. Even on his home turf, he didn't feel safe. The worst things that had ever happened to him had happened inside the shop. Fearing your mother would never return as a kid—and being right about it—was far worse than being shot at or smacked around with an oar as an adult. Worse. Much worse.

"What are you doing here?" Hud said, stopping before Goldie.

She looked like she had been run through a wringer. Her clothes were torn and dirty, and her face was the same. A trickle of blood had dried on the corner of her bottom lip, and her right eye was starting to puff up and bruise. "I had nowhere else to go," she whispered, then jumped into Hud's arms and held him as tight as she could.

Thunder boomed again, closer, and the rain fell hard and suddenly turned to hail. Ice pebbles bounced off the ground and slapped at the back of Hud's head. "We need to get you inside."

Goldie nodded, pushed a strand of her matted blonde hair from in front of her eye. "I was hoping you would say that."

Hud pulled himself out of her embrace, unlocked the door, and pushed it open. She smelled of cigarette smoke, mud, and a distant perfume that had been applied hours ago; sweet, exotic, tropical. Whatever had happened to her hadn't been pleasant. He would have been self-conscious about his own hygienic state, being covered in swamp muck and sweat, but that seemed like the last thing he should be worried about.

They both pushed inside the door as a great gust of wind riled up and kicked even more hail at them. It felt like buckshot. Hud slammed the door behind him. "Looks like we made it just in time," he said.

"I've been looking all over for you," Goldie said. She started to shiver.

Hud took her into his arms, an act he could have never hoped for as a teenager and could hardly believe now, even after their brief encounter outside the bar. "There's been a lot going on. What happened to you?"

Goldie closed her eyes and held them that way for a long second. It was as if she was trying to hold back tears, keep from breaking down completely. "I really don't want to talk about it right now."

There were no lights on inside the shop. Most of the shelves were bare. Cobwebs had begun to form, to take over the room in a slow, methodical progression of certain decay. Mustiness and neglect had a comforting smell all their own; it was home. Dim light seeped from under the curtain that separated the back of the house. Before Hud could say or do anything else, Goldie angled her face up, brushed her lips across his, and said, "We have some unfinished business to attend to."

~~~~~~~~~

A trail of clothes led to Hud's bedroom. The storm raged and pushed at the outside of the house trying to get in, trying to threaten the moment, but nothing could do that. The roof could have come off and Hud wouldn't have noticed. He gladly finished what he'd started at the hotel, ravaged Goldie's body up and down, in and out, and started all over again. They didn't talk other than to offer a direction here or give a demand there. Moans of pleasure and accomplishment filled the room. Time washed away in a sea of sweat and desire. Every teenage fantasy Hud had ever imagined starring Goldie Flowers was fulfilled, along with more direct, primal adult acts that nearly led into uncharted territory. Goldie didn't object to any move, any position. She showed him a part of herself very few women ever had. All she wanted was more, and Hud was happy to give her all she could take.

Sometime in the middle of the night, they raided the few groceries Hud had stocked in the refrigerator and returned to the bed to replenish themselves. Rain gently pattered against the window, and the wind had retreated into a breeze. It barely blew the sign out by the road. Hud could hear it creak back and forth as he had the night before and for years in his childhood. It was a comforting clock without hands or judgment.

"Are you going to answer my question?" Hud said, taking a bite of a ham sandwich.

"I thought I just told you everything you needed to know." Goldie's voice echoed in the small room.

"You haven't told me anything," he said.

Goldie sighed, lowered her head. She was propped up against the headboard, a sheet pulled up over her breasts, her legs covered, too, but her feet stuck out at the end of the bed. Her face had long been washed of tears and blood, but her hair had fallen straight, matted with exertion and the previous day's activity. "I got into a fight with Tom."

"Your boyfriend?"

"My husband."

"Nice," Hud said. He leaned over and put the sandwich on the nightstand. His appetite vanished. "You could have told me."

"Soon to be ex-husband. Number three if you're interested."

"I'm not."

"Good. You don't seem the type to give a shit about things like that."

"I like to know who I'm going to piss off, that's about it. I'm looking over my shoulder every two seconds the way it is."

She let the sheet fall away, reached over him to the nightstand and grabbed his pack of cigarettes and the lighter. Her nipples brushed his chest, sending a zap of fresh energy straight to his crotch. She lingered there a moment longer than she would have if she'd really wanted a cigarette. "You mind?"

"Help yourself." Hud paused, watched Goldie light a cigarette, and admired the perfection of her body all over again. What he wouldn't have given to have seen her naked at sixteen. "So this soon-to-be ex-husband and you got into a tussle. What about? Did you call the police?"

"I'm not filing charges. That'll just make things worse."

"Should you have a restraining order?"

"Paper won't stop a guy like Tom if he sets out to hurt me in a bad way. Besides, I'm worth more to him alive than I am dead. I'm not afraid of him. He won't hurt me. He just likes to play rough, be the tough guy, you know? He just got carried away. He'll calm down and come to his senses. He always does."

"How are you worth more to him alive?"

Goldie exhaled a chest full of smoke. "Daddy still gives me a monthly allowance. If I die, that ends. He doesn't work, so he'd be cut off wouldn't he?"

"Tom doesn't seem real bright."

"I have bad taste in men."

"Thanks." Hud hesitated, dug into his memory for a contradiction that had made him wince. "I thought you and your father were on the outs. You said so, and so did he in one way or another. Why would he still give you money?"

Goldie stared at Hud for a long second, looked him up and down, then reached across him again and stubbed out the cigarette. "I really don't want to talk about Daddy right now." She exhaled the last bit of smoke from her lungs and stopped halfway back to her spot. She kissed Hud's chest, trailed to his navel, and didn't stop until his half-erect cock was fully in her mouth.

He closed his eyes, distracted enough from the conversation not to pursue it any further. For the moment. He had questions. He knew he would go back to it. Just. Not. Now.

They continued on much like they had before, only with fewer words, and a harder, more direct way of satisfying each other. Spent, they fell asleep in each other's arms as the sun began to rise. When Hud woke up, Goldie was gone. It was almost as if it all had been a dream— or a nightmare—it was too early to tell.

CHAPTER TWENTY-THREE

The previous day's storm had been ushered in by a cold front, and the remnants of it remained long after the last drop of rain had hit the ground. In a matter of hours, the temperature plunged thirty degrees and promised the first true taste of the winter to come. A healthy layer of frost had formed on the windshield of Gee's car, a ten-year-old green Chevrolet sedan. The interior smelled ancient, like a locked-up tomb. Hud didn't know how long it had been since the car had been driven. He was surprised and relieved when it started right up.

There was no avoiding his destination. He drove straight to the county police station so he could confront Burke on his own terms, though it had crossed his mind to try and find Goldie first. He still had some questions that needed to be answered. She hadn't even bothered to give him the number to her cell phone, and he hadn't asked. He'd been focused on her . . . presence.

Hud walked into the building as confidently as he could. He had showered, put on a fresh set of work clothes, and readied himself for the day as if everything was normal. But he knew better. If Burke didn't have intentions of firing him he would be surprised. He shrugged at the thought. Gee's house was paid for, and she'd left behind a little money. Not that he wanted to live there, or reopen the shop, but he wasn't going to starve to death, nor was he going to be homeless. Burke could do whatever he wanted to. No matter what happened, Hud was going to be a cop whether there was a badge in his wallet or not.

It was early, and the interior of the building was eerily silent. He'd entered through the back door, avoiding the press and media trucks parked out front. At least his security key, a plain white credit-card-shaped piece of plastic, was still active. That was a good sign.

Burke was sitting in his office, staring at a flickering screen on his computer. "That was a hell of a stunt you pulled yesterday."

Hud had stopped at the door, then glanced up and down the empty hall. It felt as if they were the only two people in the building. "It didn't turn out like I planned."

"Imagine that."

"You have every right to be pissed at me."

"I have every right to fire you." Burke's voice was calm, even. It was unsettling.

"I expected that."

"I didn't say I was firing you. I said I had every right to."

"I heard you the first time."

Burke stood up and faced Hud. He looked like he hadn't had any sleep in two days, and he probably hadn't. Puffy bags protruded under his bloodshot eyes, and his white shirt, which was normally starched heavily and stiff, just like him, was wrinkled and limp. His blue and white striped tie bore more than one coffee stain, and his cologne had worn off long ago. Hud had to remind himself to proceed with caution.

"You created a big shit storm, you know that?" Burke said. "And if it wouldn't create an even bigger one, I *would* fire you."

Hud said nothing for a long moment, let Burke's words hang in the air.

"Well," Burke bristled, "don't you have anything to say for yourself?"

Hud nodded. "Leo Sherman's death is my fault."

Burke's right eyebrow raised, then fell back in place. "I wasn't expecting that. Explain."

"I showed up at the boat company at the wrong time. I sat and waited until Deputy Moran and Charlie Sandburg went out on a dock. I assumed that he was showing her where the reported boat was stolen from, but I was wrong."

"About what?"

"Leo Sherman was getting ready to turn himself in, but Sandberg said I may have spooked him. If I would have let things play out, CO

Sherman would still be alive, and hopefully we'd know that he wasn't Pam Sizemore's or his wife's killer."

"We don't know that he wasn't, just because he's dead."

"You're not serious?" Hud said, then bit his lip before he called the chief stupid or something else he'd regret.

"I am serious. How do you know that Sherman was going to turn himself in? That's not in Moran's report."

"Charlie Sandburg told me, the guy who's running the boat company these days."

"Yeah, I know who he is. We're trying to find him to ask him a few questions of our own."

"What do you mean 'find him?'"

"Nobody's seen Charlie Sandburg since yesterday. There's no sign of him anywhere."

"I saw him leave. He drove off in an old Jeep like nothing was the matter, though he was nervous. He knew there was trouble to be had for keeping Sherman around, but the killer kind of took that problem off the table by shooting the man."

"You let him go?" The volume of Burke's voice spiked and he clenched his fingers together.

"I had no reason to hold him."

"You could have held him for questioning. You don't know what kind of information he could have provided us. He's probably in Canada by now, hiding out in one of those fly-in fishing camps he advertises on his wall. Christ all mighty, what is it with you?"

Hud stood his ground. "Sandburg said Sherman was concerned about a turf war going on between some locals and a faction out of Chicago. He thought this thing with Pam Sizemore started there."

"We're following all of the leads we have. You know that."

"No, I've been out of touch for a little while. I need to get back up to speed; that is, if I'm still on the investigation."

"Everybody's on this investigation. No one is off-duty until the son of a bitch pulling the trigger is either dead or locked up behind bars.

This damn thing is starting to get national attention, damn it. We don't need that here, and you know it."

"People are dying. That tends to get peoples' attention."

Burke stepped forward so there was very little room between the two of them. "Don't think for one second you're going to get out of this scot-free. I'm on the hook for damage to a boat that you hijacked, and where in the hell is your vehicle? It needs to be accounted for."

"It's at the boat company. Somebody put sand in the gas tank. I guess they didn't want me to go anywhere."

"Another gift from Charlie Sandburg."

"Maybe, but I can't think why he would do such a thing."

"Maybe so you wouldn't be able to chase after him once you figured out all of the shootings were within range of the point just off the boat company."

"You think he's the killer? What's his motive?"

"If I knew that I'd be holding a press conference right now instead of talking to you, wouldn't I?"

Hud could smell Burke's last swig of coffee. It didn't settle well with him, and he stepped back. "Are we done here?"

"Sure," Burke said. "For now. And just so you don't do anything stupid, you're riding with Sloane today."

"So, I'm on a short leash . . ."

"You're lucky you're not flat on your ass. Now get the fuck out of here."

~~~~~~~~~~

"I searched Gee's room after the funeral for anything I could find that might give me some answers. I had to wait until she was dead to go in there."

"You were afraid of her?"

"I respected her request for me not to look for something that wasn't there."

"That's like offering honey to a bear isn't it?"

"One of the reasons why I left, I guess. It was easier to stay away."

"Did you find anything?"

"Nothing. I turned the place upside down. I even ventured up into the attic and down into the crawlspace."

"And you don't think you overlooked anything?"

"It's possible. Especially when you don't know what in the hell you're looking for."

"That must be frustrating for someone who's made a life out of being a detective."

"I never claimed to be any good at it. I just said I can't help myself."

~~~~~~~~~

All three detectives had their own offices but shared an open room for meetings and investigations. It was just outside of Burke's office. The room was large, with three extra desks that didn't belong to anyone, leftovers from more optimistic times. Now, they were just catchalls for stacks of papers, office supplies, and whatever else landed on them. It looked as if it had been ten years since the tops of the desks had seen the light of day. The back wall was usually bare, with the exception of some safety posters and the state flag, but now it was covered with pictures, maps, and reports, all related to the multiple murders.

Sloane and Pete Lancet were standing with their backs to the door, facing the wall, studying it silently. Sloane, who was dressed in a standard dark maroon pantsuit, glanced over her shoulder, let the look linger for a second longer than she should have after making eye contact with Hud, then turned back to the wall and said nothing. Lancet showed no interest in finding out who had just walked in. He either knew instinctively, or he didn't care. Hud figured it was the latter. Nothing like being behind, the odd man out.

He eased up next to Sloane and looked at the wall. Three pictures of the victims stared back at him. Pam Sizemore was barely recognizable. The picture looked like a class picture from high school. She had straight, shoulder-length hair, her eyes were vacant and her face thin and sunken in, even then. *"She had a condition of some kind,"* Moran had said in the cruiser before they had been shot at. That had been his last touch in the investigation. His last official touch, anyway.

Both of the other detectives ignored his presence. Hud skimmed across the documents pegged to the board—it looked like cork, and there were various sizes of water stains behind the pictures and documents that made it look like a map, but it wasn't. Hud was surprised it hadn't crumbled to pieces. He stopped on Leo Sherman's work picture, showing the man dressed in his green CO uniform, proud, square-jawed, hair trimmed in a military cut. There was no indication that he was involved in anything other than loving his job. Sherman's involvement had always puzzled Hud, especially once his wife, Kaye, was found dead. Hud glanced at the picture of her. It was half of a formal sitting picture, as if she and Leo had gone to the JC Penney for a Christmas card shoot—just her, but you could see her husband's shadow on the fake background. There wasn't a hair out of place. She wore a new white sweater and a smile that couldn't have been faked. Kaye Sherman looked happy and content, a stark contrast to Pam Sizemore.

"You here to stay?" Pete Lancet finally asked.

Hud looked down at him, past Sloane, who stood as still as a bittern not wanting to be discovered. "Burke said to get to work."

Lancet had on a different pair of cowboy boots, shiny black with silver lightning bolts coming out of the pointed toes. They went along with the black jeans and black sport coat he was wearing. His tie was lying on top of the closest table. "Call it what you want."

The air was thick, and Lancet's eyes were as hard as the two-inch heels of his boots. Hud sighed. He was in no mood to prove his worth or enter into a war of words with someone he hardly knew. It seemed pointless. "Where did Kaye Sherman work?"

"It's in the file," Lancet said quickly. "Haven't read it?"

Sloane broke her statue stance and glared at Lancet. "Knock it off, Pete. We need all of the help we can get."

"He's done enough, hasn't he?"

Sloane closed her eyes, then looked over at Hud. "You get it?"

"Yeah," Hud said. "I get it. Can't say I blame you, Pete. I've had a rocky start."

"We don't need your help," Lancet said.

Hud shrugged. "I'm not going anywhere."

Lancet's jaw set even harder, threatened to shatter. "I am." He spun around, grabbed his tie, and stalked out of the room.

Hud was tempted to go after him, put an end to the tension one way or another, but Sloane reached over and touched his elbow gently. "Let him go. We have some things to talk about anyway." Her voice was low, almost a whisper, husky and slightly seductive in a way Hud hadn't heard from her before.

He restrained himself, relaxed as much as he could, and turned his attention back to the picture of Kaye Sherman. She was the break in the pattern. She hadn't been shot like Pam Sizemore and Leo Sherman. Her murder seemed like a reaction, not part of the plan. At least to Hud. For some reason, now that he saw her alive and happy, he thought she might be the one that was hiding something. Not Leo.

CHAPTER TWENTY-FOUR

Sloane grabbed up a file from the table that Lancet's tie had been lying on. "Everything we have to date is here. You can review it once we leave." She handed the file to Hud.

"So you know you're babysitting me?" he said.

"Whatever you want to call it. Burke trusts me. Besides, he knows how Pete feels about riding with anyone."

"The lone cowboy. Impressive."

"He's just territorial. Don't worry about him. He'll warm up to you when the chips are down and he needs something from you. He put me through the wringer before he finally gave me a break when I first got my shield. I thought it was because I was a woman. It wasn't. He just doesn't like competition of any kind."

"If you say so. He started out nice as pie, then a switch flipped."

"He's like that. You'll get to know his moods."

Hud grasped the file a little tighter, turned his attention back to the board, and stared at the picture of Kaye Sherman again. "Bring me up to speed. Where'd Sherman's wife work?"

"She was an office manager for a doctor's office. Has been for years. Went to work as a file clerk right out of high school and worked her way up. Things changed over the years from one doctor to seven. It became a corporation once the new hospital went up in town. It wasn't a country doctor's office. She had skills and a lot of responsibilities. Everybody liked her."

"You interviewed her office?"

"I did. I didn't turn up anything that gave me concern. She was a victim in this thing. A senseless loss if you ask me."

"Did she have any access to drugs?"

Sloane scrunched her forehead. "Sure, I guess, though she didn't have any medical capabilities that I know of. Why?"

"I don't know; I'm just trying to link Sherman to Pam Sizemore," Hud said. "Has toxicology come back on Sizemore?"

"It's in the file. Preliminary."

"Any meth?"

Sloane shook her head. "None. Some Tylenol, nicotine, and Oxy-Contin. All moderate levels."

"Did she have a prescription for the Oxy?"

"Nope. None that we can find. That'd be hard to overlook."

"I'm not surprised," Hud said.

"Why not?"

"At first I thought Pam Sizemore was a heavy duty meth user, at least until I spent a little time around her kid. He looked the same way she did. Emaciated, frail, dark circles under his eyes like he knew chronic pain. Then I began to think she had a condition of some kind. Moran confirmed it, but we haven't discussed it in detail. Our conversation was interrupted."

Sloane stepped back from the wall and looked toward Burke's office. Hud followed suit and saw the chief through the glass wall talking on the phone. It looked like a casual conversation. Burke wasn't throwing his arms about in protest or demanding anything, at least not yet.

"Have you seen everything you need to?" Sloane said.

Hud glanced back at the wall. "Yeah, for now, I think. You have something in mind?"

Sloane grabbed up her purse, a nondescript, black, over-the-shoulder deal that could go with all her of work outfits, and headed toward the door. "I need to get out of here."

For some reason, the look on Sloane's face and the words that came out of her mouth sounded personal. Like a woman scorned instead of a detective on her way out the door to solve a crime.

~~~~~~

It was no easy task avoiding the media. The trucks and vans had started to overflow from the front parking lot to the side of the building. Hud and Sloane hurried to her car, another Crown Vic, slightly newer than Hud's and clean as the day it had been driven out of the factory. Sloane slid in behind the steering wheel and closed her door. Hud made himself as comfortable as he could with all of the electronics mounted on the dash. The interior of the vehicle was a traveling office with communication capabilities unheard of only years before.

"I'm surprised that we got away without being accosted by a reporter," Sloane said.

"Me, too."

Sloane didn't take any chances and sped out of the parking lot as quick as she could.

"You have some place in mind that we need to go?" Hud asked.

"As far away from there as possible." Sloane kept her eyes on the road and her face blank of emotion, but her eyes betrayed her. They were full of rage, narrowed, in an unusual expression that Hud hadn't seen before.

"How come I get the feeling I missed something?" Hud said.

"You didn't miss anything. Nothing. Okay?"

"Sure, if you say so."

Sloane didn't answer, just kept driving. Her eyes grew glassy, and her hands gripped the wheel so hard it looked as if she was trying to manhandle an uncontrollable car. But that wasn't it at all. The road was starting to dry, and any ice that had formed on it overnight had already melted.

Hud was puzzled by Sloane, but he knew when to speak and when to shut up. Something was going on with her; he just wasn't sure what it was. Time would tell if it was important. He was as sure of that as he was of anything else.

~~~~~~~~~~

They came to a stop in the parking lot of Johnny Long's Supper Club. The restaurant didn't serve breakfast in the off-season, just lunch and dinner. A delivery truck was parked at the rear, and three other cars were huddled up close to the back door. Hud glanced across the parking lot to the Demmie Hotel and saw that their parking lot was just as sparse. It was too early for Tilt Evans to take his station behind the bar, but just the thought of the thin old man gave Hud a taste for a bit of whiskey to get the day going. He might take the urge a little more seriously if he were by himself.

"What's up here?" Hud asked, as Sloane parked at the front door.

"This was the last place Pam Sizemore was seen alive."

"Right. At the back door with a busboy. Jordan something or other. Tilt Evans told me about him."

Sloane nodded, looked pleased. Whatever had been bothering her when they'd left the office had fallen away. She had her game face on now. "Rogers. Jordan Rogers. Burke interviewed him but didn't get anywhere."

"Probably scared the shit out of him."

Sloane didn't react. "I want to talk to him. I think he's holding out on something."

"You were in the room?"

"Why do you think Burke hired a woman?"

"You soften the blow. Look at them with mommy-eyes and pull a confession out of them. Or maybe he likes the scenery. Burke always has enjoyed the company of women."

Sloane shot him a hateful look, but said nothing.

"Sorry, that was out of line," Hud said.

"It was."

"Okay, what's his story, this Jordan Rogers kid?"

"No known priors. C student at school. Not even a traffic ticket. Folks live on the south shore year round. Father works in town at a machine shop on and off when they need a welder, and his mother drives a school bus. Hard working, ordinary people with ordinary lives, who've probably seen tougher times than we can imagine."

"How'd he know Pam Sizemore?"

"Tilt says she was a friend of a friend and she was looking for this

Jordan Rogers guy. Only when I talked to Rogers, he said he had no idea why she would have been looking for him."

"So, he's lying," Hud said.

"I think so. He knows what Pam wanted, but he wouldn't tell us. Her tox report gave me an idea."

Hud stared out the window at the building before him. Johnny Long's looked the same as it had when he was a kid, only smaller somehow, and more decrepit, antiquated in a 1950s Vegas kind of way. The scalloped trim needed painting, and some of the lightbulbs in the sign were broken. He could imagine the interior was the same. "Why would he lie?"

"If he was getting meth off of her that'd be a problem, wouldn't it? You think he'd confess to that after she's been killed? Who wants to be linked to a murder?"

"She cooked but didn't use. Is that what you think? She just sold?"

"It happens a lot. Makes sense, good business sense actually. If it was only for yourself, why would you ever leave? She had to have a motivation for cooking, especially when there wasn't a trace of it in her system."

"He has the look?"

"It wouldn't take too much imagination to see him tweak out."

"Great, I just love dealing with meth-heads first thing in the morning."

~~~~~~~~~

"I've told you already, sometimes it's like she didn't exist. She didn't leave a diary, no pictures, nothing in the house that has ever given me a clue as to what had changed in her life."

"Maybe it's best that you don't know."

"Are you suggesting that I should have stopped looking for her? You of all people? You would have done the same thing."

"I probably would have. But at some point you have to get on with your life. Maybe you should have forgiven her."

"Forgiven her? For what?"

"For leaving you."

"I don't know what to say to that. That's what I was doing. That's why I came back."

"Sure it was."

~~~~~~~~~~~~

Jordan Rogers rolled his eyes when he looked up and saw Sloane and Hud walking his way. Sloane had been right. The boy looked like a classic meth-head. He was in his late teens or early twenties, thin as a rail, with long, straggly hair that didn't look like it had been washed in weeks, and his right arm was a sleeve of poorly rendered blue-ink tattoos.

A broth of some kind was simmering on a six-burner gas stove, and the entire kitchen smelled institutional, like the hallway of a school two hours before lunch. The kitchen was as big as Gee's house, including the shop, and held the biggest collection of stainless steel tables, dishwashers, stoves, refrigerators, and walk-in freezers that Hud had ever seen.

"A moment of your time, Mr. Rogers," Sloane said, as she flipped her badge at the boy.

A manager, a short, balding older man that Hud didn't know, and Sloane didn't seem concerned about, had let them into the kitchen. The back door was open, and the delivery truck driver was carting in crates of leafy green vegetables.

"I know who you are," Jordan said. His eyes darted to Hud, and he talked fast; one word tumbled over the next. "Who's he?"

"Detective Matthews. He's riding along with me today. Nothing to concern yourself with. I just need to ask you a few more questions."

"My dad said I shouldn't talk to you without a lawyer no more."

"It's a real simple question, Jordan," Sloane said. Her voice was soft, as comforting as the smell of the broth. In almost two seconds, she had transformed herself, relaxed, let all of her hard edges wither away. Hud was impressed.

"I'm supposed to call him if the cops come around," Jordan said. His chest heaved just as the delivery driver slammed the walk-in door shut. Jordan jumped at the noise, turned away to identify the cause of it, then spun around again to face Sloane.

"One question, then I'll leave you alone, Jordan. I promise. You already have an alibi. Nobody thinks you hurt Pam. We told you that."

"I don't need no trouble."

Hud stood back and watched the kid closely. His skinny little fingers were twitching, and his left foot was tapping a fast beat. He wasn't full-out stoned, but it hadn't been long. Maybe a day or two since he'd crashed and collapsed into a long-needed sleep. It was getting close to time for another hit to tweak himself back up.

"One question, then we'll leave. Okay? I don't want you to get in trouble with your boss."

"I need my job."

"I know you do," Sloane whispered. "Times are tough all over."

Jordan looked at the door that led into the dining room. The manager lurked close by. Hud could hear him stapling papers at the maître d stand. "One question, then you'll leave?"

"I promise," Sloane said. Nothing changed. No sign of victory. She didn't even flinch.

"What?" Jordan said. "Go on, what?"

Sloane took a step closer to the boy. He watched her and froze. All of the twitching and tapping stopped. It was as if a vacuum had sucked all of the air out of the room. "If I wanted to trade some meth for some Oxy, who would I go to? I know you know. You just need to tell me where Pam got her Oxy."

It was clearly not the question Jordan Rogers had been expecting, but it hit a nerve. All of the color instantly drained from his face, and he bit his top lip. Then he took a deep breath, as if he was going to say something. But he didn't. He spun around again, only this time toward the back door, and he bolted straight out of it. Broke into a full run before Hud or Sloane could say another word.

"Shit!" Hud said, then pushed past Sloane as fast as he could and started to chase Jordan Rogers with all of his strength and determination.

CHAPTER TWENTY-FIVE

Jordan Rogers was fueled by fear and youth and ran almost twice as fast as Hud. The ground was moist, as the mid-morning sun burned off the frozen dew. A thin layer of fog hung over the lake, encasing the surrounding world in silence. The lake was smooth. No waves lapped against the shore. All Hud could hear was the beating of his heart, the struggle for breath erupting from his chest, and his hard-soled brown wingtips hitting the ground harder and faster than they were intended to. It was all he could do to keep his balance as he zig-zagged in between the trees and the shore, following Jordan's trail. His lungs burned, and he wished he'd never started smoking again.

The land behind Johnny Long's reached out and met the lake in a gradual slope. To the north, the direction Jordan had fled, was an open lot that stretched about one hundred yards. It was peppered with tall trees, mostly oak mixed with some pine, and the grass was thin on the slippery ground. The lot ended in private property, as another row of dilapidated pre-World War II cottages stared out over the lake. None of the yards were fenced in, and this gathering of cottages offered plenty of places to hide if the kid knew the area at all.

Jordan kept running and Hud kept chasing, even though he was losing the race. What Jordan Rogers lacked, though, was focus and a well-thought-out escape plan. He kept looking over his shoulder, checking to see where Hud was, how close he was behind him. It was an every-two-second exercise, which, in the end, proved to be his down-fall. Jordan slipped on the wet ground, bounced off a thick oak tree, tumbled forward, and slid face first against another tree.

Hud pushed harder than he thought he was capable of. Adrenaline kicked in. This time he was the owl and not the mouse. His prey scrambled to his feet, slipped again, then gained his footing just as Hud leapt into the air; if only he'd had wings. They collided, a flesh against flesh tackle that was Super Bowl–worthy, followed by a crack and a loud groan that echoed off the thin, vaporous wall of fog. They crumpled to the ground in a heap of arms and legs.

Every police department's interrogation room looked pretty much the same: bare walls, bright overhead fluorescent lights, a two-way mirror, a nondescript four-legged table that would have made the Shakers proud, and two utility chairs. Comfort was not in the design plans, or in the ventilation. The air was thick, unmoving, and, despite how cold it was outside, warm and stuffy inside the room. Sweat beaded on Hud's brow.

Sloane sat across from Jordan Rogers, and Hud stood next to the door doing his best James Dean imitation, with his right foot behind him, holding up the wall. All he was missing was a cigarette dangling from his mouth. His pants had dried from the rumble and tumble of the apprehension, but they were dirty. He was starting to think he had an unnatural attraction to mud.

"You want anything to drink?" Sloane asked Jordan.

The dishwasher shook his head. Mud and dirt liked him, too; he was covered from head to toe in it. Fear hadn't left his eyes. "No. Last time I was in here the other guy kept getting me soda. Then he wouldn't let me go use the bathroom when I had to. I 'bout peed myself. No, thanks. I'm not going through that again. It was a mean game that I ain't falling for twice."

"I'm not the other guy," Sloane said.

"I don't care who you are," Jordan answered. "Do I need a lawyer? I ain't got no money and neither do my folks. I need one of those free ones. And a phone call. Don't I get a phone call? How come there's no phone in here? I'm a prisoner. I have rights. I know I do. I'm innocent, you know. I am. I didn't do nothing. Nothing, you got it?" He tapped one foot, then the other. He was antsy, or still a little ramped up from his most recent encounter with meth.

"You never answered my question," Sloane said. Her voice and demeanor were calm, unaffected by Jordan's sudden purging of words. She looked like a human resources person sitting across the table from a job applicant, judging every move, every nuance for believability and worth. The look on her face told Hud that she hadn't seen or heard anything of value—yet.

Hud remained still and continued to watch with interest. He was going to take the soft, observant approach until Sloane signaled him in. That was fine with him. He didn't mind watching Sloane work. She was pretty good at keeping the kid in the chair. He couldn't bolt this time.

Jordan sneered at Sloane. Hud thought the kid was going to stick his tongue out at her. "I'm not going to answer your question, either. I'm not stupid," he said. "I'm not. I was good in school. Most of the time. I skipped sometimes. I liked to watch *I Love Lucy* in the morning. How about you? You like Lucy?"

He almost got to Sloane. She was trying to follow him, but she couldn't, or didn't want to, Hud wasn't sure which. "I don't watch much TV. So, we can just sit here for a while then. Enjoy the view since you're not going to talk to me," she said.

"I ain't going to confess to selling drugs. Not me. Nope. I'm not going to the pokey for something I didn't do."

"I didn't ask you if you sold drugs to Pam Sizemore, did I?"

He shrugged. "I don't know. Did you? I don't remember what the question was."

"But you ran. Why'd you run, Jordan?"

"I didn't have nothing to do with this. Nothing. I said that. Don't you remember? Fred Mertz reminds me of my Uncle Paulie. Big, bug-eyed, and wide. Drove a Kenworth but always told Peterbilt jokes. Why would he do that?"

"Nobody said you did anything, did they, Jordan?" Sloane continued, staying on track. "Let me refresh your memory. I asked you if I wanted to trade some meth for Oxy who I would go to."

"Same thing." Jordan crossed his arms and cast a sideways glance at Hud. He was checking to see if he was still there.

Sloane lowered her head, then flinched in Hud's direction. Jordan didn't notice, or it didn't matter to him if he did.

Hud hadn't moved a muscle. "She'd come to you, wouldn't she Jordan," Hud said, just as evenly as Sloane. "You and her had a deal worked out. You worked out a code on Twitter that only you two knew the meaning of. You probably think we're old and don't pay attention to that kind of stuff, that nobody is smart enough to check and see what you two talked about for the last six months, but you're wrong. Dead wrong. We know you had a relationship with Pam Sizemore that was all business and no play, isn't that right?"

Sloane said nothing. They both watched Jordan Rogers squirm in the cold, hard seat he had found himself in. He licked his lips. They looked like desert sand baked pink in the fluorescent light.

Hud stepped away from the wall. "We have access to phone records, too, Jordan. Nothing is private when it comes to murder. All we have to do is go to a judge and ask him for a warrant for all of your phone calls. Who you called. Who called you. What voicemails you saved. I will know everything about your phone. Everything. You can't lie, you can't hide, and you can't erase what you don't have access to anymore."

Jordan Rogers craned his neck and stared straight at Hud, with more fear in his eyes than had previously been there. It was like he was in pain, a nerve in a tooth drilled on and hit directly. He contorted his face, looked away at the flat, empty top of the table. "What happens to me if I say I'm the guy she'd come to? What happens then? I can't do the pokey."

"Depends on how you answer the next question," Sloane said calmly.

"You said there was only one question," Jordan replied.

Sloane shrugged. "I just thought of another one."

"What is it?" Resignation replaced the fear in Jordan's eyes.

"Where do you get your Oxy?"

~~~~~~~~~

"So, you and Burke hung out a lot as kids?"

"Yes. Kind of. We'd fish. I'd hang out at his house. Gee wasn't ever keen on company. I think Burke's parents made her uncomfortable. He was the closest full-timer around, and there weren't many other kids my age. So there wasn't a lot of choices for friends."

"Why did Burke's parents make Gee uncomfortable?"

"They hobnobbed with the upper crust."

"Burke's dad was the sheriff. Kind of went with the territory, didn't it?"

"Gee didn't tolerate people who put on airs. Especially the locals. It was bad enough to deal with the vacation people. They could be snobby and demanding, but we made our living off them, so there was compensation of some kind for dealing with their crap, I guess. Locals. No. But it existed. The Burkes ran in a different, wider circle. One we didn't and, most likely, couldn't run in. Not that Gee was all that social. Especially after my mother was gone. So there was always tension between me and Burke, even then. He could go to places that I never could, just because of his dad."

"Like where?"

"He always got to go to the Flowerses' big shindigs, partied at the Demmie at those faux debutant balls in the spring. Rubbed it in my face when he could."

"Why's that?"

"He knew I had a thing for Goldie."

"A thing?"

"Yes, a thing. Does that surprise you? She was beautiful. Everybody had a crush on Goldie Flowers."

"No. It doesn't surprise me. It surprises me that Burke knew. That he used it against you."

"That's what Burke does, isn't it?"

"If you say so. Tell me about Goldie."

"It was distant. How could I ever tell her that I liked her? I was a kid from across the lake who wore cheap tennis shoes and had to work at my grandmother's shop after school and on weekends. She had her pick of all of the boys around."

"You lacked confidence."

"Maybe. Then."

~~~~~~~

Jordan Rogers quit talking. Refused to say another word until an attorney showed up. Which didn't take long. The public defender was a woman, Lucy Hayeton, who looked like she should have retired twenty years prior. She smelled like cat litter and had hair that was white as a deep January blizzard. Hud had never met her before and immediately didn't like her anger, severe attitude, and adversarial approach to the situation. Not that he had expected anything less. He excused himself from the interrogation room and left Sloane to face the lawyer on her own.

Burke met him in the hall. "Are you going to charge him?" Hud said.

"Maybe. He's withheld information. Obstruction."

"That's all you've got?"

"At the moment. Until all of the data from his phone can be put into a cohesive document. Everything we need is there; I'm sure of it."

"Sure of it, but not positive. She's going to eat you alive. The kid will be out of here by the end of the day. Besides, he's not our killer. You're chasing shadows, Burke." Hud started to walk away. His bones felt like cold steel.

"Where the hell are you going?"

Hud stopped. "Home to change clothes. I need a car, too."

"Yours is in the shop."

"Fine," Hud said. "I'll take Sloane's. She's not going to need it for a while."

CHAPTER TWENTY-SIX

The thick gray afternoon sky felt familiar, like a relative who came to visit on a regular basis. Somewhere beyond the clouds, the sun burned brightly, but, like Hud's mind and heart at the moment, it was wrapped in a dark blanket, inaccessible at best. The moodiness of October had always suited him, but now that he felt the pull of it, the maddening silence of the off-season and the growing lack of daylight, he was beginning to think that there was nothing but torment waiting for him in the days ahead.

He felt like Jordan Rogers was a link in the chain that could lead him to the killer, or at least to a motive. Drug and turf wars weren't unfamiliar to him. Meth was a link, too. Pam Sizemore was caught up in it somehow, but Leo Sherman and his wife didn't fit into that picture. Not in a stereotypical way. They had a lot to lose. More and more, their deaths made little sense to Hud. Unless one of them had been in the wrong place at the wrong time and somehow got pulled into the current of things. That was possible. Unlikely. But possible.

Detroit had been rife with the plague of drugs, just like every other big city, but the landscape around the lakes was different. And, to a degree, so were the people. Hud was frustrated that he couldn't see anything more clearly than he did, and he suspected that it was his own lingering troubles that stood in the way of solving the crime, or at least of heading in the right direction. He needed something to break before someone else was killed. Another day, another murder. He felt that pressure. To catch the killer before he took a shot at somebody again.

Hud had to wonder if things would have been any different if he'd never left home in the first place. Would he know the source for the kid's Oxy? Would he have had a trustworthy network that could have given him valuable information on a regular basis? He had no snitches to rely on. No one owed him any favors. He had no one to protect, and no one to protect him. Hud was on his own, and, the way he saw it, that was his biggest problem of all. Even Burke and Lancet seemed to be working against him, allowing him to fail more than succeed. The jury was still out on Sloane, though he felt as if she was warming up to him more than anyone else in the department.

It was a quick trip to the shop in Sloane's Crown Vic, where Hud changed clothes, refreshed himself, then headed back toward the office. Halfway there he realized he'd skipped lunch and decided to stop in at the bar at the Demmie Hotel for a quick bite to eat. Besides, he wanted to ask Tilt Evans what he knew about Pam Sizemore and Jordan Rogers. With Johnny Long's right next door, it was possible he had seen or heard something that might be helpful.

Hud cast a glance over to Johnny Long's as he got out of the car. A hard breeze pushed up against him, offering a cold slap from the lake, reminding him that comfort had headed south, just like everything else in its right mind. At least with the leaves off the trees there was more light—gray light—to see all the way to the lake. Small waves rode to the shore, offering texture and movement that hadn't previously been there. There were no boats on the water or people about. It was a lonely, empty view that Hud had always enjoyed. At least until now.

The restaurant's parking lot was almost empty. Only three cars sat in it. A far cry from this morning after Jordan Rogers had run off, and then been detained. Police cars and media vans had crowded every inch of the asphalt and overflowed onto the grass.

The hotel lot was just as bare as the restaurant lot across the street, and Hud was glad of that. He wanted to eat in peace, ask his questions, then get on with his day—which included teaming back up with Sloane at some point. He pushed inside, glad to see Tilt standing behind the bar, drying glasses, tidying up the place as usual.

Tilt looked at Hud, nodded, then went back to his chore. The man's white hair was a little disheveled, and his eyes were bloodshot. It looked as if he'd been on a bender the night before.

Hud settled in on his usual bar stool. There was no one else inside the bar. "You still serving lunch?"

The jukebox was silent, the lights turned down low, and the grayness from outside had worked its way into every corner of the place. The smell of hot grease lingered distantly, and the smell of sour beer was prevalent and expected. Nothing had changed since Hud had been in the bar last. He found comfort in the sameness, even if something in the air felt off-kilter.

"For you? Sure. What can I get you?" Tilt said.

"Just a burger and a Coke would be fine."

"No whiskey?"

Hud shook his head. "I'm in enough hot water." He stared at Tilt, was more than a little concerned that the bartender seemed to be ragged around the edges. Tilt was usually put together with the precision of a military man, hardly a hair out of place. "You all right?"

"Yeah, yeah, sure. The days just get long this time of year. I'm usually the only one here, so I'm cook, chief bottle-washer, and waitress all rolled into one."

"You were a little swamped for lunch after all the commotion at Johnny Long's calmed down, weren't you?" Hud said.

"A lot of out-of-towners are out and about right now, yes. I was packed for lunch. Wasn't expecting it, that's all."

"The press?"

"Mostly."

"Burke's about to come unglued," Hud said. "We need to put this thing to rest."

"The damage is already done. Won't matter what happens now, will it?"

"You think?"

"I do," Tilt said. "Three murders in just as many days. It doesn't matter what season it is. Hell, you know how things work. Half of the reservations for rentals are made one year for the next, and another third come in over the winter. At least, that's how it used to be. Bad news travels fast these days. It doesn't take much for people to feel insecure, like they're not safe." Something caught Tilt's attention, and he looked away, out the window. "Great," he offered with a sigh. "That's all I need."

Hud followed the look. "What's up?"

"Trouble, that's what."

"Really, why's that?"

"You ever met Goldie Flowers's husband?"

"Soon-to-be ex, from what I understand."

"Yeah, whatever."

Hud stood up from the bar, squared his shoulders, and looked out the window at a beat-up ten-year-old pickup truck parked next to the Crown Vic. "I have a feeling this is no carry-out order. I'm assuming you have a weapon of some kind under the bar?"

"Yeah, I do."

"Good. You might need it."

~~~~~~~~~

"So, who were the upper crust?"

"Burke, the Flowerses, of course. Millie and Herb Vance owned the Demmie back then. They had exclusive parties on the top floor, you know, and Johnny Long, of course. He owned a restaurant in one of the suburbs outside of Chicago, too, besides the one next to the lake. They all hung together and fawned over the big-money people in the summer."

"Johnny Long or Herb Vance had nothing to with the Shamrocks?"

"No, I checked. Nothing linked back to anyone here. I thought maybe Fred Myerson owned a stake in it, but that was a dead end, too."

"He owned the Dip, right, Fred Myerson? The ice-cream place with the little zoo?"

"Yeah, him."

"Was he part of the crowd Gee didn't like?"

"No, not that I know of."

"You suspected him, didn't you? That he did something with your mother?"

"I did."

"And everyone else, too?"

"Maybe that was my mistake. Not that it would have changed anything. Most all of them are dead now, anyway. Nobody's talking because they can't, or they won't."

~~~~~~~~~~

Hud sat facing the door. He could only assume that Goldie's soon-to-be-ex-husband had come looking for him.

Tilt stood tensely behind the bar, with both hands anchored on the counter. He leaned forward a little bit. "Didn't expect to see you in today, Tom."

The man stopped just inside the door and looked around. Hud recognized him immediately. He had been the man sitting with Goldie the first time Hud had seen her at the bar. The light had been dim and shadowy, and he'd only had eyes for Goldie. No surprise there. At the moment, though, he was concerned about the man—Tom—and nothing else.

"You seen Goldie, Tilt?" Tom asked.

Tilt shook his head. "Not today. Can't say I saw her yesterday, either."

"Figured as much." Tom let his attention drop to Hud. "What about you?"

"Me?"

"Nobody else in here is there?" His voice was tinged with anger that only needed a spark to spread into a rage. He had that look about him, like being pissed off was a full-time job. Unlike Goldie, there were no scratches or bruises on his face. His head was shaved, making him look even more severe than he already did. He had a tattoo on his right forearm—a red blazing skull—and some old blue ink on his left arm that looked as if it had been there since he was a kid. He might have been ten years younger than Goldie, but it was hard to tell, all pumped on anger and frustration like he was. Tom whatever-his-last-name-was was not the kind of guy Hud would have ever imagined Goldie Flowers marrying.

Hud hesitated in answering the question, which didn't set well with Tom. "Well? Spit it out. You seen her?"

"What makes you think I even know who Goldie is?"

"Everybody knows Goldie," Tom said.

"Maybe," Hud answered. What he wanted to say was, *"Yeah I saw her last night. She was scared, hurt, and beat up."* And then he wanted to beat the living shit out of the jerk. But he didn't say a word or offer any information at all. "When was the last time you saw her?" he asked.

"What's it to you?" Tom said, stepping closer to Hud, his fists balled.

"That's probably a bad idea, Tom," Tilt Evans offered. "Goldie's not here. I haven't seen her at all for a few days. If you're worried about her, I'd check with her father or go to the police. There's no cause for any trouble here, now is there?" He laid an aged, well-worn billy club gently on the counter of the bar.

"You tellin' me to leave, Tilt?" Tom said.

"That's probably a good idea, Tom."

Hud didn't break eye contact with Goldie's current husband. He had a few reasons for restraining himself. One, he was battered enough the way it was, and two, the last thing he needed was to get into a fist-fight, draw more undue attention to himself from Burke, and end up owing Tilt damages for the destruction that would surely come in its wake. It took all he had not to engage Tom, but he'd caught Tilt's drift, too. He wanted him out of the bar as soon as possible.

Tom exhaled and stepped back. "All right, but if you see Goldie, you tell her to call me."

"I'll do that," Tilt answered stoically.

"And you," Tom said, pointing his finger at Hud, "I don't know who you are, but I don't like your attitude. Another time and place, I might just show you . . ."

Hud nodded, as he watched Tom back out of the bar. "Yeah," he said. "Another time and place."

CHAPTER TWENTY-SEVEN

"I could have handled that guy," Hud said to Tilt, as he wrapped his hands around a big hamburger.

"Sure you could've. Have you looked at yourself in the mirror lately?"

Hud shrugged. "I've got skills you haven't seen."

"I wouldn't underestimate Tom Tucker if I were you."

Grease dribbled down Hud's chin as he swallowed a bit of the burger. He watched Tilt put the billy club back under the counter, then glanced away, caught his own reflection in the mirror behind the bar. He didn't exactly inspire confidence at first glance.

"I've seen his handy work," Hud said. "He got into a fight with Goldie. He obviously doesn't have a problem with pushing her around."

"Maybe not, but if he figures out you've been sleeping with her, then it might be a little worse than pushing around for you both."

"Who said I was sleeping with her?"

"I'm old, but I'm not stupid," Tilt said. "How's the burger?"

"Best one I've ever had."

"Sure it is."

"Okay, maybe not, but it's up there with the best. Should I be looking at Tom Tucker a little closer? What's his story anyway?" Hud bit into the hamburger again and watched every flick and flinch of Tilt's weathered face. It wasn't the original question that he had intended to ask Tilt, but it made sense. "I'm more than a little concerned about Goldie, myself. She was gone this morning when I woke up. I wasn't really concerned about it until Tommy boy came in. We both have things going on."

Tilt stopped halfway down the bar and started walking back to Hud. "Tom Tucker's a small-time bully. Nothing more, nothing less. He's no killer, at least not the kind of killer you're looking for."

"And what kind is that?"

"A methodical one. There's a point. A score to settle. Something to stop," Tilt said.

"That's pretty good. I agree."

"It doesn't take much to see it, at least when you put it against someone like Tom Tucker. The day he kills anyone will be because of rage. He'll push the wrong way, hit back a little too hard. He'll kill from lack of self-control, react. He won't think. Those kind of cells don't exist in that thick head of his, the kind to plan, to think ahead, to hunt. You asked me. I think you'd be chasing your tail if you spent any time at all looking at him. But that's just my opinion. I'm not in the advice-giving business, remember? Especially to a detective."

"Point taken. I just don't know anything about him, and I should, all things considered."

"Tom's lived off Goldie from day one. He thought he hit the jackpot, but him and Old Man Flowers didn't see eye to eye. Most likely because Goldie married a trailer-trash thug just to piss off her daddy. That was easy for all of us to see."

"It worked," Hud said, finishing up his lunch, sliding the plate to Tilt.

"Might've worked a little better than Goldie intended."

"So, that's the break between the two of them?"

"As far as I know, but it's not a big break. Bill Flowers is no idiot. Goldie knows too much about his business to totally sever their ties. She was his right hand for a long time. He'll welcome her back to the fold once she apologizes, dumps Tom, and comes to her senses. If I know Goldie, she's got a plan."

Hud nodded, but said nothing. Goldie had told him she still got a monthly check from her father. *Was it hush money? For what?* "Exactly. She's a thinker. Tom Tucker doesn't seem like her type," Hud said.

"Sure, if you say so. If you haven't noticed, things have changed a lot around here since you were a kid. Got rough is what they did, and

Goldie Flowers is no exception. You should stay as far away from her as you can. She's trouble, Hud, that one is. Always has been. You just never got close enough to see it . . . If I was offering advice, that is."

"I'll keep that in mind," Hud said.

Tilt picked the plate off the counter, put it in a dish tub, and headed back to the kitchen. "I've got a few things to take care of in the back. You need anything else?"

"No, nothing at all. I'm good," Hud answered as he watched Tilt disappear through the door that led into the kitchen.

He was glad to have a moment to himself, to think about what he'd just witnessed and what Tilt had told him. It wasn't exactly what he'd wanted to hear, but somehow he wasn't surprised. And it wasn't as if he and Goldie were going to ride off into the sunset together. They barely knew each other, but Hud had thought there was something there to hold onto. He'd hoped so, anyway. He liked being with her. At least between the sheets.

The urge for an after-meal cigarette quickly came over him, and he pushed off the bar stool then glanced back at the door Tilt had gone through. He'd have to go outside to smoke. No problem there, though he longed for the old days when he could drink and smoke in the same place. Old habits come back fast. But Tilt's pictures and memorabilia on the shelves behind the bar caught his eye. He'd never looked at them closely. Curiosity and admiration propelled him forward, gave him reason to walk behind the bar and examine them fully.

The pictures were angled behind water skiing trophies and old equipment like rope handles and leather gloves. Most all of the pictures of Tilt's glory days were black and white, but some were color, faded from the sun and time. Hud had noticed them before but never really looked at them. He knew Tilt's story, was aware of his victories, but what he hadn't thought about too much was the attraction that a local celebrity had to the vacationers—and to the full-timers. There were the expected pictures of Tilt accepting trophies and ribbons from nameless buxom blondes—those had caught Hud's eyes before—and then there were other pictures of Tilt, mostly at the hotel with Herb and Millie Vance and a whole crew of people. Gee called those people the upper crust and it was easy to see why. The men were all dressed up in black ties and tuxedos, and the women were in long evening dresses with their hair piled a foot high. They had martini glasses in their hands or cigarettes or both.

Hud felt his heart skip a beat, then start to race, and he started searching like he always did, hoping beyond hope to find that one familiar face that always alluded him. The pictures were grainy, smoky, faded, so he had to take his time going from one person to the next. His fingers trembled, then went numb. His mouth dried out, and it felt as if he had fallen into an oven. A faucet dripped in the bar sink behind him. A watery heartbeat that threatened to come to a boil. And his ears began to ring, drowning out every thought but one: *Are you here?*

And the answer was yes. He saw her, and the world stopped spinning.

His hand trembled as he picked up the picture, the oils on his fingers gripping the dust and possibilities so hard that the glass threatened to shatter in his hand. She was sitting at a table, cheesing at the camera. Her eyes were bright and happy, freshly exaggerated with the mascara and eyeliner that was popular in the day. She wore her hair up, like everyone else, and she was dressed like a debutant coming out for all of society to see. Georgia Mae Matthews looked alive, happy, like anything was possible. She looked like a queen, and it was all Hud could do not to cry. *She really did exist.* He bit his lip, fought back the tears, and didn't dare take his eyes off of his mother. He had never seen this picture before.

She was with someone. There were two people sitting at a table, drinking, smoking, laughing, partying like there was no tomorrow—because there wasn't. It was his mother in all her glory, and the man was somebody he recognized, too. It was Burke's father. Sheriff Paul Burke Sr. himself.

~~~~~~~~

"Everything starts with a hunch, doesn't it?"

"I've never discounted those kinds of things. You just have to work a little harder to connect the dots, to make those gut feelings make sense, be true. You have to prove them to yourself, and then to the world."

"And that was your intention?"

"I wanted to be able to bury her in a proper grave. Is that too much to ask?"

"I suppose not. And the rest?"

"You're assuming again."

"Assuming what?"

"That I had a plan all along. That I was up to something other than that one simple ambition."

"Don't forget that I don't believe a word you say."

"I wouldn't believe me, either, if I were in your shoes."

<center>~~~~~~~~</center>

Tilt walked out of the kitchen carrying a green plastic rack full of clean glasses. He stopped suddenly, as soon as he saw Hud behind the bar. The glasses clinked together like a distant alarm.

"Why didn't you tell me you had this picture?" Hud said, still gripping the picture.

"You didn't ask." Tilt looked unsure of what to do, so he stood frozen.

"I didn't think I had to. Are there more with her in it?"

"Maybe. Probably."

Hud took a deep breath, looked away from Tilt and back at his mother. "Why was she with Burke's dad?"

Tilt looked down at the glasses. "You don't need me to answer that question, Hud. You really don't."

"Yes, I do. For once in my goddamned life I need someone to tell me what the hell is going on instead of figuring it out for myself. You knew them all, Tilt. You were in the thick of it. These pictures validate that. Tell me why my mother was sitting with Sheriff Burke."

"Those were different times, Hud."

"My mother up and disappeared one day. That has nothing to do with the times. It has to do with right and wrong. Was she with him? Is he the one?" Hud said, gasping for air. *He was always on my list...*

Tilt sat the glasses on the bar with a look of confusion on his face. "The one?"

"It doesn't matter. It's a yes or no answer, Tilt. Please..."

He nodded his head. "Yes. She was with him."

CHAPTER TWENTY-EIGHT

Burke wasn't in his office. The lights were off, and the blinds on the window were halfway closed. It had been a quick trip from the Demmie Hotel to the station. Nothing could have deterred Hud once he'd seen the picture of his mother. He had to talk to Burke. He just didn't quite know what he was going to say or how he was going to say it.

"Where's Burke?" Hud said to Sloane. She was sitting at her desk, staring at the computer.

Tina Sloane didn't flinch, didn't look up at Hud. "Not here," she said.

Her shortness was hard to mistake. She wasn't happy to see him. "Obviously," Hud said. "Where is he?"

"I don't know. Check with dispatch."

Hud started to walk away, but he stopped a half step before exiting. "Is there a problem, Sloane?"

"Why would you think something like that?"

"I know pissed off when I hear it, and I sure as hell know it when I see it."

Sloane finally looked up at him, her face hard as the wall behind her. "You left me here. We have a twenty-four-hour hold on Jordan Rogers, and I look up and you're gone. We were in there together. I needed you, and you were gone."

That wasn't the first time Hud had heard those words. "I needed to get cleaned up. I took your car. Burke knew I left. Didn't he tell you?"

"Do you ever stop to think that you're not the only one on this case? We're all on it, Hud. Me, you, Lancet. The whole damned department. We have three people dead, and the killer is still out there. People are nervous, and you're off changing your damn clothes."

Hud put up his right hand. "Save me the lecture, all right. Burke's good enough at that. Lancet's had his say, too. I know where I'm not welcome. You don't have to make it worse than it already is. I'm sorry. I should've said something to you. I shouldn't have just left. It's a bad habit." He was starting to like Sloane and didn't want to alienate her, but he didn't know what else to do. He'd come back to talk to Burke, not get more of the same attitude from Sloane.

"You were right, by the way," Sloane said, never taking her eyes off him.

Hud had started to walk away. He sighed heavily and stopped. "About what?"

"About Kaye Sherman."

"Really. Tell me . . ."

Sloane relaxed, glanced back at the report she had been working on on the computer, then back at Hud. "I talked to the doctor's nurse at the office where Kaye worked. I asked her if Kaye Sherman had access to any drugs, and the answer was yes. Kaye had to approve the on-hand inventory every month and sign off on the orders to restock the samples or accept them from the pharma salespeople who called on the office. I asked the nurse, a Lucy Platt, to check the actual inventory against Kaye's last report, and . . ."

"It was short," Hud said.

"Yes. Short of OxyContin, and two other opioids. Everything else was in line with the report."

"A little or a lot?"

"A lot. She was covering something up."

"Nobody suspected anything?"

"No, there wasn't any redundancy in the office to double-check her."

"That wasn't too bright."

"They trusted her."

Hud flashed a smile, then let it fall away. He let Sloane's words linger between them for a long moment. It was a victory. At least a marker in the right direction. "Good work, but we need to check who else had access before we take this too far."

"Thanks. I agree. I asked the nurse to email that list. I'm waiting on it."

Hud nodded. "Any connection to our boy Jordan and Kaye Sherman?"

"Nope, not that I can find yet. No contact between the two of them shows up on his phone list. I'm still waiting for email and anything to do with his computer."

"We have it?"

"Moran and Varner brought it in a little while ago."

"Good. Do you have that phone list?"

"Sure," Sloane said. She reached over to a three-tier plastic tray and handed a printout to Hud.

It was a one-page document with a list of names and the dates phone calls had been made and received on Jordan Rogers's cell phone. It also had the numbers and names of the people who had called him in the last month, if that information was available; some were marked unknown. Of course, Pam Sizemore's name and number were there. Hud had expected that. But he saw another name that he knew. Tom Tucker. Somehow he wasn't surprised.

He handed the paper back to Sloane. "We need to bring Tom Tucker in for questioning."

"Why's that?"

"I had a run in with him a little while ago. He's Goldie Flowers's soon-to-be-ex-husband. Tilt Evans said he came from the hard side of the lake. He's got an air of desperation about him. I want to know what business he had with Jordan Rogers. My guess is they weren't fishing buddies."

"I don't think that's enough."

"His name's on this list. That's enough. If you still don't think he's worth checking out, do it anyway. I'll take the heat for it."

"Sure you will. Like that boat you hijacked and left Moran on the hook for."

"I suppose she's pissed at me, too."

"You need to take one of those courses, Hud," Sloane said. "You know, how to win friends and influence people."

"Yeah, thanks, I'll keep that in mind when I've got the free time to work on my personality flaws."

<p style="text-align:center">~~~~~~~~~~</p>

Dispatch said Burke hadn't left the building. Hud began to hunt for him one room at a time. It didn't take long to find him.

Burke was exiting an office near the front of the building. Along with the county sheriff's department, the building also housed the Child Protective Services, the county welfare office, and the township administration offices; the clerk, assessor, and the trustee offices. All of the government offices in the county had been combined into one building in the early 1960s, and it looked as if nothing had changed from the day that had happened. Time in a bottle. Every piece of furniture was made of plastic and chrome. Hud was surprised they had a functional IT department.

Burke walked out of CPS with a woman Hud recognized immediately. Linda Dupree. Pam Sizemore's son stood next to her, in her shadow, his arm touching her long ratty coat as if he needed a rope to hold him up, to hang on to. The boy looked down at the floor—the linoleum was so highly waxed it looked like he was standing on a mirror—and his shoulders slumped right along with his head; it was difficult to tell whether he was sad or weak. Hud couldn't help but feel sorry for the boy. He looked lost. His coat, like Linda Dupree's was two sizes too big and hung on him like a sheet.

Hud stopped thirty feet down the hall from the trio. Burke saw him, glanced away from Linda Dupree for a second, acknowledged his presence with a nod. A hard stare warned Hud off, told him to stay right where he was. Hud didn't need to be told to hold off. He wasn't going to interfere or inject himself into their conversation. The last time he'd crossed paths with Linda Dupree hadn't worked out too well.

Linda Dupree followed Burke's glance and offered a similar look. *Stay away from the kid.* She still held a grudge. Hud had no questions for her or the boy. At least not at the moment. He preferred to avoid any more conflict with the woman, not rile her up. He might need to talk to her again. Or the kid, if he could get close enough to him. Timmy Sizemore was one of the last people to see Leo Sherman alive. Him and Charlie Sandburg, the boat company owner. There still might be some information to glean. Hud hadn't made the connection between Pam Sizemore and Sherman, but he felt like he was getting close, especially with the information Sloane had collected about Kaye. Somehow, this whole thing was going to come down to a drug deal gone bad. Hud knew it. Felt it deep in his bones. That was his hunch for the motive. Now he just needed to figure out who was pulling the trigger.

Burke said something to Linda Dupree; it was a mumble to Hud's ears. She nodded and said something back in a low whisper, then Burke tousled the hair on the top of Timmy's head and told him goodbye.

Timmy smiled, looked at Burke and made eye contact, and said, "See you later, alligator . . ." loudly, with an expectant response from Burke. The boy's voice echoed off the floor and cement walls.

Burke and Hud were staring eye-to-eye now, and the chief ignored the boy, let his hand slide from the top of his head to between his shoulder blades and gave him a gentle push toward the door.

See you in a while, crocodile, flittered through Hud's brain. Burke was supposed to say it back to the kid, but the chief's jaw had locked in refusal. He said nothing. Just watched as Linda Dupree led the kid to the door.

Hud knew he was seeing something odd. He just couldn't figure out what that something was. There was nothing left to do but wait for Burke to come to him. It looked like the chief and the boy had a thing between them. Was it new or old? *Did Burke know the kid before his mother had been murdered*? It was a question Hud had never had reason to ask before, and he wasn't sure he had reason now. He was just curious.

"I see you've rejoined the world, all refreshed," Burke sneered, coming to a stop inches from Hud. His shirt was crumpled, like he'd slept in it, and his green silk tie was dotted with mustard. Must have had lunch at his desk or on the run. Things were moving fast.

"What was that about?" Hud nodded toward the door.

"It doesn't concern you."

"He's the vic's kid. Yes, it does." Hud focused his attention back on Burke, completely aware of the tone in his voice. Challenging Burke was an old habit; he wasn't about to back off now.

"There's nothing to be found there," Burke said, glaring.

"I'll decide that."

"The kid's been through enough."

"I understand that."

Burke exhaled and broke eye contact with Hud. "I know that. It's just that he's fragile. Don't you ever stop?"

"Do you really want me to?"

Burke sighed and allowed himself to go soft for just a second. "No. That's why I hired you." His tone was normal, like they were equals—for just a second—back on the boat fishing on summer break from school.

"I was hoping you'd say something like that. I can see that the kid's fragile," Hud said. "Why?"

"Why what?"

"He looks sick. Not just heartbroken."

"He is," Burke said.

"What's the matter with him?"

"Juvenile arthritis. A rare kind, I guess. His mother had it, too."

"Is he in pain?"

"Constantly," Burke said. "I don't know the particulars, but there's no cure, and the pain will increase as he gets older."

"She was desperate," Hud whispered.

"I'm sorry?"

"His mother, Pam Sizemore, she knew his pain. She was desperate to ease it. She didn't want him to live like her."

"You think that's why she was cooking meth in a trailer with her sick kid? That's a stretch, Hud. She was a crack case, plain and simple, part of the scourge that has swept through here. Good riddance is what I say. Good riddance. That kid'll be better off in a foster home. He'll get proper medicines and care. He deserves that, don't you think?"

Hud rocked back on his heels, ready to tear into Burke, but trying to restrain himself at the same time. He didn't get a chance to say a word. A woman that he didn't know stuck her head out of the CPS office and said, "Can I see you a second, Chief?"

Burke was surprised by the interruption but said yes and turned to join her.

"Burke?" Hud said, demanding his attention.

"What?"

"I need to talk to you later, if you have some time."

"I always have time for this case. It's twenty-four seven until we put the joker who's responsible for it behind bars."

"This is personal," Hud said.

"Yeah, sure, whatever. You know where to find me," Burke replied, then stalked off in the opposite direction.

~~~~~~~~

"Did you ever think that your mother was still alive? That she just up and left? That it was too much for her?"

"No. I've always believed she was dead. I've always believed someone killed her and got away with it."

"Since you were a little boy?"

"Yes, from the moment I realized she wasn't coming back. Since I was a little boy. I knew her. I knew my mother loved me. She wouldn't just leave. Someone killed her. I always believed that. She would have never left me on purpose. I'm sure of it."

CHAPTER TWENTY-NINE

The size of the county offices had felt confining to Hud from day one. His office in Detroit had been part of a massive, dilapidated complex that had looked more like a prison than a police department. It had taken him years to learn his way around the maze of offices and cubicles. There was no worry about that here. He always knew where he was.

"Good, I'm glad you're still here," Hud said to Sloane. She was sitting at her computer where he'd left her. The aroma of freshly brewed coffee filled the room.

"You found Burke?" Sloane said.

"I did. Pam Sizemore's kid was just leaving protective services. Burke was talking with Linda Dupree."

"She's a treat."

"You can say that again. The kid has some kind of painful arthritis. You know anything about that?"

Sloane paused and glanced toward Burke's empty office before she went on. "JIA, Juvenile Idiopathic Arthritis, from what I understand. He wears splints at night so his joints don't hurt as much and is on a constant regiment of pain meds and physical therapy. It's a battle for any kid from what I understand, and he most likely won't grow out of it. If he does, there'll be lingering effects. Timmy's had the deck stacked against him from the start, and his health problems have only added to the misery. My heart breaks for that kid."

"So how does he relieve his pain? Oxy?"

"Maybe. Mostly NSAIDs I would imagine. A really strong anti-inflammatory. We can find out. What are you thinking?"

Hud took a deep breath, looked at the floor, then up at the wall behind Sloane's desk. It was covered with pictures and documents from all of the murder scenes. Pam Sizemore stared back at him from her high school graduation picture. Hud glanced over to the map, then back to Sloane. "It's not a stretch, really, to think that Pam Sizemore had some variation of the disease, too. She had a frail look about her that I misinterpreted as a meth head, but we know there weren't any signs of meth in her system. Oxy, yes, meth, no. You pushed the idea on to Jordan Rogers that she was trading meth for Oxy, and we thought it was for her. But what if that was the only way she could get medicine for her kid? It would put her in the company of some rough people, or maybe she knew them in the first place. Somehow, she got involved in something that made her a target, but that 'something' is just out of reach. There's something I keep missing."

"There's something we're all missing. I have seen it before, where meth was used as a currency for other drugs. Pot mostly. It was a stab in the dark with Jordan Rogers, but it shut him down, so there's no reason to think I was wrong and every reason to think that I was right. The time is ticking on him."

"It was a good gamble. I didn't know where you were heading with it, to be honest," Hud said, as he stood back and looked at the map again. He had a strong desire for a cigarette, but he fought it off—for the moment. His eyes went automatically to Gee's shop on the map, then to the water, which wasn't too far away. A trek one way took him to the Dip and beyond, to the boat company, a familiar path cut as a kid but avoided as an adult. The trek the other way took him down the path that skirted the Shamrocks, then out to the lake where it was lined with cottages. The Burkes' house sat on the point, offering a wide view of the lake, including the backwaters, and to the opposite ridge that was lined with crumbling cottages and trailers older than Hud, where Pam Sizemore had been shot. Across the point, on the north side, was where Flowers's big house sat, butted up against other big houses that would have been considered mansions in any city. The lake had always been a contradiction of classes. One side looked down on the next, or held it in disdain for its bigoted and highfaluting ways.

A quick image of Goldie writhing underneath his body flashed through Hud's mind. He had finally crossed the class barrier, but it still felt out of reach. Sometimes he wondered if he was dreaming the whole thing with her. He coughed, cleared his throat, then looked at each of the three red push pins that marked the murder scenes.

"You all right?" Sloane asked.

"I'm fine." Hud glanced away from the Shermans' house. "The word proximity keeps popping into my head." It was as a good thing to say as any. He wasn't about to discuss his most recent tryst with Goldie to Sloane.

"I don't follow you." Sloane chewed on the tip of a blue ink pen and eyed Hud closely, obviously trying to figure out what was going on his head.

"It's just something I thought of looking at the map. Did the ballistics report state the range of the weapon used in each shooting?"

"I'm sure it did."

"And we haven't located the spot where the shots were fired from?"

"No. You would know."

"My time away from the office has kept me in the dark about a lot of things. You know that. I'm still playing catch up." Hud touched the side of his face where the tenderness had started to recede.

"I'm sorry. You're right. No, we haven't found the spots where the shots were fired from."

"It could be a spot, not spots," Hud said.

"True."

"Or they could be in the same proximity. If we had the angles where the bullets entered each body, we might be able to divine the line of fire from that information and find the point of origin or origins, combined with the range of the rifle used, if it was the same one for both. It's some major math, and out of my league. But someone should be able to figure it out."

"I agree. Probably the state police forensics lab. We've used them before. We only have the preliminary for Leo Sherman," Sloane said, then followed Hud's gaze to the map. "You want to talk to Bill Flowers, or do you want me to give his office a call?"

"I'm still riding with you, right?" Hud said.

"Unless you know something I don't."

"Burke didn't say."

"You don't want to go this one alone?"

"No," Hud answered. "I think it's a really good idea if we both go talk to Flowers."

~~~~~~~~~~~

"No matter which way you turned, you had found no motive for your mother's death."

"That's not a question."

"No, it's not."

"I could only speculate. Once Gee told me everything she would, I thought it was a crime of passion, or some creepiness from the guy who owned the Dip. I've told you that."

"Yes, that you believed that he killed her and fed her to the lion. But there would still be bones to dispose of."

"The lake is deep."

"True. But things have a way of working themselves to the surface. It's been a long time."

"Too long."

"Why a crime of passion?"

"We've talked about her history."

"We did, but there was no proof."

"There was no proof of anything when it came to my mother, was there?"

~~~~~~~~~~~

Bill Flowers looked up from his desk, saw Hud and Sloane walking his way, sighed, took off his reading glasses and tossed them onto the paper he had been reading. "And what do I owe the pleasure of your company?" he said tersely. "Did you come to look over my shoulder, Detective Matthews? I'm sure you didn't just stop by for a cup of tea."

"Sloane and I need some information," Hud said.

"I've emailed everything to Burke. It's his job to distribute that information. Can't you see that I'm busy?"

Sloane stepped past Hud, put herself between him and the coroner. "We have the preliminary autopsies, but we need information that's not in those reports," she said, softly but with authority.

"Any information I have that isn't in those reports still needs validation, you know that Detective Sloane."

Hud took his cue from Sloane and kept his mouth shut. They needed Flowers to cooperate, not take an adversarial tact with either one of them.

"I understand that," Sloane answered. "But we don't have time until the shooter strikes again."

"You think that's a possibility?" Flowers said.

"Yes, of course. We think we are narrowing in on a motive, but to wait until we're sure, it's still a possibility that they could strike again."

"They?"

"Who knows whether it's a male or female?"

"I suppose you don't."

"No," Sloane said, "we don't."

Flowers rubbed his forehead. "We're getting pressure from every side on this thing," he said. "What do you need?"

"The angle of entry of the bullet on both victims," Sloane answered.

"That's not what I was expecting."

Hud shifted his weight from one foot to the other. He didn't mind giving the lead over to Sloane. Actually, it was something he could get used to.

Bill Flowers stood up from his desk and grabbed a manila folder off the top of a file cabinet. "The pictures can verify where they were lying. Longitude and latitude can be determined from there, if that's what you're after."

"Partially," Sloane said. "I have those pictures. I just need the angle of entry."

"I have it for the first victim," he said.

"Pam Sizemore. She had a name." Sloane offered the coroner a glare, but he took no notice of it.

"Right. Pam Sizemore," Flowers said. "Ah, here it is, thirty-seven point eight, northeast."

"Can you email that to me?" Sloane said.

"Certainly." Flowers looked like he was going to say something else, possibly object, but Sloane's cell phone rang.

The sound of it echoed in the small office unexpectedly. She jumped, then dug in her pocket as quickly as she could. "Sorry," she said, looking at the caller ID on the screen. "I need to take this." Then, without waiting for anyone to agree, she hurried out of the room.

Hud didn't flinch, didn't move a muscle. He just stood there staring at Bill Flowers. It was just the two of them, and he was glad that Sloane had been called away. "You never answered my question," he said.

"I'm sorry Detective Matthews, I've been asked a lot of questions recently. I don't know what you're talking about."

"The one you walked away from after Pam Sizemore's autopsy. I asked you if you remembered my mother. But I know you do. She was part of your crowd at the hotel."

Bill Flowers tensed up, and his face paled. "I have nothing to say regarding your mother. That's old business and bears no relevance to anything that is going on with this case or any other. I suggest you let sleeping dogs lie, Detective."

Hud stepped forward. "I'm not leaving anything lie until I know exactly what happened to my mother and why. Do you understand me? You can go to Burke and have him climb up my ass all you want, I won't stop. You can get me fired, for that matter. This is my life, and I have questions that need to be answered. You'd do the same thing if you were me."

Flower shook his head. "No, I'd know when to leave well enough alone. You can't bring back the dead. You of all people know that. The past is gone. Let it go. There's a killer loose. That needs your attention. Not ghosts from the days gone by."

Hud took another step and stopped. He was inches away from Flowers. The old man smelled like mothballs dipped in formaldehyde. "I know about Burke's father and my mother. He was the one who was going to change everything for her. But you know what? My guess is somebody had a problem with that. I don't know who that somebody was, but trust me I will find out, and when I do, I will make sure justice is served. Do you understand me?"

"You need to leave," Bill Flowers said, stepping backward with a horrified look on his face.

Sloane walked back into the room before Hud could say anything else. "Is everything all right?" she said.

"Sure," Hud said. "Just fine."

"Good," Sloane answered. "We have to go." There was a steeliness in her voice that was hard to miss.

Hud looked over his shoulder to her. "What's up?"

"There's been another shooting."

CHAPTER THIRTY

Infinite gray skies made it look much later in the day than it actually was. Maybe it was the weather, or the season, as the earth tilted away from the sun, but Hud felt like it was something more. A dark veil had fallen over the lake, and it didn't look as if it was going to be lifted anytime soon. Another shooting was the last thing they all needed.

The road was blocked by a brown and tan county cruiser. Its strobe lights flashed, sending colors of the rainbow reaching into the gloom; the color faded quickly and offered no awe, just fear. A line of red road flares sizzled on the pavement in front of the car. Hud found it hard to breathe, even though Sloane had the defroster on high, pushing air directly into his face after it careened off the backside of the cold windshield.

Deputy Varner stood next to the county cruiser and waved Hud and Sloane on with a lazy flick of the hand and a grim frown. In the declining light, Varner's face looked ashen and uncomfortable, like he wished he were somewhere else—anywhere but where he was. His breath hung in the air, turning into a thin cloud of ice crystals before it disappeared. The weight of the murders pushed the deputy's shoulders down, and his eyes along with it. The grayness felt as if failure had become a toxic gas that everyone had digested.

This time they were on the north side of the lake, opposite Gee's shop and the rental cottages. Most of the places on this side of the lake qualified as houses. Big houses. They were hidden from the road, either behind brick walls or thick lines of tall pine trees. It was hard to tell if the wealthy side of the lake had fallen into the same state of disrepair and neglect as the opposite side. A glimpse down the lanes, if the gates were open, gave a person a peek at what the good life was supposed to be on a summer day. All the gates were closed now, and most of the houses were winterized, left to rest for the season. They were all locked up as tight as burial vaults.

Beyond the cruiser, a nondescript beige sedan sat off the berm on the right side of the road. All four-door cars that Detroit manufactured looked alike to Hud these days; the days of fenders and hood ornaments were long past. The sedan was trapped inside a circle of yellow police tape. The tape flapped in the breeze.

Another cruiser sat about a hundred yards north of the car, preventing any traffic from disturbing the crime scene. The media was held at bay, too, but a long camera lens or a good set of binoculars was all that was necessary to see what was going on.

Burke had already arrived; his Crown Vic sat in the middle of the road with the engine still running. The exhaust pipe looked like a fog-making machine. A stream of vapor hit the ground, sending ghost snakes in search of tall grass to hide in. A siren moaned in the distance. It sounded slow, like an uninterested coyote in no hurry at all.

Burke was standing at the hood of the beige sedan staring at the interior.

"The chief seems confident the shooter's not close by, don't you think?" Hud said to Sloane, as she navigated her own vehicle confidently, but slowly, through the maze of the crime scene.

"Maybe he doesn't care." Sloane pulled up behind Burke's Crown Vic and stopped.

It wasn't the response Hud expected. Her hard edge took him by surprise, and he had to consider that she might be right. "This one looks different," he said.

"Maybe," Sloane said, as she popped the car into park. "Let's go see." It was as if it was another day at the office, instead of the fourth murder in less than a week. Hud flinched, then followed her lead.

"What took you so long?" Burke demanded, as they walked up to him.

"We were at the coroner's office," Sloane answered.

Burke glared at Hud but said nothing. Something told him that Burke had already heard from Bill Flowers. One more complaint. One more lecture about the past. He didn't give a shit, though he knew he had to put his personal business aside, wait to ask about his mother and Burke's father at the right time. A shiver ran down his spine as he peered inside the car and recognized the victim. If the distant siren was the ambulance, there was a reason that it was coming slowly. There was no saving the man inside the car. Half his head had been blown off.

Burke scrutinized every move Hud made as he spoke. "The car was stopped alongside the road, still running, with the window halfway rolled down. One shot to the side of the head."

"Close range?" Hud asked.

"Yes," Burke replied, glancing over to the car. "Looks like our victim knew the shooter. That he stopped for them for one reason or another. Different than the prior shootings, when the shooter shot from a distance. I'm not sure this is related."

"It's Tom Tucker," Hud said. "I saw him earlier."

Sloane had obviously decided to stay silent and walked to the rear of the sedan. She inspected the bumper, then the road and ground behind it.

"I know who he is," Burke snapped. "But we need that confirmed. Where and when did *you* see him?"

"I stopped for lunch at the hotel bar. Tucker came in there looking for Goldie. She wasn't there."

"Why was he looking for Goldie, Hud?" There was a knowing tone in Burke's voice, but there was no way the chief could have known that Goldie had spent the night in his bed. At least, he didn't think Burke could know, but that wasn't an absolute. Now it was Hud's turn to scrutinize the chief.

"My guess is he couldn't find her," Hud said. "I think we need to talk to her."

"Why's that?"

"They had a fight last night."

"How do you know that?"

"I saw her."

"You didn't have anything to do with this, did you?"

"I beg your pardon?"

"Just asking. I know how you've always felt about Goldie."

"I had nothing to do with this. We need to find her, that's all. I don't know that anything happened to her or that she had anything to do with this, but we need to start there. We need to find her."

"I'm way ahead of you," Burke said. He turned his attention to Sloane, who had her eyes glued to the ground. "Be careful of those tire tracks. We're going to need to get them molded. The state police lab's on the way."

Sloane looked up and nodded. "There's a cigarette butt here, too. White filter. Looks like a Virginia Slims with fresh lipstick on it. Might not be anything. Tossed out of a passing car, but it's probably worth looking at."

"Bag it," Burke said. "Let's get this scene documented and dispersed before we lose any more daylight."

"Where's Lancet?" Hud asked, not moving, not jumping at the command.

"Looking for Goldie Flowers. You have a problem with that?"

~~~~~~~~

Hud packed away the camera and eyed Bill Flowers as he oversaw the moving of Tom Tucker's body. It was all that remained to do, other than having the sedan towed away. Then it would look like nothing had happened there at all. The coroner had been more glum than usual, quiet and distantly removed. Hud had heard him tell Burke that he hadn't seen or heard from Goldie in a week. That was that. No show of emotion, no outward concern as he went about his work at the crime scene. It wasn't like Flowers could recuse himself. The coroner's office was on a tight budget, just like the rest of the county services, but Hud had expected something else. A sense of urgency, concern. Something. He felt it himself. To hell with the darkness. He wanted to find Goldie.

Sloane walked up to Hud as he closed the trunk of her Crown Vic. "Lancet's visited Goldie's apartment and a few of her other haunts and didn't find anything. Any idea where we might go from there?"

"Why do you think I'd know?"

"I'm just asking. What's up with you?"

"Nothing. I'm just frustrated. No witnesses, no leads, nothing."

"We might know a little more once we get Tucker's phone records."

"I hope so," Hud said. He watched Bill Flowers close the door on the ambulance, then walk over to his black Cadillac and get inside. "Yeah, I got a couple places we can check, but I need a second to talk to Burke."

"Are you sure? He's in a mood."

"When isn't he?"

"You seem to bring out the best in him," Sloane said with a feigned smile.

"Give me just a minute," Hud said.

"Sure."

He sighed and walked away from Sloane as Bill Flowers drove off slowly. The red taillights seemed to linger in the cold night like two disappearing stars never to be seen again.

"You have a second?" Hud said, walking up to Burke.

The chief exhaled a vapor cloud of disdain. "What do you think?"

"I think you have a lot going on. We all do."

Burke looked more disheveled than Hud could ever remember seeing him. The chief had inhaled the toxic gas of failure, too, and it was showing on him. "You realize that Bill Flowers thinks I should fire you once this is all over with, don't you?" he said.

"I'm not surprised. But what power does he have?"

"That's your problem, right there. That chip on your shoulder. It's always been there."

Hud drew back, surprised by the proclamation. "So you agree with Flowers, that I shouldn't be here?"

"Did I say that?"

"No, but . . ."

"Look, Hud, you have to stop searching, stop asking people questions about the past, especially with everything that's going on. I know I can't make you. Hell, I don't think you can make yourself. But, damn

it, the last thing I need is Bill Flowers on my case, too. I think you're one
of best detectives I've ever met. You've been asking questions all of your
life. You're good at it. You can't help yourself. If I wanted to fire you, I
would have already done that, you idiot. I've deflected all of the criti-
cism off you. I've defended your presence, not for my own sake, but for
yours. I know that you need to be here."

Hud saw a moment of fear pass behind Burke's eyes. It was a rare
sighting. Bill Flowers had something on the chief, had some real power
of some kind. A nerve had been touched, and now that recognition of
fear fueled Hud's curiosity even more. But more than that, there was
a glimpse of the old friend that Hud had known as a boy. The gruff-
ness and hard edge had fallen away for just a second. "Look, thanks.
It's felt like I've been fighting the current since I landed here. I know
these crimes have nothing to do with the past. Pam Sizemore, the Shermans, and now Tom Tucker, they weren't around when my mother disappeared, but I'm surrounded by her presence. She's everywhere I look,
but I can't touch her. You're right. I can't help myself. I wish I could.
Somebody knows something, and I won't be able to stop until I find it.
Her. You had to know that."

"Drop it. Can you just drop it for now?" Burke said, then turned
to walk away.

"I saw a picture today at the hotel. It was of my mother. She was
with your father." There was no way Hud was going to let it go. Not
now.

Burke stopped. His body tensed, as a cloud of breath erupted from
his mouth and nose. He didn't turn around to speak. He talked into the
darkness. "That has nothing to do with this, Hud. They are both gone."

"You knew," Hud whispered.

Burke turned around slowly. "I knew you'd find out sooner or
later." He took a step forward. "But he had nothing to do with her disappearance, I can promise you that. My father would have never hurt
your mother. Never. If you think about it, you know that's true. He protected us all the best he could."

"I want to see his files. I want access to everything."

"When the time is right."

"And you get to decide when that is?"

"Yes, I do." With that said, Burke spun around and walked off into the night.

Hud didn't do anything to stop him. He just watched until he was sure Burke was completely out of sight.

~~~~~~~~~~

"Did you really believe that you would find the truth? The whole truth? That people would tell you what they thought they remembered, or what they wanted to remember?"

"Time has a way of getting to people. You've seen it before just like I have. The truth always comes out. I had faith in that, if nothing else."

"A version of the truth."

"It was important. But there was something more that I wanted. You know that, too."

"A body."

"Yes. I needed to see something. I thought it would make all of my pain go away."

CHAPTER THIRTY-ONE

Hud sat comfortably in the passenger seat of Sloane's Crown Vic. He stared out the window as she drove into the night, trying his best not to look at her. It wasn't hard to imagine that he was just a boy, riding along with Gee as they searched the lonely winter roads around the lake for his mother.

Gee had been the pilot, and he had been the copilot, eyes peeled, looking for a sign of his mother's existence. Something. Anything. A shoe along the road, a battered suitcase, a fluttering piece of paper with her name on it. They stopped and looked at it all. Without knowing it, Gee taught Hud how to search, how to ask questions, how to be a detective. Or maybe she had known all along that Hud would outlive her, be left with the questions about his mother. All she could give him were the tools to look. If she failed, if she died before his mother was found, it was all she could do for him.

Hud didn't say anything for a long time, and Sloane responded in kind.

Darkness had fallen completely on the world, and, with the vacation season over, the tiki torches, colored strings of lights, and campfires were just a memory. Trailers and cottages flashed by in the headlights. Occasionally a pair of eyes would reflect from the berm: a possum or a skunk starting out on their nocturnal jaunts. Both were vagabonds, creatures of the night, kin to the search, the need to keep moving. Hud was glad to see something alive, stirring. He was stuck in between the past and the present, a prisoner of grief, memory, and fear. Now he was searching for Goldie instead of his mother. He needed a sign that Goldie was still alive, that she had existed. He wasn't sure that she wasn't just part of a bad dream, too.

"You warned me about Burke, about how protective he was of father's legacy. Did you know?" Hud finally said.

Sloane stiffened, kept her eyes on the road. "It wasn't my place to tell you. Burke was agitated. You knew that. I wasn't sure what he'd do, considering the pressure he's been under. I was worried for both of you."

"How did you know? I tried to access my mother's file and I was locked out. I figured everyone was."

Sloane exhaled and dropped her head briefly. Voices from the police radio filled the car with requests. Ten codes. Nothing to do with the murders. A traffic stop. A taillight out. A call for a wrecker. And then silence again. Just the hum of the wheels underneath him, finding their way in the dark.

"Oh," Hud said, reading the look on Sloane's face. There was no way he was wrong. "You and Burke have a thing? I thought I felt something, saw something, but wasn't sure. Still? Or is it over?"

Sloane glanced over at Hud. Her eyes were glassy, reflecting the light off the dashboard, the computer screen mounted on the console, the radio, enough to see turmoil and shame. Her pain glowed like an Open sign on a lonely road. "Still," she whispered.

Hud didn't know what to say. What Burke and Sloane did in their own time was none of his business, just like what he did in his time was no business of Burke's, but the relationship with Sloane bothered him. He restrained himself from making a comment about the apple not falling far from the tree. *Like father, like son*? He didn't know anything about Burke's married life, or Sloane's life for that matter. Once he thought about it, though, Hud wasn't surprised. Burke always did have more than one girlfriend, always had more than one place to lay his head. It hadn't occurred to him to wonder if anything had changed. Obviously, nothing had.

"You have to tell me what you know about my mother and Burke's father," Hud said.

"I'd rather stay out of it. It feels like family business."

"It's old business."

"It's Burke's place."

"It depends on what he knows and how he came to know it."

"It wasn't in the report, if that's what you're asking."

"I'm just asking how you know."

Sloane nodded, sighed, and said, "His mother told him."

~~~~~~~~~

"Sometimes in the summer it would be too hot to sleep. We didn't have air-conditioning. Nobody did back then; that's why they came to the lake, for the cool breezes. Fans hummed in every room, and I wouldn't be able to get comfortable, so I'd climb up on the roof. Gee didn't like it when I did, went out there, especially when she caught me smoking one of her cigarettes, but that didn't stop me.

"I could see down into the dip, hear the lion pacing back and forth in its cage, or a boat out on the lake puttering home with the radio on. The water amplifies voices, sounds at night. I was always up there on the nights when the Flowerses had their big parties, hoping to hear Goldie's laugh. It was as close as I could get.

"The sky seemed wider then, too, full of stars, and on nights when the moon was full, I wondered and hoped that my mother was looking at it too, that we were sharing something, even though deep down, I knew that wasn't possible. By then, I knew if she hadn't come back it was because she couldn't. I could never imagine her making the choice to stay away, even though that's what everyone wanted me to believe."

"That she'd run off with the new man?"

"Yes. But you know I didn't believe that. She wouldn't have left me, us, not without a fight. I never gave up on that, on her. I believed that she would fight to get back to me, because I would have fought to get back to her.

"A few times I would go up on the roof and a car would pull across the lot and stop just prior to coming in. I'd get hopeful, you know, until I realized that it was a police car, that it was Burke's dad. I thought he was stopping to watch over us. It made me feel a little better to know he was out there."

"That was then. How about now?"

"Now I have to wonder what he was really looking for."

~~~~~~~

They passed by Gee's shop slowly. There were no cars in the parking lot. All of the lights were off inside, just like Hud had left them. "Looks good to me," he said.

"You really thought she might be here?" Sloane pulled the Crown Vic off the side of the road and parked it there with the engine left to idle.

"Waiting for me," Hud said. "Looking for me. Yes. I can help her. I hoped she would be here."

"Burke said you'd always been hung up on her."

"It was easy, that thing you can't have."

"Until you can."

"Then it screws up everything." Hud glanced over to Sloane and regretted saying what he had, but there was no apologizing. He hadn't known that Goldie was married. Hadn't cared. But Sloane had to have known that Burke was married, what she was getting herself into. "It's not too difficult to connect some dots, think that Goldie hunted down Tom Tucker and blew his head off. It could be her cigarette butt you found."

"That's got to be uncomfortable."

"It's a possibility that I don't want to face. But I can veer away from her as a suspect pretty easily."

"Who to, then?"

The Crown Vic's engine rumbled, ready to go at a moment's notice. Every piece of equipment inside the car vibrated. It felt like a boat restricted to a no-wake zone.

Hud stared out the window toward the lake. "The Tom Tucker killing wasn't so different after all, if you think about it."

Sloane looked at Hud like she didn't believe him.

"He knew his killer," Hud continued. "Or, it appears that he did. But that's not the first time that's happened since this thing first started."

"Ah, Kaye Sherman," Sloane said.

"Exactly. The back door was open. There was nothing taken, no sign of a struggle. Her head was smashed against the counter."

"An emotional response. Rage," Sloane said, "that got out of hand. A reaction. Not a premeditated murder . . . not a sniper shooting."

"But a crime of passion."

"You're back to that. Which would explain two murders, but not the other two, Pam Sizemore and Leo Sherman."

"The shooter had time. Knew what was coming. At least with Leo Sherman. Maybe Pam Sizemore, too," Hud said, still staring at the lake.

"Are you suggesting that there are two killers, that maybe we're wrong in combining it all into one case?"

"You just considered that possibility for the first time, didn't you?"

"I did, but I don't think it's probable."

Hud turned his attention away from the darkness that led down to the lake. "In the summer, you can't see the water from here," he said. "But once the leaves come off the trees, you can. You can see from one end of the lake to the other from the right spot. Look, I don't think there are two killers on the loose, either. But I also don't think Goldie Flowers is that one killer. I saw her face, felt her fear. Something sent her to me, and I think it was her abusive husband. I think she wanted to feel safe."

"Or maybe it was something else. She could have been using you," Sloane said.

"What for?"

"To hide in plain sight."

"You really think that?"

"We can link Tom Tucker to Jordan Rogers and Jordan Rogers to Pam Sizemore. We know that Kaye Sherman was lying about the amount of drugs in her office. Drugs seem to be at the heart of all of this, and her husband is in that mix."

"What's that got to do with Goldie?" Hud said.

"You think she didn't know what Tom was involved in?"

"Maybe. Probably. There was a rift between Goldie and her father. He might have known about Tom, too. The drugs could be the cause of the rift. Tom Tucker might have been desperate, or been a dealer for all we know. We just started looking at him. He might have been willing to do anything to keep Goldie in the style to which she was accustomed. But I still don't see how that sent her to me? She said they were breaking up. I figured it was because he was physical with her, but what if his business was dying? Charlie Sandburg, the guy that owns the boat company, said there was a turf war going on and that Leo Sherman was trying to help Pam Sizemore. What if that's what this is? What if the competition just got rubbed out? I've seen it before in Detroit. But you wouldn't expect that here. Not like it used to be. But now you would. Drugs are part of the economy. There's no denying that."

"Help Pam Sizemore out how?"

"He didn't say. I'm not sure he knew," Hud said. "But there's a link between the Shermans and Pam Sizemore."

"Drugs for the kid?"

"Maybe. It's all we have at the moment." Hud looked back at the lake. "We need to talk to Charlie Sandburg, but first I think we need to go to the highest point on the lake. Where you can see everything. Where a 30-aught-6 had the range to reach both murder scenes. The ridge where Pam Sizemore was shot, and the backwaters where Leo Sherman was shot."

Sloane closed her eyes, as if she were trying to imagine just the place.

"There's only one place I can think of," Hud said.

"Yeah, me too," Sloane answered. "The old Ferris wheel."

"Exactly," Hud said. "Let's go."

CHAPTER THIRTY-TWO

The boardwalk hadn't started out as a collection of games of chance, cotton candy stands, and thrill rides. Instead of greed and profit, the boardwalk, and the towering Ferris wheel that announced its presence from miles away, were born of tragedy. Or at least that was how Hud had heard the story.

A ramshackle carnival had rolled up on a perfect summer day in 1926. After finding an open field next to the water, the collection of rides and vaudeville acts set down stakes, hoping to draw a crowd. Cottages were starting to be built around the lake, an overflow of the prosperity of the roaring twenties. The peace dividend from World War I had paid off handsomely and the Great Depression wasn't on anyone's radar. Fun was in the air; it smelled of cotton candy, popcorn, and opportunity.

About two days into the carnival's stay, one of the Ferris-wheel buckets came loose, tossing two young girls and their pregnant mother to the ground. Luckily, the bucket hadn't been at the wheel's apex when the bolts gave away, but even from halfway up all three of them suffered broken bones and severe trauma. The unborn child was lost. The carnival was shut down immediately by county officials, and sometime during the night, the owners and everyone else sneaked off. What rides were left behind were repaired, legally acquired by the landowner, and a new venture popped up almost overnight around the Ferris wheel. The boardwalk expanded during the Depression, despite the desperation of the economy, drawing people with pennies and nickels for a high sight of the lake and other distractions from their hopeless reality. Gee had gotten her first kiss on the original wheel, looking out over the lake, a place she loved and would never leave, and Al Capone was rumored to have visited the boardwalk after a secret stay-over at the Demmie Hotel, but that was more likely a tall tale than truth. Postcards had been printed up and sold three for a penny, all featuring the Ferris wheel, the only one permanently mounted for hundreds of miles.

The Ferris wheel had been replaced twice, once after World War II, and then again in the early seventies, before the energy crisis hit and the economy tanked again. Now, after years of neglect, the giant metal circle sat silent and unmoving, rusting away, threatening to fall into the water where it would surely give in to the ravages of time. Its lights had been darkened forever. There would be no replacing it again; such an endeavor was too expensive.

All of the shops were empty, too. The boardwalk was a ghost town of snooker shanties that moaned and trembled as the wind whistled through shattered windows and open doors; a mother's scream echoed from 1926 and joined the chorus of broken dreams, lost hope, and the certainty of demise. Only raccoons, rats, and snakes made the place home now.

The Ferris wheel was the tallest and most obscure perch Hud could think of for a sniper to use. From it, two of the shooting spots would be in range of a 30–aught-6. "We should've checked this place out sooner," he said.

"Maybe in the daylight?" Sloane swung her flashlight upward to the top of the wheel, cutting through the darkness like a sharp knife. "If I see anything with beady eyes, I'm shooting first and asking questions later."

Hud flickered a smile and silently agreed.

The bright white beam cut across red rust growing on disconnected metal rods and braces that dangled in the wind. A few of the lower buckets had been removed, or fallen into the lake, but the rest of them looked to be intact. Paint had peeled away, but there were still eerie outlines of clown faces on the buckets. The sky was obscured by clouds; moonlight and starlight were hidden, making the lake look blacker and deeper than any abyss that Hud could imagine. He tried to avoid looking at the water. It was an unmarked grave, dangerous, begging him to dive in and search the bottom for a human bone, a ring, a tooth, anything that he could hold onto, no matter the weather or time of day. He had never been afraid of the lake, of water, until his mother had disappeared.

Hud eased his own flashlight across the ground, looking for a shell casing, anything that would have suggested that the shooter had been there. The silence of an October night surrounded them, blanketed them, all the while leaving them unprotected. They spoke in soft whispers. There were no more sirens in the distance, no traffic noise, no boats on the lake for a nighttime cruise. It was too cold, to desolate for a joyride of any kind.

Crisscrossing beams of light didn't turn up anything, at least nothing that jumped out at Hud and demanded that he investigate further. There were too many cigarette butts, soda cans, and various other types of trash lying around for him to single anything out. It would be like hitting the lottery if he did find something useful. A thorough investigation would have to wait until daylight came around again. He thought he'd enlist Deputy Moran to help him if it came to that. Help calm the waters. She was still most likely pissed at him for leaving her at the scene of Leo Sherman's shooting.

Frustrated, Hud swung the light up to the top of the Ferris wheel and let it rest there. A seat sat where he expected it to. Then he scaled the light down slowly, like he was taking steps, calculating the reach from one bucket to the next. He sighed out loud.

"You're not seriously thinking of going up there, are you?" Sloane said.

"Only if I have to." He brought the beam back to the ground, then walked to the edge of the seawall. The opposite shore was dark, just like the one to the south of him. But there was a building with lights on to the north of them. It was within walking distance. He looked upward at the top of the Ferris wheel and then back to the building. "Which do you think is taller? The Ferris wheel or the Demmie Hotel?" he asked Sloane.

She shrugged. "The Ferris wheel, but only by a little if you're on the roof?"

"Yeah, that's what I was thinking," Hud said. He stared at the hotel a little longer. It was a beacon in the dark, one of the few businesses that stayed open year round and catered mostly to the locals. Hud had felt comfortable there, was glad that Tilt Evans was still behind the bar, serving up wisdom and offering advice, even if it was to stay away from Goldie. "What was Pam Sizemore's last Twitter post to Jordan Rogers?"

Sloane sidled up to Hud and stood shoulder to shoulder with him, staring at the water, then to the hotel. "Last call."

"Yeah, that's what I thought it was. Last call. But maybe we mistook that text for something it wasn't."

"What do you mean?"

"We thought it was a drug deal set up, that she was almost out, the end of a batch. Come and get it while it lasts. But maybe that wasn't it. Maybe it said exactly what was meant to be said."

"Okay, but what are you thinking? I'm not following you."

"Last call. Like in a *bar*. Jordan Rogers worked next door at Johnny Long's; they met at the bar at the hotel after he got off work. Tilt told me that when I asked if Pam Sizemore ever came into the bar. They'd come in at the end of the night. Maybe that's where they made their exchanges."

"We can ask Jordan."

"We can, but that's not my point."

"What is?"

"Tilt Evans would know what was going on. He wouldn't miss something like that. He knows everything that goes on inside that bar. I'd bet my life on it. There might be a reason why Tom Tucker came to the bar looking for Goldie. I thought it was for another reason. I thought he was looking for me, but maybe he really came in to talk to Tilt, but I was there so he couldn't. Wouldn't talk freely with a cop there—either one of them. I think we need to talk to Tilt." Hud turned away from the Ferris wheel, and started to hurry to the car.

"I'm calling for backup," Sloane said, following after him.

"That's probably not a bad idea," Hud said. The wind picked up his words and carried them away. They were no longer whispers, and each syllable bounced off the lake, amplifying and flying in all directions. He could only hope that no one was listening.

~~~~~~~~~~

"So, Burke's father had motive to kill your mother?"

"What if they were having an affair and she finally wanted more? That she didn't want to be a mistress anymore? She said everything was going to change and she hadn't meant it in a bad way. She was happy before she died."

"Did he have a black car?"

"It wasn't Burke's car that she got into on that last day. I knew the Burkes' cars. I would have recognized it. I didn't know the car that she got into."

"So that doesn't add up."

"That doesn't mean he wasn't driving, or that he had someone else pick her up."

"Someone else would have been involved, complicit. Even if they had dropped her off somewhere where he was, they would have spoken up. Maybe not then, but years later. You know how that works. Secrets always bubble to the surface. People talk. No one has."

"I don't know whose car it was."

"It would have been uncomfortable, considering how close you all were, if Burke had left his wife for your mother."

"It wouldn't have looked good. Burke's parents were thick with the society people. His position was electable, so morals held value. I'm sure appearances meant a lot. There was a lot at stake if things got out of control, don't you think?"

"Your mother fell in love with him of all people?"

"Sheriff Burke had the means and the knowledge of how to make someone disappear."

"The sheriff was a killer? You think he took her down some lonely road, killed her, dumped her in the lake, then went home to his wife and son and lived happily ever after?"

"You sound like you don't think that's possible, that a cop can't cross a line."

"Not true. I had my suspicions about you, that you killed your snitch in Detroit. Have you forgotten?"

"I'd never forget something like that."

~~~~~~~~~

The neon Open sign buzzed in the window of the Demmie Hotel bar. Hud and Sloane sat in the Crown Vic surrounded by the dark of night, alone in the parking lot. There was only one other car, and Hud knew that it belonged to Tilt Evans.

The dispatcher's voice droned on over the radio, and they both listened intently. "There is no record of any criminal activity for Clyde "Tilt" Evans," the woman said. "Only two traffic tickets, and both of those were issued several years ago."

"Where were they?" Hud said into the mic.

"Hold on." Static, then silence, then more static. After a long few seconds the dispatcher said, "Chicago. Both tickets were issued in Chicago."

"Chicago," Hud whispered.

"What is it?" Sloane said.

"I don't know. I guess I had never associated Tilt with Chicago. He's always been here," Hud answered, then said 10-4 back to the dispatcher while he looked at the hotel with a fresh set of eyes.

"We all came from somewhere."

"We probably don't know as much about Tilt as we should," Hud said as he grabbed the door handle and opened it.

"Aren't you going to wait for backup?"

"No." Hud flicked his head to the bar. "The lights just went off inside. It's hardly closing time . . ."

A cold wind pushed past Hud as he exited the Crown Vic in a quick sprint with his .45 sliding upward to the ready position. He half expected to hear a shot, feel the burn of lead pierce his skin, but that didn't stop him. Running toward the truth never had.

CHAPTER THIRTY-THREE

The door to the bar was unlocked. Hud hesitated, looked over his shoulder at Sloane and saw her pale, white face edged with fear. He knew at that moment that she'd never been in a situation like this, one full of uncertainty and the possibility that they might face resistance, gunfire, maybe death. Being a county detective in a seasonal tourist community had given her little experience when it came to such a thing. Winter burglaries were her specialty. Not hunting down a cold-blooded killer. Hud would have been more confident with Deputy Moran at his side, with her kickboxer attitude and relentless fierceness. Not somebody who had succumbed to Paul Burke's charms and then come to regret it.

"Stay close," Hud whispered, trying to boost her courage. He had no idea if Tilt was capable of murder, or of all of the things that had happened since Pam Sizemore. It was a long line of incidents to link together, and he hadn't had the clarity of mind, or the time, to attempt the feat, but Hud was fairly certain that Tilt Evans knew more about what was going on than he was telling. And now he was showing something by turning off the lights early, like he had made the Crown Vic and decided to run and hide. That was just speculation on Hud's part. Nothing might be wrong. There could be a million reasons why Tilt had decided to close the Demmie Hotel bar down early—but it was out of character. He never closed early, at least since Hud had been back. Tilt's presence had been as constant as the North Star.

"You're sure about this?" Sloane asked.

"We don't have a choice." Hud inched the door open and peered inside. Light from the jukebox still flickered colors of the rainbow across the floor and ceiling, eating away at the darkness. It looked like a slow dance at a high school prom, only one with the odors of beer and grease permeating every chair, table, piece of cloth, and square inch of the bar instead of acne cream and anticipation. The rest of the lights were off, and there was no one to be seen—but that didn't mean no one was hiding behind the bar. A freezer in the kitchen hummed, and a Budweiser clock ticked; a plastic team of Clydesdales and a red wagon slowly toured the hours, never arriving at their destination.

Hud knew Tilt kept a billy club behind the bar, and he assumed that was just the first weapon within reach. Warding off trouble took a strong spine, which there was no doubt that Tilt Evans possessed, but it also took solid backup. A gun of any kind spoke loudly when it came to settling disputes that a billy club wouldn't. Tilt had never spoken of a gun, had always shied away from talking about his military experience in Vietnam, but there was no doubt the man knew something about firearms. At least he had at one time.

"Let me clear the room," Hud whispered.

Sloane nodded, agreed to stay back and cover him.

Hud pushed slowly into the bar, sweeping the entirety of it with his .45. He didn't announce himself or call for Tilt. He figured there was no sense in that. If he was wrong, if Tilt walked in and asked him what the hell was going on, then a simple explanation would suffice. Especially if Tilt was innocent, not involved in the shootings in any way. But if he *was* involved, then there was no use in taking any chances. Hud would rather look like a fool than die a careless death.

He eased his way to the bar, and then behind it after making sure that neither Tilt nor anyone else was crouching behind it in wait. A sigh of relief escaped his mouth once he was certain that the bar was empty. He flipped on his flashlight just to make sure he hadn't missed anything. Sloane stayed put, covering the door.

Nothing looked out of place, with the exception of a white bar towel crumpled on the floor and two dirty beer glasses in the sink ready to be washed. Hud shined the beam across the bar to the corner where he had first seen Goldie, only to see it how he expected to: Empty. He trailed the light slowly across the room, checking each table for anything out of place. He found everything in its place, just like it would have been at closing time. From there, Hud's attention was drawn back to the bar and the shelves behind it.

He caught a glimpse of his own reflection in the shadowy mirror, his bruises still obvious, the swelling mostly gone. His face looked like the face he was accustomed to looking back at, less battered, but there was still pain lurking under the skin, a reminder of the hit he'd taken from the oar and the shards of glass exploding from the windshield. He heard the report of the rifle distantly, in his memory, close enough to cause him to tremble, to wonder if the person who pulled the trigger knew him, wanted him dead, out of the way. Or was it meant to just scare him off?

With the flick of his wrist, Hud scooted the beam of light to the shelf where he saw the picture of his mother and Burke's father. He stopped and stared at a bare spot instead, questioning whether that was the right place. Quickly, he searched the rest of the shelves. All of the pictures, trophies, and trinkets from Tilt's past were untouched, where they were supposed to be, a shrine to youth, vigor, and the championship season that had given Tilt his name.

There was an outline left behind from the missing picture. A thin coat of dust had been stirred up and not cleaned off. A trophy had been knocked over and not set back up. Someone had been in a hurry to take the picture, to make sure it disappeared.

Hud stood back from the spot, looked over his shoulder at Sloane, who was exactly where he had left her, comfortably stiff in her position as backup. He couldn't explain his moment of stasis, why he longed to see the picture of his mother again. The flashlight in his hand quivered, and the beam shook like weak lightning. And in that moment, Hud saw the picture next to the empty spot where the picture of his mother and Sheriff Burke had been. He had to step up and look closer.

This picture looked to have been taken at the same time as the one with his mother, at a big fancy party where everyone was dressed up. The men wore black ties and all of the women were decked out in formal evening gowns. And like the previous picture, this one was in black and white, but there was no mistaking the identity of the two people dancing together, smiling at the camera like there wasn't a worry in the world, like happy endings really did come true. The man was Tilt, tanned and triumphant, and the woman, just as beautiful and perfectly put together as he remembered her, was Helen Burke, the chief's mother. She looked completely comfortable in Tilt's arms.

~~~~~~~

"Do you believe that some men are born to kill, like say a lion? That they are predators and are only doing what they know to do? That they can't help themselves but to kill. It is as natural as breathing to them. They carry no guilt or regret, just the urge to do it again . . ."

"I don't see why not."

"You've seen that behavior?"

"Sure I have. The streets are a jungle all their own. You know that. Not just in Detroit. Everywhere."

"And that's why you think Burke's father was capable of killing your mother?"

"I don't know. I never saw him as a predator, but he only lives in the memory of a little boy. What did I know about things like that back then? I didn't know what a predator was."

"You knew Burke as a boy, his son. Was he a bully?"

"Aren't you really asking me if he was a predator?"

"Sure, I suppose I am."

"He liked the girls. More than one at a time. We talked about that. He always played the field, was chasing after one girl or another. Does that make him a predator, or was he just horny? I don't know."

"What about you?"

"Am I predator?"

"Yes."

"My quarry would be justice if I were. How am I supposed to know?"

~~~~~~~

Hud shined the flashlight at the base of the door that led into the kitchen and saw a single drop of fresh blood. It would have been easy to miss in the dim light, with untrained eyes, but he zeroed in on the red dot straight away. The out-of-place towel had set his vision searching for anything else out of place. He put his finger up to Sloane, letting her know that something was up and to maintain silence. There was no way to know if anyone was in the kitchen.

The blood was at the base of the swinging door. After making sure that the drop *was* blood, Hud flipped off the flashlight, let his eyes adjust, then eased open the door far enough so he could peek in, see if there was a body on the floor or someone holding a gun on him. But there was neither. Instead there was more of a mess than Hud had anticipated. A stainless steel prep table sat on its side, with tubs, bins, pots, pans, and silverware scattered everywhere.

He flipped on the flashlight, wedging it between the door and wall to keep it open while he brought himself up in a crouch. His .45 was leveled toward the back of the kitchen, just below the beam of light. There was no sign of anyone, just the aftermath of a melee, a fight, an attack, it was hard to know exactly what had happened. Tilt was gone, and the backdoor of the kitchen was standing wide open. Hud stood up and swept the light across the floor, followed a trail of blood to the door, then covered the rest of the room, looking for that elusive body, or evidence of one left behind, but there was nothing. Nothing but blood.

Hud moved back to Sloane. "Looks like something went down in the kitchen," he said "How far away is backup?"

She shrugged. "I've had the radio turned down."

"I'm going out," Hud said. "Meet me back at the car."

"Are you sure about that?"

Hud didn't answer. He made his way into the kitchen as carefully as possible, making sure not to step in the blood. The small kitchen smelled like a vegetable salad with bleach dressing and an underlying layer of constant grease. The fryer lid was open, and heat radiated out of it as Hud passed by. There would be no late-night tenderloin for anyone on this shift.

The trail of blood was consistent, drops not puddles. A nose broken, perhaps, or a minor gunshot wound, it was hard to tell. Or whether the person wounded was running or walking. And then it stopped, vanished. No matter where he looked, there was no sign of the blood.

Satisfied that he hadn't missed anything, all Hud knew was that he wanted out of the kitchen as soon as possible. He had a bad feeling inching up the back of his spine. More than that something was wrong. It was familiar. Like a setup. He'd barely survived the last one he'd found himself in.

Hud didn't know what to expect when he stepped outside. Another oar careening toward him. A gun barrel pointed at his head. Or a shot out of the dark.

The .45 led the way, sweeping into the cold darkness, his finger on the trigger, ready to react at any sound, any hint of movement. But there was nothing to see or hear. Just Tilt's car parked in its normal parking spot, like it always was. Hud stopped and took a breath. The air was still, and all he could hear was the beat of his own heart. Adrenaline rushed through his veins, urging him to tense up, to overreact, to overlook something. He took a deep breath, glanced past Tilt's car to the Crown Vic to make sure Sloane had returned, was all right. She was. Her face reflected back to him from the driver's seat, lit by the computer, the dashboard.

"All right, Tilt," Hud said softly to the lake, to no one, to the universe. "What the hell happened here and where in the hell are you?"

Darkness surrounded him, engulfed him. There were no stars overhead, no lights on anywhere near that he could see immediately. It was like the entire population had taken the final exodus from the lake, the doom and gloom too much to bear, the prophecies of its demise had finally come true. But that was hard to believe. Backup was on the way, and there was plenty of life in motion beyond the hotel. He just couldn't find it.

Hud took a breath, relieved that there was no immediate danger that he could see or feel, and took a broader look around him.

He stepped out to the edge of the water and looked across the lake, let his eyes fall first to the spot in the darkness that held Gee's shop, then trailed down to Burke's parents' house on the point. It sat directly across from the hotel. A distant light burned in the window. Or maybe it was a porch light. It was hard to tell. Too far away.

The picture of Tilt and Helen Burke flashed in his mind, and he had to wonder the same thing he had wondered about Burke's father and his mother. Were they sleeping together? Having an affair? Then? Now?

He took another deep breath as another question, another realization, roiled to the forefront of his consciousness. If Tilt was hurt, gone, in danger, was Helen Burke safe, in trouble? Would he go to her?

CHAPTER THIRTY-FOUR

Hud slid into the passenger seat of the Crown Vic, juggling as many thoughts as he could. Before he could say a word, Sloane said, "Are you all right?"

"We need to find Tilt Evans."

"I'm already ahead of you. I put out the call. County and state are looking for him. It'd be easier if we had a description of a car to give them. You're sure that's his?" Sloane flicked her head to the lone car sitting in the parking lot.

"Yes, I'm positive. Just like I'm positive that we need to find Goldie Flowers."

"Okay, I think you're right about that." Sloane nodded and took a deep breath. "Lancet called while you were in the kitchen. Pam Sizemore's kid *was* a patient at the doctor's office that Kaye Sherman worked at. There's another link in the chain. Your theory about the reason for the drug swap looks like it might have some weight."

Hud closed his eyes, pushed away the images of blood drops and turmoil inside the bar, and thought about what Sloane said for a long second. The present was replaced with the past. Red faded to black and white as Kodak pictures danced out of the darkness of his mind. His memories mixed together into a sour recipe of anger and loneliness. Somewhere close by he could smell a hint of jasmine perfume. "A mother will do anything for her kid if he's in pain, no matter the cost to herself," Hud said as he opened his eyes and came back to reality. "In my mind anyway. Just because we found meth in their trailer and things were a mess with Pam and Timmy, living in a way we don't approve of, doesn't mean that she wasn't a good mother."

"How would you know that?"

"I talked to the kid. All he wanted to do was go home, go back to his mother. If she were a monster, a chaos queen, he would have been slightly relieved, more comfortable in some place stable. I didn't sense that at all. The kid loved his mother and she loved him. All you had to do was talk to him to know that."

"And that love might have got her killed?"

"Maybe." Discomfort suddenly coursed through Hud's entire body. He felt like he was sitting on a roller coaster, waiting for it to launch. His teeth clenched almost out of his control, and his fists balled tight. His body was so tense that it threatened to snap in half. Pain in his face returned, along with the memory of rage and isolation. He knew the kid's state of mind, his panic, his loss.

"Are you all right?"

"Yeah, I'm okay. Just . . . wait. Look, we need to go, we need to get going."

"Where do we need to go?"

"To Burke's parents' house. I think his mother and Tilt are connected in a way that we might not have known about before now. At least, that I didn't know about. If Tilt's in trouble, she might be in trouble. He might have gone to her. It's the only place I know to check for him. He never spoke of a personal life, a life outside of the bar, so even that's weak, but we need to check on her. What else are we going to do? Drive around looking for a needle in a haystack? Or go back to the office?"

"No, you're right. Okay," Sloane said.

Flashing blue and red lights appeared in the rearview mirror, drawing Hud's attention away from Sloane. He stopped, took a breath. "Looks like backup is here. Lights, no siren. That's nice. Glad no one saw them coming . . ."

"This whole thing is out of everyone's comfort zone," Sloane replied sternly.

Hud knew the tone and was reminded that he was a passenger in her car, and, in truth, in the investigation. "You're right. Look, my guess is we're the closest ones to the Burke's house. We need to go. Don't put out our destination on the radio, and they need to kill the goddamn lights."

"Burke'll go ballistic."

"Let him. He'll come for me. I can take it. You know that."

"Why not tell him?"

"Aren't you the one who warned me about him?" Hud snapped. His concern for her tone or position fell completely away.

Sloane stared at Hud, her face awash in the lights from the cruiser that had parked behind them. "Yes," she whispered. "But I didn't mean it like that . . ." She stopped. Just stopped. Then nodded, like she knew exactly what Hud meant, and maybe more. "Okay. I'll do it your way." Simple beauty and complex understanding twisted her face into a level of resignation that Hud had never seen before.

The radio started to chatter louder, talking directly at them. Backup was Deputy Moran, which was a mild relief to Hud. Varner had a bad attitude, and the rest of the department was virtually unknown to him. It was difficult to process the lack of time he'd spent on his job here. At least he knew what to expect in Detroit. He still didn't know where he was or who he was dealing with on a regular basis in his own hometown.

"We don't have time to explain to Moran what's going on. Just tell her to follow us."

There must have been more than desperation in his voice that motivated Sloane. She nodded, picked up the mic and did exactly what she was told.

While she was doing that, Hud dug into his pocket, pulled out his cell phone, and speed-dialed Lancet.

He answered on the first ring. "What do you want, Matthews?"

"I need you to check on something for me," Hud said, doing his best to ignore the hard-ass tone in the detective's voice. He expected to hear something like "Do it yourself," or "I don't work for you," but instead he heard nothing but distant cellular static and Sloane and Moran talking back and forth in his other ear.

The Crown Vic finally started to move, and they lurched into the

darkness toward Burke's childhood home. Being a passenger was difficult for Hud. He had never trusted anyone behind the wheel but Gee.

"What?" Lancet said.

"I need you to get some background on Tilt Evans for me. More
specifically anything relating to Chicago. Is he from there, maintain
any relationships there? He might be the hub we've been looking for.
If we can establish a clear motive, we're one step closer to shutting the
shooter down. I don't know about you, but I'm getting a little tired of
waiting for a bullet to blow the back of my head off."

"You really think Tilt Evans might be that guy?"

"No, I didn't mean to imply that. I don't know. My gut says no, but
all of the information swirling around in my head says, who knows?
It's possible. If there's a Chicago connection, he might be involved,
or know who is. We need to check him out deeper. Sloane and I are
tracking something down now. It might not be anything or it might
be something. I think we have a short window of time before our
shooter strikes again. They've gone quiet after each incident. This isn't
a rampage, though it might be a reaction to what's happening every
day. They might be trying to quiet anyone who knows who they are."
Hud was hoping to appeal to Pete Lancet's inner detective, get past the
departmental rivalry that existed whether he liked it or not.

"I never did like that arrogant son of a bitch," Lancet said back to
Hud.

Hud didn't say anything right away, didn't defend Tilt. He wasn't
going to debate Tilt's character with Lancet. "Look at the Shamrocks,
too. See if there's any ownership link to him, or anyone named Evans. I
dug for a little while but came up empty handed. It was a brick wall. But
I didn't know what I was looking for. I could have been looking right at
what I needed and didn't know it."

"That place is abandoned now. Why's it matter?"

Hud took a deep breath. "Look, there's always been a direct connection between Chicago and this place. A lot of shady business went
on at the Shamrocks, you know that. We all know that. But that business went away and was replaced with the business of drugs. Drugs were

always here, but more for pleasure than feeding an epidemic like it is now. Charlie Sandburg told me that Leo Sherman was concerned about a turf war between the locals and an outfit out of Chicago. We need to find out who's running that outfit. Who's in that outfit. The Shamrocks and Tilt Evans are the only things I've run across that intersect with Chicago. It's a long shot, but a path I think we need to go down."

Lancet sighed heavily into the phone. "You realize it's after hours for most places, don't you."

"The Internet never closes."

Frustrated static. Silence. No immediate response.

Sloane was dividing her attention between driving and Hud. Moran was close behind them, with her lights off. A request from Sloane.

"I'll see what I can dig up, but I gotta tell you, Matthews, I think you're chasin' rabbits in the dark," Lancet said.

"I've chased a lot of rabbits in my life."

"All right, I'll get back to you, but it ain't gonna be lickety-split, and Burke ain't gonna be none too happy about me wastin' time on the Internet." And then click. The connection was lost, or cut, one or the other.

Hud pulled the phone away from his ear, looked at it to make sure it was still working, then stuffed it back into his pocket. "That guy is something else."

"I told you he'd come around. You'll get used to him." Sloane's eyes were fixed on the road now, trying to look past the headlights into the darkness, into what lay ahead of them. "You've said Leo Sherman was concerned about a turf war. I just thought about this. How would he know about that?"

"Good question. He probably came up on meth labs out in the woods, that kind of thing, and interacted with Burke in some capacity when it came to the drug situation around here. He was boots on the ground. Knew about what was going on around the lake more than anybody else. I bet you see a lot of things driving around checking fishing licenses. We could find out, but if Leo Sherman was the type of CO I think he was, then he would know. Trust me. He would know."

"Right, of course. But what if it was something else? Something more personal than just doing his job? Maybe he found out another way?"

"Like what?"

"Like protecting his wife. Maybe he found out what she was doing, helping Pam Sizemore and who knows who else? What if this outside outfit didn't like her presence, had found out about what she was doing? He was trying to save her. Leo Sherman was trying to save his wife just like Pam Sizemore was trying to save her kid from suffering. You were in the Sherman's house. It was nice. They had a good life. Something worth protecting. Maybe Kaye Sherman got involved in something that was out of her league and she couldn't get out on her own."

"It makes sense."

"And it makes sense that Jordan Rogers or Tom Tucker would know about Kaye Sherman's involvement. Jordan would know."

Hud stiffened in the seat and looked over at Sloane with recognition of what she was saying. "If Tom Tucker was the local dealer, the source that Chicago was trying to wipe out, then Jordan would be dealing with him."

"The shooting was execution-style. Someone was afraid he was going to talk, break. They had to get rid of him, silence him like you said."

Hud shook his head. "They knew each other. It was an ambush before it was an execution."

"All right, I can see that. But then what? Afterward, that person came back to the bar, got into a scuffle with Tilt Evans for one reason or another. And now Tilt's gone, too. All we have is some blood left behind. Like you said, Tilt most likely knew everything that was going in his bar. He was a risk, too. He might have had his own suspicions who the shooter was."

"We need to find Tilt," Hud said. "And like I said, Helen Burke's house is the only place I can think of to start. Lancet might be right. We might be chasing rabbits down a hole."

"Or you might be right," Sloane said. "You might just be right."

"I drove around the lake one last time before I left for college. I was alone, didn't tell Gee where I was going. I had my cigarettes, a little bottle of whiskey, some good tunes, but I wasn't feeling especially nostalgic. It was the end of summer, before Labor Day, a normal day on the lake. I think I was hoping for a miracle, that I'd find something before I had to leave."

"I'm surprised."

"By that?"

"By the fact that you were hoping for a miracle."

"It didn't come. There was no voice from the sky offering the answers I needed. I stopped at the Dip. I was going to confront Fred Myerson, accuse him of killing my mother, but I didn't. I couldn't."

"What stopped you?"

"I had no proof. There were tons of people around. It would have been a crazy thing to do. I left and never went back."

"What happened to him?"

"Cancer got him."

"Another dead end."

"It was a high probability that someone took the truth to their grave. Sometimes, I thought I could live with never knowing what happened to her."

"But that never lasted?"

"No, it was only because I had no other choice. I had to live without knowing. I had to live without her."

〜〜〜〜〜

"Slow down," Hud said, as Sloane was about to turn down the lane that would take them to the Burkes' house.

"Why?"

Hud sighed. "We should at least do a visual of the Shamrocks as we go by, make sure the place is dark, quiet. We'll come back to it after we make sure Helen is all right."

"That's probably not a bad idea." Sloane brought the car to a crawl, and Moran followed suit behind them.

There were no lights on in any of the small cottages, just like Hud had expected. But even in the thick darkness of night, without any help from the stars or moon, it was easy to see that something was there that shouldn't have been. A car sat in the parking lot, and when Sloane swung in behind it, there was no mistaking it. It was Burke's car.

CHAPTER THIRTY-FIVE

The world beyond Sloane's Crown Vic was covered in nervous darkness and filled with the fog of uncertainty. Hud and Sloane had both tried to raise a response from Burke, one on the radio, the other on the cell phone. Neither of them received an answer. They stared at each other, lost, reluctant to step outside the car, though Hud knew that if the shooter wanted to strike, it wouldn't matter. There would be no missing this time. The roof of Hud's mouth felt like it was going to cave in. Burke was out there somewhere.

Hud took a deep breath and reached for the door handle. "Call Lancet, get as much backup here as you can. Tell them to come quietly. This isn't the Charge of the Light Brigade." He hesitated, then said, "This might not turn out well. Are you ready for that?"

"Ready as I'll ever be." Sloane's eyes were vague and distant. "Do you think you're going out there alone?"

Hud nodded. "I think you need to stay close to the radio."

"I have the handheld."

"You'll broadcast to every ear that might be listening. You know how voices carry across the lake in the night air. Besides, I know this place. I mean, it's different, doesn't look the same as it did when I was a kid, but I know it. I spent a lot of time around here. I wore a path between the shop and Burke's house."

"We all spent time around here, Hud." There was something in Sloane's voice that didn't match up with what she said. Resentment, melancholy, nostalgia, something that he didn't have time to decipher.

"You're right; I just have a hard time remembering you as a little girl dressed up all frilly and prissy."

"I wasn't allowed to play like a boy."

"But now you can."

"If you say so." Sloane sighed, looked at the ceiling of the car. "You're right. I'll stay back, keep an eye and ear out, but not for long. I don't like being a sitting duck."

Hud palmed the .45 in his other hand. "Let me know if you hear from Burke."

She nodded as he pushed out of the car and headed toward Moran's cruiser. Sloane didn't say a word, no call me if you need me, nothing. All she had to offer was a stare that turned into an uncomfortable glare. Hud thought he was keeping her safe.

~~~~~~~

"So why did you agree to talk to me?"
"Because I knew you'd ask the right questions."

~~~~~~~

The air was cold and a slight wind pushed off the lake. His ears were tuned to high alert, listening for any sound out of place: a snap of a twig, a round being chambered, someone breathing heavily, a chirping October cricket. All sounds he'd heard before, but now they would mean more. He felt like he was walking out of one setup and into another. This situation had felt bad, twisted, like something was out of place, from the moment he'd seen Burke's Crown Vic. There'd been no radio communication, no contact from the chief that Hud had heard since they'd left the Tom Tucker crime scene, but he'd been in the bar looking for Tilt, on a path of his own. He hadn't needed Burke, and Burke hadn't needed him.

As Hud moved toward Moran's cruiser stealthily, familiar images flittered through his mind. Blood on the floor. Tilt dancing with Burke's mother. A little boy screaming for his dead mother to return. None of which seemed connected or have anything to do with anything . . . but yet, Hud wasn't so sure. He couldn't be. Not now that there was no sign of Burke. *Where are you?*

Moran rolled down the window as Hud stopped and crouched next to the door. "You look better than the last time I saw you," Moran said.

"I need you to go down to the house and check on Mrs. Burke," Hud said.

She looked at him with confusion that quickly transformed to annoyance, then faded away into duty-bound resignation. Nothing came from her pursed lips. At least she knew how to pick her fights. Hopefully, her other kickboxing skills wouldn't have to be put to the test. "All right," Moran said. "What am I looking for?"

"You know the bartender at the Demmie?"

"Tilt Evans? Yeah, everybody knows Tilt. The world's greatest skier, except no one has ever seen him ski."

"I have. He *was* really good back in the day." Muscles weakened, bones became brittle, and youthful arrogance settles into tension and fear. Hud was tempted to give Moran a life lesson, but he knew he not only lacked the time but the authority. It wouldn't matter what he said to her.

"All right, if you say so," she said.

"Keep an eye out for him. Goldie Flowers, too. Make sure Helen Burke's safe. She's probably going to wonder what the hell is going on when you show up at her door. Just keep her occupied until you hear from us. She's like Burke. Her bark's bigger than her bite. For some reason, I hope Burke's there, too. Though I can't figure out why he'd leave his car here."

Moran nodded. "Me, either. I'm a little worried." Her mouth twisted up like she wanted to say something else, but she restrained herself. She put the cruiser in gear and inched out of the parking lot and down the lane toward Burke's childhood home in total darkness. Only the interior glowed. The deputy looked as if she was trapped inside a hard brown-and-tan bubble. They both knew it didn't offer any protection. Just the opposite. It had been a target once and mostly likely would be again at some point.

Hud stood back and watched the cruiser disappear, get swallowed up by the darkness, then scuttled to the closest Shamrock cottage armed with the .45 in one hand and a flashlight in the other.

Up close, it was easy to see that time had been more unkind to the resort than Hud had originally thought. There were ten cottages, all the same, ten-by-twenty at the most, with clapboard siding that had at one time been painted a bright green; the color of an Irish shamrock reaching for the sun. But the paint had faded, peeled, or been completely worn away by nature's relentless fury. Some of the windows and doors were completely off their hinges, open, clattering in the wind, allowing animals and other vagrant creatures to come and go as they pleased. The Shams would have been a perfect place to hide a meth lab. The downside to the choice of the location was the closeness to Helen Burke's house and her watchful eye. Anyone with any sense at all would have found another place to cook their drugs.

Hud worked his way along the cottages, sweeping in doors and checking open windows as he went. Occasionally, he would look over his shoulder to check on Sloane, make sure she was still there, watching over him, waiting to jump into action if she were needed. Her presence gave him a little bit of false confidence.

October was the gateway to the season of decay, but nothing had prepared him for the rotten smells he encountered. The air was doused with the aroma of slow death, flesh disintegrating one cell at a time, in no hurry to become one with the soil underneath it. Even the wind couldn't combat or push away the rot.

Hud didn't linger in any one place too long. The smell was worse than any morgue that he'd ever been in. The intensity of the experience nearly gagged him, made him turn away. He hadn't seen one sign of Burke since he'd started looking.

By the time he'd reached the last cottage, Hud had started to doubt that Burke was there. At least not alive, capable of making any noise.

If it weren't for the presence of the chief's Crown Vic, Hud would have thought that he'd set himself, and everyone else, on a wild goose chase. But the car *was* there, and there was no explanation or clue as to Burke's whereabouts—unless he was home with his mother. It was the only hope that Hud had left.

After sweeping the last cottage with a quick burst of light, Hud determined that it was vacant too. Plaster peeled off the walls, the stuffing had been pulled out of the furniture and made into a nest of some kind in the not so distant past. There was no sign of a human, living or dead. He stopped, sighing, to gather his thoughts. The next thing to do, after checking Burke's car, was to have Sloane radio Moran and see if Burke was at his mother's house.

Resigned and relieved, Hud started for Burke's vehicle, replaying in his head everything that had happened since they'd left the Demmie and arrived at the Shamrocks. He glanced up at Sloane watching over him, and stopped just out of the shadow of the last cottage. *"We all spent time around here, Hud."* Sloane had said. He had never been able to place her at Burke's house, and he had no memory of her father or mother, either, for that matter. But it all made sense: her mother was protective, wanted her to be a girl, kept her away from the boys. And her father was a cop, too, part of the club with Burke's father's gang. Her father would have known everybody on the county force even though he wasn't on it. They all worked together.

And then the questions began to flood into Hud's mind. Did Sloane's father know my mother? Was Burke's father just an affair? And perhaps Sloane's father was the man who was going to change everything. He was married. In the mix. Did he party at the Demmie with the rest of the upper crust? Did he drive a black car? And most importantly, what did Tina Sloane really know, if anything, about his mother?

Two things happened almost simultaneously as Hud stood there trying to find footing in his thoughts: Sloane flashed her headlights on and off, attempting to get his attention, and Hud's cell phone hummed in his pocket.

He had the ringer turned off. He figured the phone call was probably Sloane, but hoped that it was from Burke. His stomach roiled like a storm had just cut loose, and his face throbbed from the blow of the oar. Pain and a week's worth of blood and madness washed over him, and he was certain that, no matter what happened, he would never be able to relieve himself of the stench of the murders. They had changed him, shown him a side of his home that he didn't know existed. He wished for the happy place of his memory that didn't exist anymore. It wasn't just the Ferris wheel that threatened to crumble into the lake and disappear; everything did. Even him.

Hud stared at the Crown Vic, the flashing headlights, and reached for his phone. It wasn't Burke or Sloane. It was Lancet.

"Hey," Hud said as softly as he could.

"You all right?"

"Just in the middle of looking for Burke."

"Anything?"

"Not a sign of him, but Moran's down at the house. I hope he's there."

"I haven't heard anything, either. I'm worried."

Sloane flashed her lights again, only this time closer together, more emphatic. She was getting impatient. Hud had the phone cupped to his ear, his back to the car, so no one could see that he was on the phone. "So, what's up?" he said.

"Look, I came across something that I think you need to know. It's troubling."

"What?"

"You sent me on that information chase to Chicago . . . and I think I found something. More than something."

"Okay."

"Look, I have some friends in Chicago, and I called in a few favors, did a little digging on the Internet, like you said, but I got some access to some county records that you probably couldn't have gotten to before now. Things have changed."

Hud tried to listen past the gloating in Pete Lancet's voice. There was something else there, too; a quiver, nervousness. "We need a break."

"Not this kind," Lancet said. "I was able to break through the wall that was hiding the shell corporation, the one that owned the Shamrocks. It's been condemned recently by the county, and because of that I was able to use that information to track down the origin of ownership. There were two names. Two recognizable names. Burke's dad was one of them. He was part owner of the Shamrocks from the mid-1960s, and the other name was . . ."

Hud cut Lancet off, knew what he was going to say before he said it. "Sloane. The other name is Sloane."

"Yeah. How'd you know?"

CHAPTER THIRTY-SIX

Hud stood staring at the Crown Vic, his feet firmly planted on a bed of decaying leaves. Sloane hadn't given up. The flashing headlights continued, nearly blinding him. They had the intensity of a lightning storm, and he felt vulnerable, like he were standing in an open field, stabbing a metal rod angrily at the heavens. He knew he only had seconds before Sloane gave up and came to tell him whatever it was that was so important to her. Seconds to decide if he was right about his suspicions, if they were warranted at all. *Had she been playing me for a fool all along?*

He had no idea where Sloane had been when Pam Sizemore was shot. But she *was* at the Sherman's house when the oar came swinging at his head. It could have been her who had knocked him for a loop. Same with Leo Sherman. Hud had no idea where she was when the CO had been shot in the backwaters. There were a hundred different places she could have been hiding with a 30-aught-6 rifle. It *was* possible that she could have killed all three of those victims.

Tom Tucker was a little different, the opportunity tighter, but possible, once he thought about if everything checked out, if Sloane had had enough time to leave the office after interrogating Jordan Rogers and going to see Bill Flowers. Hud had no idea where she was then. He'd assumed she had been at her desk the whole time, waiting for him. There was no reason to question her whereabouts then, or time to call Lancet back and have him check out Sloane's schedule. He had to trust his gut. There was time for her to kill Tom Tucker after he had left the Demmie. Barely. But some time. So, was Tina Sloane a cold-blooded killer? If so, why?

He had to question her motive. If Burke's father and her father had been in a long-standing partnership together, it wasn't a stretch to think that that business, illegal or on the up-and-up, had been passed on to one or both of them. Could Sloane have been the Chicago connection, the other side of the turf war? If the Shamrocks had been condemned, did that partnership venture into drug distribution—or had it been there all along? A channel developed and refined in the drug heyday of the seventies? Vacationland and recreational drugs go together like ice cream and cake. Why wouldn't the business evolve from pot to meth when times got hard? Syndicates got used to making money. One drug or the other didn't matter to that kind of business.

As a cop, Sloane would have been in the best place possible to monitor how close she was to getting caught, to the drug connection being discovered. Unless Burke was involved, too. There was that question. *How much did Burke know?* How deep did the business go? Hud was too far on the outside to know, but he could see her motive a little clearer. What he couldn't see was a reason for Sloane to have killed Pam Sizemore. What had set her off? What had started the series of murders? Did Leo Sherman go to someone in the department after discovering his wife's involvement? Was it compassion or business? Did he lead Sloane to Pam Sizemore? Put her in a position that required Pam to be silenced because she knew the connection?

Or was Sloane innocent and Burke the shooter? Had he had the same opportunity that she'd had? A snippet of the conversation he'd had with Sloane flitted through Hud's mind, from when she'd come to the shop to warn him about Burke. It had felt strange then, and it felt even stranger now. *"... So he could keep an eye on you ..."* It was her explanation about why Burke had hired him. Maybe she had been telling him more of the truth than he had realized. Maybe they were in it together? Maybe it was so they both could keep an eye on him. Burke knew that Hud would start poking around in the past.

Time for speculation and planning ran out. Sloane got out of the car. Hud didn't move. He didn't know what else to do but stand there. He held his .45 in his right hand, readying himself for whatever came next. Of all the things he had done in his career as a detective, he had never successfully negotiated his way out of a confrontation with a killer. He had tried that with his snitch, and it had nearly cost him his life.

Sloane stopped at the corner of the Crown Vic cautiously, sizing him up. She was nothing but a rigid silhouette of herself. All of the bland details of her attire, of her attempt to fade into the background, all perfectly meshed into the darkness behind her. She was almost invisible, her goal accomplished.

A moth fluttered across the headlight of the car, looking larger than it was. Hud could barely see Sloane's face. Shadows hid her eyes and the intention in them. He couldn't see her hands, either, whether they held her trusted Glock, whether he was in the line of fire. If she was the shooter, she wouldn't miss this time. He was sure of that.

"Did you find anything?" Sloane said. They were about twenty feet apart. Her voice carried easily on the wind. She didn't seem too concerned about being conspicuous, about being heard.

Hud's cell phone buzzed in his pocket. He ignored it, decided to walk closer. He had no choice but to take his chances looking her in the eye. "Nothing. Any word from Moran about Burke?"

"He's not there." Her face came into view in a shroud of grayness. It was as hard as granite. Her eyes, almost black, were full of scrutiny and uncertainty. She unsettled him more than he had expected.

He stopped a few feet in front of her. "Where's he at?"

"I wish I knew. What's the matter? You look sick," Sloane said.

"Those cottages smell like death."

"You'd think you'd be used to that."

"I could never get used to that kind of foulness," Hud said.

Sloane looked at his right hand, at the .45. Hud followed suit but didn't see her Glock in her hand, didn't see a weapon at all. That was a relief. She didn't have her gun openly ready. *Why would she?* Doubt filtered into all of the damning scenarios in his mind. Maybe he was overreacting, seeing connections that weren't there. He hoped that was the case.

"Who were you on the phone with?" she asked.

Hud sighed, cocked his head, disappointed that he had been unable to hide his conversation from her. "Lancet. He found out some information about the Shamrocks that he thought I ought to know." He watched every muscle in Sloane's face for recognition, for a reason to react. The granite wall remained solidly in place.

"And?" she said.

"I think you know what he found."

Sloane stepped forward. Her face changed. Her blank professionalism turned into personal recognition. They were ten feet apart now. "It's not what you think."

Hud stepped back in response. "Then maybe you better explain it to me. Because right now what Lancet told me only raises questions and doesn't answer anything at all. You need to tell me what the hell is going on, Sloane. I'm in no mood to be blindsided again."

"Everything is crumbling, isn't it?"

Panic was hard to read at night, especially with conflicting amounts of light and darkness. Hud wasn't sure what to make of Sloane's reaction. He didn't want her to feel trapped, backed into a corner like a wild animal, with no way to escape. "I can help you," he offered. "If you're involved in something over your head, I can help you."

Sloane shook her head. "No, you can't. You know that. Don't lie to me, Hud. That's what I've liked about you since you came back. I believed you when you said something."

"Did I make the same mistake believing in you?"

Sloane didn't answer, just stared at him.

Somewhere in the distance, the first note of a siren droned high into the cold night air. Brittle oak leaves, hanging on for dear life, rattled behind Hud. The .45 felt heavy in his sweaty palm, and his finger twitched an inch away from the trigger.

"Was it you?" Hud said. He had no choice but to ask Sloane directly, openly. There was no resisting the questions tumbling in his mind. A shiver ran up the back of his leg, shook his hamstring, warning him to run, to take cover. But it was too late for that.

"I don't know what you mean."

Hud stared at her, deciding whether or not to believe her denial. It was too dark to tell.

"Okay," he said. "Why didn't you tell me that your father and Burke's father owned the Shamrocks? Let's start there."

"What makes you think I know anything about that?"

"At the moment, I think you know a lot more than I do." Hud's cell phone buzzed in his pocket again. Insistent, like Sloane flashing the headlights at him. He ignored it again. "What was so important that you needed to get my attention?"

"We should go. There's nothing here. We need to find Burke."

"Right," Hud said. "I'm not going anywhere at the moment."

Sloane glared at him, then looked at the .45 again. "Do you think that's necessary?"

"I do. You didn't answer my question."

"My father's business isn't relevant. He's dead. So is Burke's father. Their sins are not our sins."

"But Burke's father's legacy is important to him. Remember? That's what you told me. How about your father's legacy, Sloane? What are you protecting? What is *your* father's legacy?"

"You're on dangerous ground, Hud."

"Is that a warning? I've been shot at, smacked upside the head, and dusted off by just about everyone since this whole thing began, and here we are. Do you really think that I'm going to back down now?" Hud stepped in closer, stopped five feet from her. The wind caught her perfume. Just a hint. The promise of something tropical, a journey far away, never to be taken. "You really need to tell me what's going on, Sloane. I can help you," he repeated his offer one last time.

The siren grew louder, closer, more defined. There were two, not one, and distantly, another one cried out, trying to catch up with the others. A bead of sweat formed on the ledge of Sloane's top lip. Hud had no idea what was going on, had no access to a radio, but something told him that Sloane knew where the sirens were heading.

"They're coming here, aren't they?" he said. "Time's running out."

"No," Sloane said. "It already has. I can see it now. There's only one way out of this." She lowered her chin for a brief second, then stepped forward.

Instinct demanded that Hud raise his .45, aim at her head, tell her to stop, but he resisted the urge, fought believing that Sloane was the shooter for as long as he could. Doubt and disbelief were a mistake he had made before. His wrist rotated upward, and he stepped forward just as Sloane lunged into him, planting her right foot and swinging her upward facing arm at the same time. It was like a door closing shut on Hud's wrist as their arms met. He wasn't ready for that kind of attack, and his .45 slipped from his grasp, sailed out of his hand, and tumbled into the darkness.

Sloane wasn't finished. All of her hand-to-hand combat training was fully engaged. Before Hud could fully process that his gun had been knocked out of his hand, she punched him with the other arm, full force, fist balled, in the same side of the face that the oar had previously found. He tumbled sideways but remained on his feet. Sloane punched like a man. Not like the frilly princess her mother had hoped she would be.

There was enough time for her to pull the Glock out of the small of her back. "This stops now," Sloane demanded.

Hud didn't surrender or wait to comply. He fell the rest of the way to the ground and extended his leg out at the same time, putting as much force into his legs as possible, a direct blow at the back of Sloane's calves. The force of the sweep knocked her forward. She hadn't been expecting it either, but she held onto the gun.

Survival meant throwing any concern for her health and safety aside. Hud scrambled toward Sloane, jumped and tackled her. She was strong, determined to hold onto the Glock, to win the fight. Fingernails and teeth became weapons. The night air was full of sirens and heavy breath, sweat, the smell of death, and the determination to live. But as hard she fought, Hud was finally able to pin Sloane down, grab her by the throat, and put as much pressure on her windpipe as she could bear. The move forced her to release the gun. Hud grabbed it up with his free hand and jammed the barrel against her forehead. "I swear, you move a muscle and I'll blow your fucking head off," he said in between pants, trying to gain his breath.

Blood trickled out of the corner of Sloane's mouth as Hud lessened his grip on her throat. He was straddling her, had her arms pinned with his legs, could feel her laboring underneath him. She didn't offer him anything but a hardened glare.

"I'll ask you again, Sloane. Why'd you do it?"

"You know why," she spat.

"Enlighten me. Did Leo Sherman come to you and try to soften the blow for his wife? He found out what she was doing, didn't he?"

"Because of that he was close to finding out more."

"That you were the Chicago connection."

"Yes. It was supposed to be simple: get rid of Pam Sizemore and send a message to Tom Tucker at the same time. Pack it in, this is over. You're small time."

"But Sherman blew things up. This is his land, and he loved it, was willing to fight for it."

Hud cocked his head toward the lake, listened to the storm of wails offering promise and saw lights in the darkness for the first time. Behind him a nearby engine roared. He wondered if he needed to still be worried about being shot in the back by some unseen sniper.

"Why'd you kill Kaye Sherman?"

"Confrontations get messy. You know that, Hud. And it gave me room to breathe."

"It put the focus on Leo. Until you had to shoot him, too."

"You were getting too close. Don't you think he would talk?"

"Tom Tucker, too. He knew you."

"He figured it out."

Hud stiffened. "What'd you do with Goldie?" Sloane tried to turn her head, but Hud wouldn't let her. He forced her to look him in the eye. "Tell me what you did to her, goddamn it. Tell me."

"She was with Tucker. That's all I know. I expected her to be with him. I had to leave. I was running out of time. She was with him when I left."

"Dead."

"She was there."

Hud trembled inside. He almost had everything he wanted, but he still didn't know where Goldie was, whether she was dead or alive.

The darkness enveloping the Shamrocks suddenly erupted into bright white light. The ground rumbled with police cars, fire trucks, and ambulances. The air smelled of urgency and diesel. Nothing had stopped or parked. All of the vehicles were speeding forward toward Sloane and Hud.

"You figured it all out, Hud," Sloane said. "I knew you would from the first moment I saw you. I knew you would." Defeat edged her voice, and she closed her eyes briefly. "You were determined to find the truth, come hell or high water. I should have aimed better when I shot at you. But I missed, and here we are. Daddy would have been disappointed with me for that."

Hud exhaled, felt a moment of relief. She was right. Everything had led him to this moment, and Tina Sloane had finally been stopped.

A car stopped behind them. Close, maybe thirty feet away. Hud didn't dare take his eyes off of Sloane, but he was becoming more comfortable that the struggle was over. Resignation rested on her face, as her future became more and more obvious. She couldn't outrun all of the flashing lights and guns that had just shown up.

A door slammed. Footsteps approached. Then a voice rang out that Hud recognized immediately. "Get off her!" It was Burke.

Hud tensed, then realized he had backup, that there were more eyes on him and Sloane than he could imagine. He started to loosen his grip on Sloane.

"But you were wrong about one thing, Hud," she said.

He looked over his shoulder as Burke stalked toward them, screaming, yelling. "What," Hud said, "what was I wrong about?"

"She wasn't going to run off with Burke's father ..."

He knew what she was talking about right away. "... Yours? She was going to run off with your father?"

"And destroy all of our lives."

"But that didn't happen," Hud said, surrendering to the revelation. The depth of what Sloane said staggered him, caused him to lose sight of where he was, what he was doing. "You were protecting him all along." It was a whisper, a truth so deep that he couldn't bear the thought of it. Sloane's father had killed his mother. And justice would never be served. Not real justice.

It was the break Sloane needed to break free of him. It only took a few seconds for her to reach for the .45 she'd knocked out of Hud's hand.

He reacted, saw what was happening, and in that moment of the need to live, to fight on, to push past regret, he pulled the trigger of the Glock before she could even touch the gun. The shot hit her between the eyes, stopped her forward movement. Blood splattered into the blinding light, offering the color of life to the condemned ground. The report echoed above all the engines, the sirens, and coasted over the lake, disappearing on the push of the wind so quickly it was like the sound had never existed at all.

"Why'd you do it?"

"I had no choice," Hud said, as he stood up and looked at the two-way mirror. The interrogation room was hot and sweaty. Burke had turned off the air flow.

Deputy Moran shook her head. "Everybody saw you shoot her."

"It was self-defense."

"There are witnesses this time. No one saw her go for her gun."

"They saw what they wanted to see. The truth will come out. You wait and see. It always does," Hud said. "It always does."

CHAPTER THIRTY-SEVEN

They found her bones when they tore down the Shamrocks. The floor in cottage number three had been patched and cemented. She had been entombed under a thick slab that would have seemed like it would last forever, outlast the person who put her there.

Confined by the legal system and facing the reality of no bail, Hud Matthews was escorted to his mother's funeral in handcuffs. The ride there was slow and long, and he was glad that Burke hadn't put him in a cage, had allowed him to sit in the passenger seat like a normal human being instead of an alleged cop killer.

"You're not going to let me see the report, are you?" he said to Burke.

"You know I can't do that." Burke tossed him a sideways glance, and there was no hint of regret in his voice.

Hud stared out the windshield, was glad that the day was bright, the mid-autumn sky free of any clouds, of any perceivable threats. The temperature was comfortable, and he had the side glass cracked at the top so fresh, cool air pushed into his face as they rode along. "You have to tell me what's in it."

"Look, I know how important this is for you. We shouldn't be here together. You know that, but Sloane . . ."

"Had you fooled, too."

"You could say that." Burke sighed. "I will tell you this. My father always suspected Sloane's father of having something to do with your mother's disappearance. But he didn't push too hard, according to his notes, according to his file."

"You didn't want me to see that."

"No, you'd start asking questions."

"About your father. You knew?"

Burke slowed the car and edged it over to the side of the road. "I knew he had some business deals that were shady. Damn it, Hud, look at the house. It's in the best spot on the lake. They lived high on the hog, partied with the wealthiest people around. My dad didn't make that kind of money, and my mom didn't work. It had to come from somewhere. I found out a lot when he died. We washed our hands of it all. I swear to you."

"But Sloane didn't?"

"We didn't talk about it."

"Come on, Burke, don't fuck with me. Not now."

"I already knew too much. My hero wasn't such a hero. He couldn't go after Sloane's father for anything because it would expose him, too. They would lose everything. It would have been the same for me if I went after him. My hands were tied."

"That's what Sloane said to me. That their lives were going to be destroyed." Hud lowered his head, took a deep breath and faced Burke. "My life *was* destroyed. I lost everything. And here I am sitting in a police car, handcuffed, accused of being a murderer. Tell me how that's fair? Everybody was protecting themselves, afraid of doing the right thing when the right time came to do it. Including you. You covered your ass. Thanks for being my friend, Burke. Thanks a lot."

"I was at the Shams looking for evidence that would help you, but you pulled the trigger first. I couldn't find anything. That's why I wasn't there at first. I was talking to my mother, seeing if I had missed anything. She was never receptive to talking about the past. You know that. You put yourself where you are. Don't blame me for that."

"I had no choice. It was me or her." Hud's voice was elevated, and he realized that he was yelling inside the car.

"I'm sorry. I can't talk about that. You understand," Burke said calmly.

Hud nodded, sighed. "I guess I do, but there are things you can tell me. Please, I need to know about my mother. You have to understand that."

"I do."

"I'm glad. So, you think Sloane's father killed her?"

"He's my main suspect, just like he was my father's, but I intend to prove it. He couldn't, or wouldn't. I will. I have modern science. Forensics. I know we can prove that Sloane's father killed your mother," Burke said.

"Regardless of the personal cost?"

"I'm not sure I have much choice. Do you?"

"Not really. Do you remember what color of car Sloane's father drove back then?"

"What's that got to do with anything?"

"I saw her wave, get into a car, and drive off. It was the last time I saw her. It was a black car. You have to find out if he owned a black car."

"That shouldn't be hard to confirm."

"I think he killed her, too. He had motive, time, and all the knowledge to cover up a murder. It's something," Hud said.

"It is."

Hud rolled the window down the rest of the way and breathed in a deep breath of air. He could see the lake, calm, smooth, and placid. A deep V of geese flew overhead, riding the wind south, outrunning the dreariness of the coming winter and the hopelessness that surrounded everything on the ground. The promise of warmth and safety awaited them in a different place. He wished he could go with them. But that was impossible now.

"How'd she die?" Hud asked, his eyes still focused on the water. She hadn't been there. He'd been looking in all the wrong places all of his life. It was hard to count how many times he had walked by cottage number three and not given her a thought. But he always looked for her face in the water. Always. But all he ever saw was her in his own reflection. It was all he had.

"A single blow to the back of the head," Burke said, as gently as he could. "Bill Flowers was certain that she died instantly, if that's any consolation."

"It's not. But there's no way to tell for sure."

"No."

"And no motive, at this point?"

"Only what we can speculate."

"Killing her was the only way to keep what he had. He was a cop, too. He had a lot to lose, just like everyone else." Hud bit his lip. "All she wanted was what everyone else had. That's all. She just wanted us to be happy. And it got her killed."

"Yeah, I think you're right. Something like that. I don't know that we'll ever find out for sure." Burke looked at his watch, then at Hud. "We have to go or we'll be late."

"All right."

The car eased away from the side of the road, and Hud looked at the lake for as long as he could. Once it disappeared from sight, he looked ahead, toward what was coming. "How's Goldie?"

"Recovering. I don't know how she made it back to the hotel. She crawled there after she was shot. Tilt Evans saved her life, took her to the hospital."

"After Sloane shot her."

"That's still under investigation."

"I'm sure it is. I thought something else had happened there. I thought Tilt was involved in all of this. We went to your house to make sure your mom was all right."

"Me, too. I thought Tilt was involved." Burke paused. "You knew about them, too."

"I suspected. Just like I thought your father was with my mother. I never considered Sloane's father, that my mother would run off with him. Why would I?"

"Everybody was having a go at everybody else. It was the swinging seventies," Burke said.

"Yeah, sorry I missed the party."

~~~~~~~~~

The funeral took place at the Flowerses' funeral home. Bill Flowers had seen to everything, taken care of the costs, the preparation. He met Hud and Burke at the front door.

The inside of the old Queen Anne–style house was cavernous and hadn't changed since the last time Hud had been inside it, thirty years ago. Even the green brocade carpet was the same. Bouquets of flowers lined the hallway to the chapel, and from his vantage point, Hud could see a simple oak casket sitting in the middle of a room full of empty chairs and more funeral flowers than he'd ever seen.

"I thought you might want a moment alone," Bill Flowers said solemnly. He was dressed head-to-toe in black, and there was no hint of animosity in his voice.

"Thank you," Hud said. "You're sure it's her?"

"Absolutely positive."

"Okay." It was a whisper. He started to move forward, his hands out in front of him, still cuffed, but his feet felt like they were weighed down with cinder blocks. He quivered, and his knees buckled. His heart raced, and he had trouble catching his breath. Both Burke and Bill Flowers caught him before he fell forward.

"Whoa," Burke said. "Are you all right?"

"Yeah, yeah. It's just that it's been a long, long time. You're really sure it's her? I can't see her?"

"Yes, it's her. You'll have to trust me," Flowers said. "You don't want to see her. Just remember her how she was."

"All right," Hud said as he stepped forward. It felt as if he was floating, like he was in the middle of a bad dream and a good dream all at once. All he had ever wanted was to say goodbye, to know what had happened to her, to know where she was. He had just wanted to see her one last time. But that was impossible.

Hud stood before the casket, touched it softly just as a tear fell to the floor. "I knew you never left me. I knew you loved me and Gee too much to do that. I never left you, either . . . I'm sorry. I'm sorry. I wish I could have saved you . . ."

~~~~~~~~~~

"Will the defendant rise," the judge said.

Hud did as he was told and said nothing.

"How do you plead against the charge of first degree murder of one Tina Sloane?"

"Innocent, Your Honor. I am innocent."

ACKNOWLEDGMENTS

I am fortunate to enjoy the company of great friends and colleagues who contribute to every book I write. I am grateful for the expertise of the following people: Special thanks goes to Mark Stroud, Liz Hatton, Patrick Kanouse, Matthew P. Mayo, and Lynne Raimondo, for the suggestions, time, and encouragement that you gave me on this novel. Special thanks also goes to my editor, Dan Mayer, and the entire production, marketing, and publicity teams at Seventh Street Books. Continued appreciation goes to my agent, Cherry Weiner, and to my wife, Rose, who lives the day-to-day writing life alongside of me and enjoys every second of it. Thank you.

ABOUT THE AUTHOR

Larry D. Sweazy (www.larrydsweazy.com) has been a freelance indexer for eighteen years. In that time, he has written over 825 back-of-the-book indexes for major trade publishers and university presses such as Addison-Wesley, Cengage, American University at Cairo Press, Cisco Press, Pearson Education, Pearson Technology, University of Nebraska Press, Weldon Owen, and many more. He continues to work in the indexing field on a daily basis.

As a writer, Larry is a two-time WWA (Western Writers of America) Spur Award winner, a two-time, back-to-back, winner of the Will Rogers Medallion Award, a Best Books of Indiana award winner, and the inaugural winner of the 2013 Elmer Kelton Book Award. He was also nominated for a Short Mystery Fiction Society (SMFS) Derringer Award in 2007 (for the short story "See Also Murder"). Larry has published over sixty nonfiction articles and short stories and is the author of ten novels, including books in the Josiah Wolfe, Texas Ranger western series (Berkley); the Lucas Fume western series (Berkley); a thriller set in Indiana, *The Devil's Bones* (Five Star); a mystery novel set in the dust bowl of Texas, *A Thousand Falling Crows* (Seventh Street Books); and the Marjorie Trumaine Mystery series (Seventh Street Books). He currently lives in Indiana with his wife, Rose.